The COLUMBO Collection

WILLIAM LINK
(Maxine Picard Photography)

The COLUMBO
Collection

William Link

Crippen & Landru Publishers
Norfolk, Virginia
2010

Crippen & Landru Publishers Cincinnati, Ohio 2010

Copyright © 2010 by William Link

Introduction Copyright © 2023 by Joseph Goodrich

The drawing of Peter Falk as Columbo is by A1 Hirschfeld. ©A1 Hirschfeld; reproduced by arrangement with Hirschfeld's exclusive representatives, the Margo Feiden Galleries Ltd., New York. WWW.ALHIRSCHFELD.COM

Cover design by Deborah Miller

Crippen & Landru logo by Eric D. Greene

ISBN (trade softcover edition): 978-1-932009-94-1

Printed in the United States of America on recycled acid-free paper

Crippen & Landru Publishers
P. O. Box 532057
Cincinnati, OH 45253 USA
Email: Orders@CrippenLandru.Com
Website: www.CrippenLandru.com

Contents

To the memory of Richard Levinson (1934-1987). My collaborator and best friend since the first day of junior high school.

To Margery, with love as always.

Special thanks to my niece Amy Salko Robertson.

To my family, both West Coast and East.

To the new generation: Anabelle, Bennett, Fin, Miriam, Hallie, Jonah, Asher, and Jordan.

To Rosanna, Chrissy, Antoine, and Leo, and now young Margot.

To my dear friend Jay Benson, whose good humor and phone calls always brighten my day.

To my good friend Marvin Miller who, like Merlin, makes miracles happen.

To the talented and lovely Shera Falk, the real Mrs. Columbo, who proves that there is always a terrific woman behind an exceptional man.

And to the incomparable Peter Falk, whose alchemy took a character on paper and made it flesh and blood and unforgettable to millions of people all over the world. A marriage made in television heaven. Thank you for everything, Peter.

Introduction: Just One More Thing (or Two)

By Joseph Goodrich

Look around, and what do we see?

It doesn't make for easy or pleasant viewing.

Crooks and con men stroll the corridors of power. Constitutional rights are abrogated by reactionary judges. The global pandemic has stolen an untold number of lives and damaged economies around the world. The environmental crisis is being ignored. The dark forces of Fascism threaten the existence of democracy. In short, the lunatics have taken over the asylum.

Thank Heavens for Columbo!

Mysteries are perforce moral tales. They offer the reader entry into a world where crime is punished and order is restored – if only momentarily. Given the state of perpetual anxiety we inhabit these days, a figure like the good lieutenant feels more necessary than ever. In difficult times we seek reassurance and comfort. We find it in Columbo.

The rumpled working-class everyman of a detective is more popular than ever. The pleasures of the evergreen TV series created by William Link and Richard Levinson are easily enumerated: crisp and clever plotting, fine performances, the satisfaction of seeing justice enacted.

New and old fans will take pleasure in these adventures; each of them prompts an almost visceral memory of Peter Falk at work on the small screen. The hallmarks of the series are all there. The well-placed villain. The unconventional and (shall we say) criminally underestimated policeman. The perfect crime taken apart bit by bit. Cold-blooded murder committed and solved (mostly) in the City of Angels.

First published in 2010, the collection sounds a melancholy note today: both Link and Falk have joined Levinson in "that undiscovered country from whose bourn no traveler returns." How fortunate that, with the flick of a switch or the turn of a page, we can join their greatest creation on his quest for killers, a pencil to write with, and a really excellent bowl of chili.

Welcome back, Lieutenant. It's good to see you again.

Joseph Goodrich
Jackson Heights, NY
June 2023

Just one more thing....

In his foreword to the original edition, William Link speculated on the source of Columbo's name. Try as he might, he couldn't locate it. But then – after the book was published – he did. Which only goes to show that memories can't be forced, they can only be gently invited to appear.

It seems Bill woke up one morning with two words on his lips.

And therein lies a tale.

As Bill explained it to his wife Margery, whom he'd abruptly awakened: In 1960, he and Dick Levinson escaped the glare and sweltering heat of New York City by seeking out the deliciously air-conditioned darkness of a move theater. But they didn't go to just any movie. Talent seeks out talent. They bought tickets for a film by Link's favorite director: Billy Wilder. The movie in question? *Some Like it Hot.*

No doubt you've seen it. Tony Curtis and Jack Lemmon witness a gangland murder in 1920s Chicago and run for their lives, disguised as members of a female jazz band. It's often considered the greatest comedy Hollywood ever produced.

But that's not the point.

Do you remember the name of the character played by George Raft?

No?

Bill Link did – and realized that was where he and Dick Levinson had found their detective's last name.

After all those years, it had come back to him. A nice bit of poetic justice, it turns out, as Raft's character was a stone cold killer. His name snapped Bill awake one morning and revealed for all time the answer to the burning question: Where did you get the name for your detective?

The name of George Raft's character was:

"Spats" Colombo.

Granted, there's a slight spelling difference, but what's a letter or two in the scheme of things? The Lieutenant and "Spats" are both of Italian heritage and both, shall we say, involved in matters of law and order. Opposite sides of the same coin. Heads and Tails.

And speaking of tales, that's where this one ends.

The origin of Columbo's last name?

Mystery solved.

I hate to bother ya, but...

Columbo's first name isn't Frank.

FOREWORD

IT'S AMAZING, BUT THIS IS the first time I've been asked to *write* about Lieutenant Columbo, the character I created with my late best friend and collaborator Dick Levinson. Okay, so where do I start? Well, how about at the very point of origin, the spring of 1960?

Columbo would probably have never been created if there hadn't been a writers' strike. Dick and I had arrived in Los Angeles a year earlier and immediately went under contract to Four Star Television. Sometime that spring, we were abruptly told to turn off the lights and leave our office because the Writers Guild had been unable to negotiate a new agreement with the Alliance (the studios).

It looked like it was going to be a lengthy stoppage so we returned to our favorite city, New York, and sublet an apartment from Stuart Rosenberg, who would go on to direct *Cool Hand Luke* and many other motion pictures and television shows. Dick and I were both bachelors at the time and we looked at this huge, multi-roomed, rent-controlled apartment, on the corner of 72nd and Broadway, with a good deal of awe. Rosenberg had a vast, wonderful library brimming with great novels and the rent was reasonable. What more could two out-of-work writers ask for? We found out later that he had been a lit teacher in a previous, non-showbiz existence. We also found out years later that, coincidentally, he and Peter Falk were friends. In fact, in his very first movie, Rosenberg had directed Peter in *Murder Inc.*, for which Peter would earn an Oscar nomination.

We hunkered down in the apartment and were immediately confronted with the eternal writer's dilemma: what to write?

Happily, we were also readers and students of the microscopic, sometimes duplicitous, boilerplate in contracts. The Writers Guild stipulated you couldn't write for filmed television during the strike, but you had free rein for the live variety.

Luckily for Link and Levinson, there was the *Chevy Mystery Show,* a summer replacement for the vacationing singer Dinah Shore. Mysteries were right up our alley. We had sold many short stories to *Ellery Queen* and *Alfred Hitchcock* magazines. In fact in the late '60s, we went on to create the private eye series *Mannix*. This turned out to be our first big television hit, which ran for eight years on CBS. We sat down, with the bookshelves filled with Proust and Thomas Mann staring malevolently down at us, and knocked out a spec script called *Enough Rope*. Our agent said the Chevy show would never buy it. We insisted he submit it. He did. It was bought within three days.

We flew back to the coast and saw our script performed live at NBC Burbank studio. The strike now settled, we moved back into our office at Four Star.

Something kept buzzing around in the back of our heads: *Enough Rope* could be converted easily into a stage play, and the theater had been one of our passions since childhood. I remember my mother taking me to see my very first play, *Life with Father*. I was in my Sunday go-to-church attire: navy blazer, white shirt, necktie, and flannels. In those dear, departed days, the theater was an event and you dressed accordingly. I saw many plays and musicals with family and friends because Philadelphia was one of the tryout towns before the shows ventured to face the critics' arbitrary bayonets on Broadway.

We left Four Star and metamorphosed the script into a stage vehicle—which was immediately optioned by Paul Gregory, a very successful Broadway producer at the time. With the theatrically dynamite cast of Joseph Cotten, Agnes Moorehead, and the great character actor Thomas Mitchell, the play ran for a year and a half all over the U.S. and Canada.

When the play (now retitled *Prescription: Murder* or *Rx Murder*) opened in San Francisco, we realized to our surprise that during the curtain calls, Mitchell, playing the cop, received the most enthusiastic applause, not the star and popular movie actor Joseph Cotten. This was indeed a conundrum.

We had seen the cop, Lieutenant Columbo, as just another of our clever, but nothing-to-write-home-about, homicide lieutenants. Sure, Mitchell was a superb actor and some of his lines and moves got big laughs, but come on! The star was Joseph Cotten. And yet the cop character as written had an undeniable appeal, a special Everyman quality. A man who hid his cleverness under a bushel, whose charm appealed to the audience.

Years later I met the actor Bert Freed at a party. I told him that he had been the very first Columbo in the live, NBC production. He was astonished. "You talking about that big hit TV series with Peter Falk?" He was dumbfounded. He had had such a successful career as a character actor in so many shows that he had totally forgotten that Sunday night stint as the cop.

We call this Actor's Amnesia.

We sold the play to Universal which put us under a seven-year contract, after which we stayed on. Our years at Universal were probably the most creative of our lives. After Dick's terribly premature death in 1987, I stayed on, becoming an almost permanent fixture, writing and producing for twenty-five years all told. The most popular thing we accomplished there was the launching of the *Columbo* television series, starring the inestimable Mr. Falk.

We have been asked in many interviews how we chose Peter. Interviewers are astonished when they find out he wasn't our first choice. Bing Crosby was. Were we out of our collective gourds? Hold on. Think about the Crosby persona: cool, intelligent (when he wasn't playing a doofus with Bob Hope in their *Road* pictures), pipe-smoking (instead of a cigar), funny. But Crosby turned down the script with a nice letter, saying he'd rather play golf than act at this point in his life. We were stumped: who would we go to next?

And then destiny paid a visit in the form of a phone call from Peter Falk. We had known Peter in New York in late 1958 when we had the same agent. At the time, Peter was just beginning his career with stage and television roles and we were beginning ours after Army service. We used to have occasional breakfasts with him at a drugstore on Broadway. He was an extremely likable, down-to-earth, bright guy.

I remember taking the phone call that morning in our office at Universal. "I just read that script of yours," he said in that now famous gravelly voice, "and I'll kill to play that cop."

How he had gotten the script we didn't know. But the more we thought about him, the more perfect he seemed: very New York, not a handsome leading man. We didn't want handsome. Falk was an excellent actor: intelligent, not particularly well-groomed on-screen or off, with a terrific, offbeat sense of humor. How come someone so perfect had been totally off our casting map?

I remember sitting in the screening room watching the first dailies of our television adaptation of *Prescription: Murder*. Falk "came off the screen," as we Hollywoodites like to say. His hesitant, gruff, humorous, but basically very human persona was exactly what we wanted in our cop. An Everyman in a raincoat with cigar.

We shot two two-hour World Premiere films with Peter, *Prescription: Murder* and *Ransom for a Dead Man*. Both debuted at number one in the ratings. NBC was ecstatic. And network ecstasy is about as rare as finding a best-selling romance author who can really write. Or an honest financial accounting from a studio.

Herb Schlosser, who was then the head of programming at the network, was suddenly adamant about doing a series with the character, but Falk wasn't interested. He had already failed in a series (*The Trials of O'Brien*) and he much preferred doing just a few shows a year in a 90-minute format. But of course his indifference could have been a ploy to get more money.

A numero uno actor usually got exactly what a numero uno wished. And thus, *Columbo* became a limited series (six hour- and-a-half films a year) and an instant hit. A TV Guide cover proclaimed "America Discovers *Columbo*." A few months later the rest of the world did too.

Winston Churchill once said that success is never final. In *Columbo*'s case he was right on target. Universal informed me recently that the show plays off and on in almost every country that has television, once a day in France, twice a day in Monaco.

Perhaps it's time to dismantle a few myths. Peter Falk does not like cigars. He was a cigarette smoker until he gave them up more than ten years ago. The raincoat was not provided by the studio wardrobe department, it was Peter's, bought on 57th Street in New York when he ducked into a clothing store during an unexpected rain squall. The Smithsonian even requested the raincoat. Columbo does not have a first name, even though a popular Canadian board game said it was Phillip! When Peter is asked, he always retorts that Columbo's first name is Lieutenant.

Fans have written me: When will we meet this wife Columbo is always talking about? The short answer: never. Dick and I made a pact with Peter at the very beginning of the series that the wife would always remain off-screen. Why? To keep the audience intrigued, of course.

Fred Silverman, who was then head of NBC, put an ill-fated *Mrs. Columbo* on the air. We were asked to be involved, but we declined.

Where did we get the name Columbo? That is a question Dick and I were asked in probably a hundred interviews over the years. We just didn't remember. There had been a nightclub in Philadelphia named Palumbo's. There was a crime family in New York with a man named Joe Colombo at its head but we had never heard of it or him.

A few years after Dick died, I was browsing in Maurice Neville, a bookstore in Santa Barbara. I stumbled on a volume, the *Collected Works of A.J. Liebling*. Liebling was a first-rate journalist for *The New Yorker* who wrote essays about his two lifetime passions: food and boxing. I paged through the book and suddenly the name Columbo jumped out at me like a punch to the solar plexus.

Liebling had written an essay about one of my favorite fighters, Rocky Marciano, who retired undefeated as the heavyweight champion of the world. It seemed Marciano's next door neighbor and boyhood pal became his fight trainer. Guy by the name of Allie Colombo. It's true that one has a "u" and the other has an "o", but we had never seen Allie's name written.

Is this where we got the name? I remember having seen a rerun of a Marciano fight on TV in Stuart Rosenberg's apartment that spring. During that fight, Allie Colombo's name was mentioned. But can I really say, a half-century later, that that was the genesis of Columbo?

You might ask why I decided to write these stories. Good question, but the answer is very simple: Columbo was the most popular character Dick and I ever created. So why not continue his adventures between the covers of a book? It would be a first, and we always prided ourselves on being first with what we wrote. When we penned the original script we had no idea how the play and what followed would end up entertaining millions.

You have in your hands the publication of the very first Columbo short stories. So just settle down in your favorite chair, put on your detective hat, and enjoy the raincoated, cigar-puffing sleuth back on his usual homicide beat.

William Link
Los Angeles, California
February 2010

AUTHOR'S NOTE: In the following stories LAPD Detective Columbo investigates murders in various jurisdictions, which I am told is out of the ordinary. So, the author, myself, has taken what is jokingly referred to as author's convenience. This allows the good Lieutenant to investigate wherever he pleases. This is extremely unusual as you and I, dear reader, know, but we also know that Columbo is a highly unusual cop. So let's give him a long enough leash so he can bring these dastardly murderers to justice.

To WILLIAM LINK,

IT WAS A PLEASURE TO
DRAW LT. COLUMBO!
ON BEHALF OF EVERYONE
IN THE WORLD, THANK YOU
FOR THIS ICONIC CHARACTER.
HE IS A HERO WE NEED NOW
MORE THAN EVER!

JOE DATOR
10/31/2020

With awards crowding shelf after shelf in his Los Angeles home, William Link was no stranger to accolades. But, as a life-long cartoonist whose own work had been publicly exhibited, one tribute had special significance for Bill: Artist Joe Dator's "Rediscovering Columbo in 2020," which appeared on *The New Yorker*'s website in October of that year.

Dator's illustrated essay captured the essence of the series — how one unprepossessing working-class cop fought and vanquished the rich and powerful adversaries who smugly assumed they could pull the wool over this scruffy sheep's eyes. Among other delights of writing and acting, *Columbo* offered the most entertaining class warfare imaginable.

Bill adored Dator's warm and witty salute and sent the artist a note of appreciation. Dator responded with the following drawing. It is reprinted here with his kind permission.

No doubt about it: Lieutenant Columbo — envisioned by William Link and Richard Levinson, embodied by Peter Falk — is a detective for the ages.

TRANCE

THE ANNUAL POLICE CHARITY EVENT for a local disadvantaged children's home began late Saturday afternoon. The performances started at seven with a packed house of cops and members of their families. Columbo was there with his teenage niece, Julia. His wife unfortunately had a church raffle that evening and couldn't come with them.

There was a ventriloquist and a singer and then the star of the evening—Marc Whitfield, hypnotist extraordinaire!

Whitfield was a handsome, six-foot, theatrical-looking man in his forties with black hair and incongruous silver sideburns. He radiated authority—much more, unfortunately, than most of the men watching him. His intense, deep-set, coal-black eyes raked the room looking for, what some suspected, would be his "victims."

The audience erupted with laughter when he chose Sergeant Bart Sawyer and Sergeant Ernie McMillan, two of the most popular men on the force. Their disparities made them almost a comedy team.

Sawyer was crisply good-looking and well-built, but McMillan was cute with a round face and a growing paunch. He had been warned he would face disciplinary measures if he failed to get his weight down.

Whitfield guided them to folding chairs before he said to McMillan, "Ever ride a bike when you were a kid?"

"Yeah. Got one for Christmas when I was twelve."

"Good."

He took less than a minute putting both men "under" as he called it with a few soft, intimate words and a little tap of his finger to each of their foreheads. They slumped slightly in their chairs, their heads drooping down on their chests as if they had begun to enjoy what Whitfield had told them would be a "deep, peaceful sleep."

It was then that he brought out a luscious young woman and led her to a chair near the two men.

"Ms. Monica Hall," he announced to the audience. "Ms. Hall is a well-known model here in town and New York."

The woman's entrance was followed by Whitfield's assistant wheeling a bicycle out on stage.

Columbo's niece nudged his arm. "Have you seen him do this before, Unc?"

"Nope."

Whitfield asked his two subjects to rise. "Sergeant McMillan," he said in a quietly forceful voice, "do you see that beautiful new sports car?" He indicated the bicycle. "Wouldn't you like to take it out for a spin?"

McMillan dutifully mounted the bicycle.

"Now I want you to pedal very slowly around the stage. Please be careful."

McMillan began a wide, shaky circle around the hypnotist and Sergeant Sawyer.

"Now, Sergeant Sawyer — do you see that sports car speeding near you? Isn't it your duty to stop that reckless driver and give him a ticket?"

The audience, mesmerized, a few wives tittering, suddenly broke into laughter as Sawyer waved his hand for McMillan and the bicycle to stop. He wrote out something on an imaginary pad and handed it to McMillan, who gave him a justifiably angry look. The audience applauded, seemingly unheard by the two participants.

"Very good," Whitfield congratulated Sawyer. He instructed McMillan to leave the bike. "Sit," he said to McMillan, who went back to his chair.

"Now, Sergeant Sawyer, I *know* you want to restrain that reckless driver you just ticketed. Your further duty would be to handcuff him, would it not?"

Sawyer removed the cuffs from his belt and proceeded to handcuff McMillan, who sat calmly unperturbed with a simple smile on his face.

"And now, Sergeant Sawyer," Whitfield continued, "you need to hide the key. Do you see that woman police officer to your right?"

The audience laughed, not quite anticipating what Whitfield was up to.

"Why don't you go to her and let *her* hide the key."

Sawyer went slowly over to the woman and handed her the key. With a sly, lascivious smile she dropped it down inside her bodice.

Big laugh from the audience.

"What's he up to?" Julia asked Columbo, who shrugged.

The hypnotist whispered something to McMillan before he spoke to both of them. "You are going to wake now. You will feel perfectly relaxed and refreshed like you've just returned from a wonderful day at the beach."

He snapped his fingers under McMillan's chin and slowly he emerged from his trance. McMillan grinned as the audience applauded. And then he noticed that his hands were cuffed!

Somebody shouted, "Hey Ernie—you better pay that ticket!"

Laughter. Another shout: "And you better get back on the scale!"

Now Whitfield snapped his fingers under Sawyer's chin. After the man came slowly awake, he said, "Could I have your handcuffs, officer?"

Sawyer felt around behind his belt, perplexed. "I—I don't have 'em," he said lamely. Then, smiling, to Whitfield: "You're going to get me in real trouble. What did you do with them?" Then Whitfield pointed and he saw them on McMillan, and the audience exploded in laughter.

"The key to the handcuffs," Whitfield said. "Where could it be, Sergeant Sawyer?"

Sawyer went directly to Ms. Hall. Before she could prevent him, he tried to reach down the front of her blouse.

"Sergeant!" she modestly exclaimed. She extracted the key herself, gave it to him.

This engendered the biggest audience reaction of the evening.

"This guy's really good," Columbo said to his niece.

"Do you think maybe they're playing along with him, Unc? That maybe they're not hypnotized at all?"

"Nah. Sure looks real to me."

Sawyer unlocked the handcuffs on his friend. Whitfield thanked both of them to tremendous applause and cheers. He dismissed them, thanked Ms. Hall, and bowed to the audience as the clapping continued.

"Think he'll give me his autograph?" Julia asked him.

"Nothing wrong with trying."

Columbo had dropped his niece off after a bite at Barney's Beanery. He had almost reached his house when his police radio clattered on. "Lieutenant Columbo?"

"Yes?"

"Proceed to 723 North Lynwood. Report of homicide."

Columbo stifled a yawn, no rest for the weary. "On my way."

723 was a garden court apartment, little lavender lights in the shrubbery casting a strange glow that made the leaves look wet. There was a convoy of black-and-whites and a medical van parked on the street out front when Columbo arrived.

He entered the apartment, swallowing a yawn, where all the activity seemed centered. The hand on his wristwatch edged midnight.

Members of the tech team were all over the living room and bedroom. Most of the furniture looked brand new and there was a brave moth flying around a pale floor lamp. One of the men pointed Columbo to the bedroom.

Sergeant Pagano greeted him as he came in. There was a body near a double bed and the police photographer was taking pictures. The victim appeared to be a woman, a splash of blonde hair vivid against the colorless carpet.

"You at the show tonight?" Pagano asked him.

"Yeah. The dispatcher caught me going home."

Pagano laughed. "You don't look too happy about it. What's the old saying?

Through rain and snow, through—I forget."

Columbo smiled. "They say that about mailmen, Sergeant."

"Oh! You're right. Anyway, reason I asked about the show. The victim here, female, late thirties, strangled—name of Ilene Louise Whitfield."

Columbo blinked, his tiredness suddenly evaporating. "Whitfield. That hypnotist tonight—his name was Marc Whitfield. The wife?"

"We're checking, trying to get hold of him."

It was then that the tangle of investigators parted, and Columbo saw Sergeant McMillan being questioned in a corner of the room.

"McMillan," he said, puzzled. "What's he doing here?"

"Says he found the body. For some reason, he doesn't know why he came over here after the show. He saw the dead woman and split. A neighbor saw him wandering like in a daze outside, called us."

"Back up," Columbo said, more than puzzled now. "He doesn't know why he came over here? Did he know the woman?"

"Says he never saw her before in his life." Now Pagano

looked puzzled. "We shined a light in his eyes. He really looked like a guy on drugs or in some kind of trance."

Columbo strung the word out, "Trance ... interesting."

"Interesting how?"

Columbo moved closer to the body. "Whitfield hypnotized him tonight. But he came out of the trance and...." His voice wandered off.

"And?" Pagano prodded. He saw Columbo was staring down at the carpet.

"What are those?" Columbo asked, kneeling down now and peering at something. "They look like beads."

"They are. When the woman was strangled, her necklace broke and the beads got scattered around on the rug."

Columbo got heavily to his feet, walked over to a closed closet door near the bed. He got a handkerchief from his pocket and covered his hand. He opened the door and peered inside. "How do you like that," he muttered. "One of the beads even rolled in here."

"Columbo," Pagano called, like to a truant child, trying to mask his exasperation, "it's getting late and we got a murder to solve."

Columbo came back over to him, stuffing the handkerchief back in his pocket.

"So what's worrying you?" Pagano asked.

"Nothing. Just wondering if my wife won anything at the church raffle tonight."

Pagano shook his head: this guy was too much. "Listen, go home. Go to bed, get some sleep. We've got this thing covered for now."

Columbo nodded, still in one of his deep-dish thinking moods. He nodded again at Pagano without really seeing him, and went slowly toward the living room. Then he suddenly stopped—and turned back.

"You think," he said, "you think somebody could kill somebody while they were in a trance?"

Pagano laughed. "You should know about trances, Lieutenant. You've been in enough of them yourself."

Columbo grinned. "Yeah. That's where I get most of my best ideas. G'night, Sergeant."

The next morning Columbo faced Sergeant McMillan in the interrogation room. Columbo was in a pretty good mood, his wife having won five bills last night which would go toward a new 42" TV for the living room.

McMillan looked sleepless and anxious, his perpetual cheerfulness seemingly shattered at the garden court apartment. All Columbo knew about him was that he was long divorced and had a daughter in college.

"Tell me about this trance," Columbo asked, sitting down. He never lit a cigar in the little room, it always annoyed the person in the hot seat. There was a word, interrogator, he thought, but no word for the guy across the desk. Interrogatee? Strange.

"I don't know. I left the auditorium after the show and got in my car. And—and it seemed like I was driving around forever — and then it seemed I had to be somewhere. Isn't that strange?"

"Did it seem like you were being directed or something?"

McMillan nodded so hard his chin bumped his chest. "Yeah! Exactly. I knew what I was doing but I didn't know *why* I was doing it. Does that make any sense?"

Columbo's hand went pensively to his mouth before he realized he didn't have a cigar. "This Whitfield fella put you in a trance in his show. But he woke you up."

"Yeah, and I felt great. One of the guys later told me what he did. Pretty funny."

"Yeah, it was."

Columbo leaned back in his chair, looking up at the long tube of fluorescent lighting in the ceiling. It was sort of restful. "This is important, Sergeant. Before Whitfield woke you up from the trance ... I saw him whispering something to you."

McMillan seemed startled, some color surfacing in his pale, pudgy face. "You know ... in a way, I was aware of everything he was making us do in his act. Like I was sitting in the audience watching myself. And I *do* remember him telling me something."

Columbo moved his chair a little closer. "What did he say to you?"

"I—I don't remember."

"Did he tell you not to remember what he said?"

McMillan's hands twisted on the table. "I don't know. Maybe."

Columbo got up, realized there was no room to really pace much. He made a circuit around the table and returned to sit down in his chair. "Do you think," he said, "that Whit-field could have given you what they call a post-hypnotic suggestion?"

"I heard of something like that. But what would he tell me?"

"That you should go and kill his wife?"

Now McMillan's fingers fought each other like snakes. Embarrassed, he dragged his hands to the edge of the table, let them drop like expended combatants to his lap. "I would never do that, Lieutenant. Never!"

"And you had never been to that apartment before?"

"No. And the woman was an absolute stranger to me."

"And you were drawn to the place." Columbo paused, thinking. "How did you get in?"

"I guess the door wasn't locked."

Columbo put his hands on the table. "Why'd you go in the bedroom?"

"I don't know. Instinct? When I saw the body I ran out. Not very far, down the little walk, actually. One of the neighbors, a woman, saw me, and took me back to the apartment."

"Because you told her about the body."

"I guess."

"Okay," Columbo said, getting up. "That'll be all for today, Sergeant."

McMillan blinked at him. "You're not putting me under arrest or anything. Are you?"

Columbo shook his head. "You're free to go. Assume your regular duties." He went to the door.

"Hey Lieutenant, wait. You really think Whitfield told me to kill his wife?"

"I don't know. But if he did—that would make both of you implicated in the murder, wouldn't it?"

Before McMillan could answer he was out the door.

Marc Whitfield's condominium was in one of the older buildings on Wilshire near Westwood that still managed to look contemporary. Columbo rang the doorbell on the ninth floor and waited only a few seconds before Whitfield opened it.

It was noon but the hypnotist was still in a dressing gown, his theatrical hair tangled and ungroomed. He looked uncharacteristically unsure of himself, depressed, a far cry from the authoritarian master hypnotist of the previous evening. Columbo showed him his credentials and followed him into the living room, designer shades blocking out the strong sunlight.

"Sit down," Whitfield said. "You'll have to excuse me, but I'm still trying to get my head straight. I just can't believe Ilene was murdered. And your people said McMillan, of all people, found her!"

Columbo watched him bring a hand to his forehead before he asked, "You and your wife lived separately?"

"Yes. We had our ... differences and she moved out. Rented an apartment about fifteen minutes from here."

"Were you ever there, Mr. Whitfield?"

"No. We really hadn't been on speaking terms for a while. I wanted her to come back so we could work things out, but she refused."

"If I could ask—what seemed to be the difficulty?"

Whitfield drank coffee from a cup on a nearby table. "I had an ongoing profession and she was trying to get started in an acting career. There was a resentment." He smiled grimly. "Never have a wife who wants an acting career, Lieutenant."

"Oh no, sir. My wife's quite happy keeping house, gardening, doing things at the church."

Whitfield's hand, returning the cup to the saucer, was shaking. "I still loved her. That's why something like this is so devastating." He suddenly jerked upright in his chair. "Why are you asking me these questions? You're supposed to be out there, looking for Ilene's murderer."

Columbo smiled. "You know, I saw your show last night, Mr. Whitfield."

He nodded glumly.

"I wanted to ask you—Sergeant McMillan—who found your wife's body? You think he was still in a trance?"

Whitfield stared at him. "I know we're the third planet from the sun, but you, Lieutenant, are in a whole other solar system. I brought him *out of the trance*! You said you were there, don't you remember?"

"Oh sure, sure, I remember that. But can't people go back under some time later?"

"Only if they're instructed to do that by the hypnotist. It's very unusual."

"Well, well that's what I'm getting at, sir. You whispered

a few things to him before you woke him up, and I'm wondering what they were."

Now Whitfield leaned back, on the verge of laughing, his grim mood dissipated. "Whispered to him? What? That he should go murder my wife?!"

"I didn't say that, sir. What exactly *did* you whisper to him?"

Whitfield poured himself more coffee from a canister on the coffee table. "I told him when he woke up to notice the handcuffs. I wanted that laugh from the audience."

Columbo mulled this over.

"You seem—dissatisfied, Lieutenant. What's the problem?"

"I don't know—seemed like you told him a couple more things."

Whitfield got up, raised the motorized window shades with a remote. Sunlight flooded the room with the sudden bright noise of traffic on Wilshire.

"I wish we had taped my performance last night," Whitfield said, returning to his chair. "You would have seen that I spoke very briefly to Sergeant McMillan. As a policeman you should know that witnesses like yourself sometimes expand time, sometimes even compress it, rarely give a totally accurate account."

More mulling. "Why do you think the Sergeant left the auditorium and went to your wife's apartment—a place he says he had never been before?"

"If I was a mystery writer, Lieutenant, instead of a hypnotist, I could maybe give you an answer to that question. Why don't you ask Sergeant McMillan?"

"I already did. He talks about being in some kind of trance that made him drive there."

"You want some coffee?" Whitfield said. "I'm afraid it's a little cold, but I can heat some up."

"No thanks. How would he know where to go?"

Whitfield smiled, totally at his ease now. "You mean I also whispered my wife's address to him? And told him exactly how to get there, even though I didn't know myself?"

All Columbo could do was shrug.

Columbo met Pagano for lunch at his chili joint on Santa Monica, sitting at his favorite table.

The first thing Pagano said after he sat down was, "McMillan knew Ilene Whitfield."

This was unexpected news to Columbo, who was digging in his shirt pocket for a cigar even though he couldn't smoke it. "How did he know her?" he asked Pagano.

"This was something we suspected but we couldn't get anybody to talk about. Now the murder's blown the whole thing wide open."

Columbo knew the Sergeant was savoring this revelation, so he didn't hurry him along.

"McMillan was involved with a prostitution ring right here in Beverly Hills. Very high-priced hookers working at the most expensive hotels."

"McMillan ... " Columbo mused, thinking of the man's friendly, overweight persona. "Seems really out of character."

"Yeah, that's why it took us so long to nail him. It turns out this Ilene Whitfield scouted the women, ran their business while McMillan made sure law enforcement was kept in the dark."

"So that's how he knew where Ilene lived."

"Right. But we still don't have a motive if he killed her."

Columbo put the unlit cigar in his mouth. "Where is he?"

"We didn't hold him this morning, but you can be sure we'll be picking him up posthaste," Pagano said. "You see where I'm going with this?" signaling the waiter for service.

"Oh yeah. He could claim Whitfield gave him a post-hypnotic suggestion to kill his wife. He was just an innocent instrument programmed by proxy by the real murderer. We on the same page here?"

Pagano nodded enthusiastically. The waiter came and took their orders. Chili for both, onions on Columbo's.

"We gotta get a legal opinion on this," Columbo said. "*And* a psychological one too."

Pagano smiled. "That's why I invited our shrink Dr. Laventhal to join us for lunch."

It was only after they had finished their chili that Doctor Loraine Laventhal arrived. She was a sleek brunette in her forties with black plastic hornrims that seemed to weigh down her not unattractive face.

There was a minimum of small talk before the Doctor ordered a sandwich and they got down to business.

"What do you know about hypnosis?" Columbo asked her, holding the cigar in his hand.

"Don't light that," she said.

"Oh, no way, ma'am, it's not allowed."

"To answer your question, Lieutenant, I'm hardly an expert on hypnosis. What do you wish to know?"

"If somebody's given a post-hypnotic suggestion do they necessarily have to carry it out?"

Doctor Laventhal waited until the waiter had set down her sandwich before she replied. "It would depend on what the suggestion is."

"What if the suggestion was that the subject should go kill somebody?"

She considered this. "As I said, I'm not an expert — but I think it would depend on the subject's moral-ethical orientation and control factor."

"Meaning?" Pagano asked.

"Meaning if murder was abhorrent to that person he would not carry out any harmful post-hypnotic suggestion under any circumstances."

Pagano looked at Columbo. "Congratulations. We're right back where we started. So McMillan was in an illegal business with the woman. But why would he want to kill her? And what would be Whitfield's motive in trying to make him do that? And how could he count on McMillan doing it?"

"I gotta tell you, Sergeant," Columbo said. "You ask some very good questions."

Columbo stood in the hot sun outside the Ferguson Funeral home in Westwood. An older man came out and went to his car in the adjacent parking lot. Then Whitfield, dressed in various elegant tones of black, came out. He stopped dead, spotting Columbo.

"What are *you* doing here? Isn't this at least off-limits when a man's arranging his wife's funeral?"

"That's why I didn't want to disturb you inside, sir. I waited out here and boy, is it hot!"

Whitfield shook his head, strode past him on the way to his car in the lot. Columbo tagged along, trying to keep up. "You mind if I come with you, Mr. Whitfield?"

Resigned: "If you must."

They got into Whitfield's car, an old, spanking-clean, black Mercedes sedan.

"This is some clean car," Columbo said.

Whitfield pulled out of the lot into L.A.'s usual dense traffic on Westwood Boulevard.

"And it looks like you just had it washed. Some people, I guess, would never think of doing that when a loved one was murdered."

Whitfield took this in stride. "A man comes every week, takes the car to be washed. So I'm not as heartless as you imply. Now *what* are you doing here?"

"Just part of the investigation. Did you know your wife ran a prostitution ring with Sergeant McMillan?"

Whitfield almost swerved off the street, cars honking in the opposite lane. He gave Columbo a very brief, incredulous look.

"I take it you knew nothing about that?" Columbo asked.

"You're out of your mind."

"Didn't you get a little suspicious when she suddenly had a lot of money?"

"I told you we were at odds. After she moved out I rarely saw her."

"I mean, didn't you have any inkling she had something going on?"

Whitfield sighed deeply. "I must've had my head up my can." A thought occurred to him: "Partnered with McMillan. There you go—he probably had a good reason to kill her."

Columbo's look was guileless. "Why do you say that?"

"Aren't there always problems that business partners have? Comes with the territory."

"Not necessarily, sir. But if he was in a trance—"

Whitfield interrupted. "Back to that, are you? Well, for the sake of argument, let's say he *was* in a trance. It would give him a perfect opportunity to kill Ilene because he had a motive."

Columbo was following along. "Uh-huh, uh-huh. But then we got the same old question, sir—why did you put him in the trance. And all that whispering."

Whitfield was fed-up, but he managed a smile. "I'm going to my lawyer's office in Century City. Any place I can drop you off—within reason?"

"Hey!" Columbo exclaimed. "I forgot—I left my car back at the funeral home."

Whitfield's smile had only a modicum of meanness. "Well, I can't take you all the way back there, I'm late already."

"Don't worry about it, sir. I can get one of the boys to pick me up."

"Fine." He still wore the smile, a trifle condescending now. "I guess it's always nice to have 'the boys' at your beck and call." The smile twisted. "Maybe they can solve this thing for you too."

Columbo was back in the interrogation room with McMillan. This time the cop was in a prisoner's orange jumpsuit and he looked in need of a shave and a lawyer, although he probably had the latter by now.

"Ernie," Columbo said with a wince of genuine sympathy, "why did you get into this prostitution thing in the first place? You had a good record, you were well-liked, you had everything."

"My daughter. I had to get her into a good college, and you know what they cost these days, forty grand or more a year with books and dorms and all the other shit. Besides—Karen took the divorce damn hard. She's been with a shrink for the past two years. They charge through the roof, too. I know that's no excuse, Columbo."

He made no comment. "How'd you meet the victim?"

"We booked a prostie and she told me she had once worked for Ilene Whitfield. So—so we got together, Ilene and me. I had to watch it, though."

"You mean because you were a working cop?"

McMillan looked at Columbo as if he was terminally naive. "That and something else. The husband, the hypnotist, was obsessively jealous. Ilene couldn't make a phone call without him trying to listen in. Once she thought he had even tapped the phones in the house."

Columbo drummed fingers on the table. "That's why she moved into the apartment?"

"Yeah. They were on that fast freeway to Freedom Land."

Columbo, flexing his fingers: "Change of subject, Ernie. When you went into the bedroom that night—what were you aware of? I mean even in your trance."

His eyes rolled back in reflection. "I don't know. The body, of course. The eyes were bulging so I figured strangulation and there was no blood I could see. And — and there were beads on the floor. Like from a pearl necklace."

"She was wearing a necklace," Columbo said. "It broke

when she was strangled and the beads fell all over the carpet. . . There was nobody else when you walked in?"

"Are you kidding? Nobody. But I'll tell you, I got outta there like the goddamn place was on fire."

Columbo got up, stretched. "Thanks, Ernie. I'll try to do what I can to help you."

McMillan almost got up himself. "Does that mean you don't think I did it?"

Columbo smiled. "Jury's out. And there's not even a jury yet!"

Whitfield was hosting a small gathering of friends and relatives at his condo after the memorial. There was a bar tended by a white-coated African-American and a table with a vast array of catered cold snacks and soft drinks.

He was talking to a distant cousin when he saw Columbo come in, stand in the foyer, surveying the guests like he was trying to get his bearings.

He excused himself to the cousin and went over to him. "I don't remember inviting you," he said.

"I don't think police business requires an invitation."

Whitfield detected a new note of hardness in his tone. "Come with me," he said, matching his tone.

He led Columbo, weaving around some of the mourners, into his study, firmly closing the door. He dropped down in the chair behind his desk, picking up a letter opener and slapping it a few times against his palm. "So why have you gate-crashed my wife's memorial?"

Columbo was looking down at the traffic on Wilshire.

"Lieutenant? ... You know what I think?"

"No, sir."

"I think *you* think I murdered her."

Columbo turned from the window, his face expressionless. "Why would you think something like that?"

"You've got the perfect suspect, Ernie McMillan, and for some inexplicable reason you're hounding *me*. Is it because he's a cop and you guys protect your own?"

Columbo gave this some thought. "Tell you what, Mr. Whitfield, since you brought it up—just for the record, where did you go after your performance at the theater?"

Whitfield smiled, still slapping the letter opener. "Good. You're finally letting it all hang out. 'For the record,' as you put it, my sister was at the performance. We went back to her house for an hour or two. Somehow your people tracked me down there and informed me that my wife had been murdered."

"Interesting. Would you have your sister's phone number?" Whitfield got up, galvanized. "I can do better than that." He went quickly to the door, opened it, and called something out to someone in the assemblage.

A few moments later, a small, unassuming woman dressed in black came into the room. She was younger than Whitfield but not by much. It was obvious she had none of the preening authority of her brother.

"Norma, I'd like to introduce you to Lieutenant Columbo. He's investigating Ilene's murder."

Columbo nodded at the woman. "I know this isn't the best time, ma'am, but I'd like to ask you a few questions."

The woman nodded back.

"You were present the night your brother performed at the police event?"

"Yes ... I was. What's this all this about, Lieutenant?"

"Just getting a timeline, ma'am. And after the performance you and your brother left the auditorium and went where?"

"To my home." Her voice was small like her stature, but surprisingly strong.

"And how long were you two there?"

She thought. "For a while. Until Marc got that terrible call from the police that Ilene ... that Ilene was dead."

"Go ahead," Whitfield said, "ask her if I was in her presence the whole time."

"Were you, ma'am?"

She looked confused. "Yes. Of course. What *is* this all about?"

Before Columbo could answer, Whitfield said, "The Lieutenant is hunting around for a murder suspect, and it seems I'm on his list."

The woman stared angrily at Columbo. "How could you *possibly* think such a thing? My brother loved Ilene. I know they had separated, but that doesn't mean he wanted to kill her."

"I understand that, ma'am. I think your brother is maybe jumping to some conclusions here."

She shot daggers at him: "I think *you're* jumping to conclusions. Is this the way you people operate?"

Whitfield took her by the arm, pivoted her toward the door. "I don't think the Lieutenant has any more questions to ask you. *Do you*, Lieutenant?"

Columbo was back at the window. "No. I want to thank you, ma'am. You've been very cooperative."

She firmly asserted, "My brother's a good man." Then she went out and Whitfield closed the door.

"Satisfied?" he asked.

Columbo was watching the traffic again. "You think your sister would take a lie detector test?"

Whitfield, back behind the desk, abruptly flung the paper opener down on the blotter. "You're a real son-of-a-bitch, you know that?"

Columbo came over to him. "She's your sister, Mr. Whitfield. She loves you, so maybe she'd lie for you. You know how families are. My aunt Anna, she sees her husband fall down the stairs dead drunk. She tells people he's as sober as a judge. And she'd swear to it on the Holy Book."

Whitfield's face closed. He sat silently for a long time. Then: "I'm sure Norma would agree to take a polygraph test. I'll speak to her."

"I'd really appreciate that, sir. Save me from getting a court order."

Whitfield was silent again. Then: "So I'm your guy. I'm feeling a big target burning on my back."

"I'm looking in all directions, sir."

"What did I call you? Incorrigible. Good luck, Lieutenant. You're going full speed down a dead-end alley."

Pagano caught Columbo in a corridor of the precinct house. "You got Sullivan testing some woman on the lie box. A Norma Whitfield. Whitfield's sister, niece?"

"Sister."

Pagano gave him a hard look. "What's the deal?"

"Let's say I'm interested in where Whitfield was around the time his wife was murdered. He claims he was with the sister."

The hard look turned cynical. "*Claims*, Columbo?"

"Just covering all the bases, Sergeant."

Later that afternoon, Columbo learned that Norma Whitfield had passed the polygraph test. In the opinion of their expert, she hadn't lied about her brother being with her after the performance that night. The hypnotist had his alibi.

The sky had turned dark. Columbo was driving, a few anticipatory raindrops stinging the hood. For some reason, he found himself heading along San Vincente Boulevard near Ilene Whitfield's garden apartment. Some buried instinct was drawing him like a magnet, but he knew he wasn't in a trance. There was a recurring image of a broken necklace in his mind and he couldn't figure out why.

There was a cop outside the apartment, who gestured to Columbo that the door was unlocked.

Columbo went in. The living room looked much the same. The rain had started in earnest now, noisily pelting the roof.

He went into the bedroom, also much the same except that there was no body and the beads were no longer on the carpet. He stood for a long moment on the threshold, the rain beating down on the shrubbery, his eyes fixed on the closed closet door. There was virtually no space under the door, so there was no way a bead could have rolled into the closet unless it was open—or just partly open.

The cop followed Columbo into the apartment. "Can I help you with anything, Lieutenant?"

"No. No, thanks, Officer. I just wanted to check something out. Does that phone over there work?"

"I believe so."

Columbo made a quick call to a member of the tech team. The rain was coming down much stronger when he hung up.

"You want to wait till this squall tapers off?" the cop asked as he watched Columbo going to the door.

"Nah, no problem," Columbo said, raising his voice over the storm, "I got a raincoat."

Whitfield entered the interrogation room, Columbo right behind him. He sat down and asked, "Why have you brought me down here? I heard my sister's polygraph checked out."

Columbo sat down across from him. "It did, sir. A-OK."

"So is this just some more of your police harassment?"

"Nothing like that. This is a little more serious."

Whitfield laughed. "That, coming from you, sounds like a gross understatement."

Columbo didn't smile. "You murdered your wife, Mr. Whitfield. You're an intensely jealous man. I think you were jealous of her because of what you thought was a clandestine sexual relationship she had with Sergeant McMillan—not knowing it was strictly a business relationship. And she had already crushed your ego by moving out."

"What are you now—an amateur psychiatrist?"

"You picked McMillan as one of the subjects in your performance, gave him a post-hypnotic command to go to your wife's apartment. It was your idea of a perfect payback—your wife is found murdered and he becomes our chief suspect. Even if you came under suspicion you—"

"Which I did," Whitfield interrupted.

"—you were covered. Your sister gave you an alibi that held up when she passed the lie detector."

"Get around that if you can," Whitfield challenged him.

"Oh that's an easy one, sir. You hypnotized her that night after you two came back from the performance, told her you were with her at her house. She always trusted you so she was a perfect subject. Once she was under, you went to your wife's apartment and strangled her. The way I see it, you were about to leave when you heard McMillan outside. I think you looked around in panic, saw the closet door was open and you hid in there. He came in, saw the body, and fled—which gave you a chance to split before the police came."

Whitfield was suddenly paying very close attention. "Dare I ask if you have any proof?"

"When you strangled your wife her necklace broke. One of the beads rolled into the closet. When I saw it in there it got me thinking that maybe the killer hid in there when he heard McMillan coming in."

Whitfield's smile was forced. "I really get bored repeating myself—*any proof!*"

"Oh yes, sir. I just had my fingerprint man check the knob on the inside of the door."

"And there was a print?"

"Uh-huh."

Now the smile had vanished. "And you matched it with mine."

"Uh-huh. On a knob in the house you said you had never

visited. When you left your sister's house, you didn't have any gloves with you."

"And may I ask where you got my fingerprints?"

Columbo stood up. "After the show that night? My niece got your autograph in her autograph book. Your prints are all over the page."

Whitfield used both arms on the table to wearily raise himself from his chair. "You know what you are? Relentless. That should be your goddamn middle name."

A DISH BEST
SERVED COLD

IT WAS THE CAPTAIN'S birthday and Manuel (Manny) Paz bought him his favorite beverage, a bottle of single-malt Macallan scotch. It nestled in its carton and the liquor store even tied it up in a bright red ribbon.

Manny took the back alley over to the Captain's house in the early afternoon with the bottle in a briefcase. Walking was difficult, his healed hip wound still made it a problem. Overhead, jumbo jets now and then moved seismically, thunderously, since the nabe was under the flight path of Los Angeles International. When he approached the kitchen door, he paused, looking up at the row of tall palms that bordered the street. They always reminded him of a platoon of Army men standing at parade attention.

He knocked on the kitchen door and it was almost a minute before Captain Lamont let him in. Lamont was dressed as always in his faded fatigues, still seemingly grimy with the dried sweat from Iraq.

"Happy birthday, Captain," Manny announced, shaking hands with his friend. He removed the package from the briefcase.

The Captain touched it. "Is that what I think?"

Manny grinned. "Get two glasses and we'll find out!"

The Captain took two tumblers from the kitchen cabinet and Manny followed him into his little study off the living room. It was a cramped bungalow, full of cheap furniture and bitter memories. The Captain's wife had divorced him during his tour in Iraq and Manny never had had the courage to ask him how come she hadn't taken the house. How could a woman be that cruel, cutting herself loose from a man while he was serving his country in a terrible war? It reinforced Manny's resolution to never marry.

In the study they got down to "serious business," as the Captain liked to describe it. Lamont got the bottle from the carton, disposed of the ribbon, and Manny made sure he did the pouring, filling the Captain's glass well over half.

"Hey, hold on," the Captain warned. "Any more I'll be asleep by suppertime."

You'll be asleep long before that, Manny thought. He held his own tumbler up to the light, checking that the sleeping tablets were well-dissolved in the liquor. A stray ray of sunlight from a chink in the blinded window turned the liquid a beautiful golden brown.

"You paid a pretty penny for this," the Captain said, delighted.

"It was well worth it, wouldn't you say, Captain? Drink up. Plenty more where that came from."

They both drank, Manny just a tiny sip, ensuring he wouldn't get drugged before his mission was accomplished. He thought he could almost feel the adrenaline pumping through his arteries, keeping him awake, jittery-alert like it had on the patrols. Like it had on that fatal night over there.

He noted now that the Captain had gray-black stubble on his lean, wolf-like jaws. That played perfectly into his plan: someone who planned on taking his life didn't get up that morning and shave.

"Have you got anything planned tonight, Captain?"

"Well, my niece is taking me out to dinner. Says we're going to the best restaurant in town, but won't tell me what it is. So I better not drink too much, Manny, or she'll have to take me on a stretcher to this 'best restaurant.'"

Manny's small smile was tight. "You can always take a little nap before she picks you up. Sleep it off, Captain."

"What are you doing tonight, Manny?"

"Well ... there's a good fight on the tube."

The Captain downed what was left in his tumbler. "Boring! You'll come with us, no excuses."

"Oh, no, I couldn't, sir—"

"Bull. You're my best friend. We've been through quite a bit, Manny, you and me. Thank God we're out of that hell hole."

Now he poured himself a few fingers more of the scotch. "You get over here at seven sharp. Nineteen hundred hours, Sergeant."

Manny smiled, not as tight this time as he noticed the Captain's eyes were clouding and his speech had slightly slowed. "When my Captain tells me to report, you know I'll be there on time, sir."

"And—and stop with that sir stuff, Manny. We're—we're well... out... of the military."

He was definitely faltering, and Manny wondered if maybe he had been hitting the bottle earlier today, starting his birthday celebration alone.

They chatted only a few more minutes before Captain Lamont suddenly slumped, the empty tumbler falling from his hand, rolling under Manny's chair.

Manny got up, went slowly over to the sleeping man, used a thumb to open one eye. Dead to the world. And soon to be dead forever.

Quickly, he slipped on gloves from the briefcase, removed the Captain's prized Colt .45 from the bookcase. He knew it was loaded since the Captain always kept it that way. He secured the .45 in the Captain's left hand. Then, carefully, he moved the heavy gun's barrel to the Captain's forehead. He waited now for one of those jets. It wasn't long until a plane roared overhead, and Manny eased back the trigger.

There was blood now all over the fatigue jacket and on the wall behind the corpse and all over the carpet, but the hand still held the Colt, lying now in the Captain's lap. Live by the gun, die by the gun.

On an adrenaline high, still wearing gloves, Manny took a new carton of scotch from his briefcase and placed it on top of the liquor cabinet. He carefully picked up the Captain's glass from the floor so as not to disturb the fingerprints and rinsed it out. Then he opened the carton and removed the scotch bottle. He unscrewed the cap and poured a little scotch in the glass and placed it and the bottle on the table next to the body. He grabbed his glass and the Macallan bottle and dumped them into his briefcase, removing a tube of sleeping pills. He spilled tablets on the table next to the glass and left the tube there.

He flexed his stiff fingers in his gloves, looked over the still-life scene he had arranged. Nothing forgotten. Satisfied, he slowly limped over to the door. He looked around the room one last time.

Everything had to be orderly, in its place. That was what Captain Lamont always demanded of his unit. And that, at his end, was exactly what the Captain got.

Columbo arrived at the crime scene the next morning. He quickly felt a vague uneasiness about the place. There were planes roaring in the sky: he was almost as afraid of planes as he was of guns. His wife was flying back East to Brooklyn next week to see relatives and he was even afraid for her. Feet safely on terra firma, that was the way he preferred it.

At first it seemed like a cut-and-dried suicide: Iraq war veteran takes his life, probably a sad victim of post-traumatic stress disorder. But second thoughts began to simmer when he questioned the dead man's niece, Tracy, in the living room of her uncle's house.

Tracy was a strawberry blonde, like his own niece, with the same pale skin that was an upfront display screen for their sometimes racing emotions.

"Yes, Lieutenant, he was a troubled man, but he wasn't deeply depressed or anything. I mean, I was taking him out last night for a great dinner. He was looking forward to it. It was his birthday."

Columbo didn't think it was the proper setting to light a cigar. "Sometimes people hide their depression."

"Not Uncle Lawrence." She had hazel eyes, again like his niece, which flashed with a sudden thought. "You said you're from Homicide. Why are you here investigating a suicide?"

Columbo shrugged, seemed somewhat embarrassed. "Well, I was driving to the station and I saw some investigators going in the house." He smiled. "My wife says the only nosier person she knows is our priest!"

Tracy laughed, then became serious again when a few members of the tech team came out of the study, talking quietly among themselves. "Well, I guess there's not going to be much for you to do if murder is your specialty."

Columbo shrugged. "I guess that's right, unless we find some evidence to the contrary."

She was somber now. "Don't people like you have instincts? What's your instinct, Lieutenant?"

"I'm not much on instincts these days. I was sure my wife didn't want one of those flat screen high-def TVs and boy, was I wrong!"

Tracy didn't seem to be listening. "One thing bothers me," she said.

"What would that be?"

A blotch of color had come up in the pale skin of her face. "He told me once he thought somebody might want to kill him."

Manny, in his gardener's clothes, was trimming a client's box hedges when a man in a raincoat came around the side of the mansion. He had his wallet open with a badge showing.

"Lieutenant Columbo, LAPD. You would be Manuel Paz?"

Manny put down his gardening shears and flicked some grass from his jacket. "That's right. Can I help you?"

"Well maybe, maybe not. You were a good friend of Captain Lawrence Lamont?"

Manny nodded gravely. "I was. I served in the Captain's unit in Iraq. I—I still can't believe what happened."

Columbo nodded, suddenly sneezed. "Yeah, tough. Neither can his niece. She told me you were the Captain's best friend and you worked on the estate here."

Manny felt his eyes narrowing. "You're here on police business?"

Columbo sneezed again, dug in his raincoat for a piece of Kleenex. "Sorry. I guess it's the flowers or something. I got terrible allergies. Could we maybe go over there?"

Manny smiled. "No problem."

They found a haven away from the flowering shrubbery on the front lawn.

Columbo blew his nose. "Reason I'm here, sir, is, well, we found some irregularities in our investigation."

"Irregularities?"

"Well, the victim's niece said her uncle was afraid his life might be in danger."

"But he wasn't in Iraq any more, Lieutenant," Manny scoffed.

"No, no, he thought someone *here* had it in for him."

"Strange. But that's not an irregularity."

Columbo was sweating now in the strong sun, wiping at his forehead with the Kleenex. "Tracy, the niece, wanted an autopsy and that's where something irregular turned up. Could we maybe go under that tree over there where there's some shade?"

Manny grinned: This guy was a real mess. "Sure. No problem. You sure you don't want to take off that raincoat?"

"Nah, I'm fine."

They took shelter under a large elm. "So, Lieutenant," Manny prodded, "what's with this irregularity?"

"Well, it seems Captain Lamont was drinking scotch laced with some sleeping pills. They caught that in his blood stream."

Manny lit a cigarette, cupping his hands against an imaginary breeze. "Still sounds like a suicide to me."

"Yeah, but he fired his .45 pistol into his brain. Why would he do that if he thought the sleeping pills would do the job?"

"Why do some guys wear a belt *and* suspenders? I hate to joke about something as tragic as this, but you get my point, don't you, Lieutenant?"

"Oh yeah, I get it all right." Columbo opened a button on his raincoat. "And there was no suicide note, either."

"Is that unusual?"

"No. But a lot of men leave them."

Manny was looking back to where he had been trimming the hedges. "I really have to get back to work, Lieutenant. Any more ... irregularities?"

"Not yet. No."

Manny tried to keep his voice level, unemotional. "What do you mean, not yet?"

"Never had another case where the victim tried two different ways to take his life. I'm going to have to really put on my thinking cap."

"Will I be seeing you again?"

"Maybe."

Manny, smiling, pointed at the cop's sweating white forehead. "Then I suggest that next time you wear some sunscreen."

Columbo wandered through the corridors of the Veterans Hospital off Wilshire near Westwood. He was directed to the ward where a young soldier under a blanket, propped against pillows, was reading a Stephen King paperback. A chart at the foot of the bed read: *Pvt. Billy Goodnight.*

Columbo nodded at the private, flashed his badge, and told him his name. "Have you heard your unit commander, Captain Lamont, committed suicide?"

Goodnight slowly closed the book. "Yeah, yeah, I did." He had a strong Southern accent.

"How well did you know the Captain?"

"I guess as well as you know anybody under combat conditions."

"I've been trying to get some information on him from the Army, but they seem to be taking their time getting back to me."

Goodnight's smile was this side of cynical. "Well, when an officer leaves his men to face an enemy attack, I don't think they want that spread around. Three of our buddies were killed. I lost my legs. Just like the Captain now, they ain't ever coming back."

Columbo pulled up a chair so that he was face to face with the young man. "Leaves his men? Isn't that some kind of serious court-martial offense?"

"Sure. But the sector commander liked Captain Lamont. So he just disappeared, somehow wound up back here in CONUS."

"CONUS?"

"Continental United States. I heard he was suffering from post-traumatic stress disorder. I would be too if I was responsible for getting three of my best men killed."

Columbo nodded, getting to his feet. "How close were you to Sergeant Manuel Paz?"

"We're good friends. He was just visiting me here last week. Damn fine fella."

"He was wounded in that attack just like you?"

"That's what got us both out."

Columbo took a slow, meditative journey down to the foot of

the bed. "The Captain's niece told me he was afraid someone wanted to kill him. Would you say your friend Manuel fits the bill?"

"I'd say him and probably somebody else."

Columbo's voice sharpened: "Really. Any idea who that might be?"

Goodnight laced his hands behind his head and leaned back against the pillow. "Sure ... me."

Columbo said nothing, waited for him to go on.

"Captain Lamont got away with murder," Goodnight said. "If there's any justice in this whacked-out world, he deserved what he got." He smiled. "But I've been out-of-commission in this ward for a long while—wouldn't guys like you say that's a damn good alibi?"

Manny was making himself lunch, dropping a wad of butter in an iron skillet and adding a few thick slices of ham. Never having married, he was used to eating alone, sometimes watching television or reading a magazine.

He was flipping the meat onto a plate when his doorbell rang. Now who the hell could that be? The mailman with a registered letter or something?

It was the cop, what was his name? Still in that raincoat and it looked like the same suit too. What the hell were they paying these guys these days? Not enough to buy a decent plainclothes outfit to look presentable.

"You again," Manny said. "I was just sitting down to lunch."

"Oh, sorry," Columbo said. "Smells good. I hate interrupting people when they're eating."

"Then why do you come around at lunch time?"

Columbo shrugged, with a hapless smile. "I was in the neighborhood on some other business and I figured maybe I'd catch you in."

Manny sat down at the kitchen table with the plate. He spread some mustard on his ham, added pepper. "Anything new on your case?"

"I'm not even sure we've got a case here." He looked over expectantly at the coffee percolator. "If you're going to have some coffee, would you mind if I joined you?" Another shrug. "I don't want to impose or anything."

"*Why* are you here?" He suddenly remembered the name—Columbo.

"Well, just a few little things are still bugging me. Do I call you Sergeant?"

"I'm a civilian. The name is Manuel. Manny Paz."

"Yeah, yeah, I know. Captain Lamont's neighbor, a Mrs. Lorenzo? Very nice woman, a widow. Her husband died last month so she was really shocked when somebody else died right next door."

"Could you get on with it, Columbo? I got a doctor's appointment."

"Oh yeah, sorry. My wife says I got this awful tendency to ramble—"

"Why are you here?" He was beginning to lose his appetite, pushed his plate away.

"This Mrs. Lorenzo was home around the time we think the Captain took his life. But she didn't hear the shot and the house is real close."

"Is she old, has a hearing impairment?"

"No, she's only in her fifties. You mind if I smoke?"

"Yeah, I do. I'm *eating*."

"Oh right, yeah. I'll wait till after I leave. Where was I? Oh— the gunshot. Mrs. Lorenzo says there's always planes from LAX taking off and flying overhead. Maybe the noise of one covered the shot."

Manny got up, put on the percolator. "Probably that was it."

"Yeah. I mean, I don't think Captain Lamont waited till he heard a plane before he fired. Why would he do something like that?"

Manny poured them both coffee and brought the mugs to the table. "Beats me."

Uninvited, Columbo pulled out a chair and sat down opposite Manny. "Hey, thanks for the coffee. I can really use it." He sipped at his cup. "The bottle has me going too."

"What bottle? What are you talking about?"

"The scotch bottle the Captain was pouring his drink from ... His fingerprints were on the glass, but not on the bottle. Now you got to admit that's pretty weird."

Goddamn! Manny thought. I was wearing gloves when I took the new bottle from its carton. How was I supposed to think of everything after I killed him? And this was obviously the kind of stuff this clown got off on!

Manny sighed, deliberately displaying his frustration. "And this is why you came all the way over here? To ask me why there were no fingerprints on the bottle?"

"No problem. I was in the neighborhood, wasn't I? And I always think two heads are better than one." He grinned.

"I'm not a cop, Columbo. I was a soldier for twenty-two years. Nobody takes fingerprints when you're fighting a war. So I can't help you with your bottle problem. If it is a problem, which I doubt."

Columbo nodded understandingly. "You lost some friends over there, Iraq?"

"Yes. We all did."

Columbo sipped more coffee. "Did Captain Lamont feel bad about the mistake he made?"

Manny narrowed his eyes, almost involuntarily. "Why do you ask me that?"

"Well, you told me you and the Captain were good friends. I was just wondering how you could be good friends when he did something like that."

Manny got up, poured himself some more coffee. "You've been looking at his 201 file?"

"And talking to some people at the Army's Office of Public Affairs. Your captain must have been carrying a pretty big load of guilt."

"Maybe that's why he took his life. I'm sure that must've occurred to you."

Columbo took out a cold cigar stub, placed it in the corner of his mouth. "Oh yeah, it did. Trouble is, too many things occur to me, that's what always fouls me up."

"This whole thing looks pretty clear to me. He brooded over what he had done and decided he couldn't live with it anymore."

Columbo got up and poured himself more coffee. "Sort of funny, though, how you could still like the guy after what he did...."

Manny decided not to answer, finished his own coffee.

"What were you doing that afternoon?" Columbo asked.

Manny had been ready for this: "I was at the movies in Century City."

"Really? At the movies. Which one, you remember?"

"The new Tom Cruise."

Columbo sat down again at the table with his mug, still chummy, very casual. "Yeah, me and my wife saw that one too." He laughed. "You like the scene where Cruise throws off the bad guys by taking a bus instead of his motorcycle?"

"There's no such scene in the picture. You got it mixed up with some other one. Or—"

Columbo's eyes flicked at him. "Or?"

"Or you deliberately made that up to see if you could trap me."

Now the eyes went blank, innocent. "Trap you? Why would I do that?"

Let it all hang out, Manny thought. This guy's got no fuel in his tank, no goddamn cards in his hand, but he still keeps upping the ante. "Your job specialty is investigating murders and you think Captain Lamont was murdered. And don't tell me you don't think that."

"I won't say it's not been in the back of my head," Columbo said. "But I wouldn't let it worry you, Mr. Paz." He got up from the table and took his mug back to the sink. "Thanks for the coffee. I really appreciate it, I really do." He went to the kitchen door. "I *really* needed that coffee."

Tracy was doing some cleaning in her uncle's house, the police having told her to do what she wanted but to leave the suicide room intact. She was vacuuming in the living room when the doorbell rang.

It was that Lieutenant Columbo. For some reason she was slightly intimidated by the man even though he was unpretentious, sort of blue collar, and looked like he was always chewing something over. She noticed he had some letters in his hand.

"These were in the mailbox," he explained, a little sheepishly as if he had intercepted their personal property without permission.

"Oh—oh, thank you, Lieutenant. The poor man is deceased but the bills keep coming."

"I couldn't help seeing, ma'am, that there's a business letter from a local Toyota dealership."

"Uncle Lawrence was thinking of buying a new car."

"Unusual, wouldn't you say? A potential suicide looking for a new car?"

She blinked at him. "Yes, now that you mention it—it *is* a little unusual." She turned off the vacuum.

"You mind if we go in the study? But if you're still too sensitive about going in there, I can—"

"No, it's no problem. But your people said I shouldn't disturb anything."

Columbo smiled. "I hope that doesn't include me."

The room was unchanged, slightly musty now, the bottle and glass still on the table, bloodstains like dull flower blossoms on the upholstery of the Captain's chair, the wall, and the carpet.

"Didn't you examine everything in here already?" Tracy asked.

"Oh yeah, we did. Very thoroughly. No, I don't want to examine anything. I want to do what we call a re-enactment."

For some reason she was amused. "What's that?"

"It's just going over what we theorize might have happened before your uncle took his life. I know this might be a little ... distasteful, but could you sit down in the chair?"

It was, a bit, but she managed it. "What now?"

"I want you to get up and go over to the cabinet there where all the liquor bottles are."

Puzzled, she got up, went over to the cabinet, turned to look at him. "You want a drink?" she joked.

She hadn't seen Columbo so dead serious, hadn't even lit his cigar. "You see the carton there, the scotch carton?"

"Yes. There's nothing in it."

"Pretend there's a scotch bottle in it, okay? Take it out and bring it over to the table."

"I think I'm back in my high school dramatic club." She removed the imaginary bottle and took it over to the table, set it down. "It wasn't very heavy," she joked.

"*Now* I get it," Columbo murmured, talking to himself. "He still had the gloves on. Had to."

"Lieutenant? What gloves?"

He was lighting a dead cigar. "You're a fine actress, Tracy. And I thank you for playing along with me, I really do."

"Lieutenant Columbo—*what about gloves?*"

"The man who killed your uncle wore them. And it turns out to have been his one mistake."

"What man? Can't you tell me any more?"

A rare, satisfied Columbo smile. "In due time, Tracy. In due time."

Manny was trimming some rose bushes when he saw the cop coming across the lawn, a hand in the air warding off the sun.

"Columbo," he said when the cop came clumping over, "I told you to wear some sunscreen, didn't I?"

"You're right, you did. But I got so many things on my mind these days, I just didn't remember. You wouldn't have some on you, would you?"

"No." He smiled. "No coffee, either."

Columbo was looking up at the hot bright sky, breathing in the beautiful day, but Manny wasn't fooled. This guy was a formidable adversary and he could not let his guard down.

"So what's up?" he asked. Sarcastic: "Just in the neighborhood again?"

"Nah. Afraid it's the same old police business."

"And I'm the suspect, right? The *prime* suspect? I asked you that before but you ducked the question."

"If I remember, I told you not to worry, didn't I?"

Manny stood, wiped sweat from his face. "You remember everything, Columbo. I'll bet you can even remember the weather last Tuesday."

"That's easy in L.A., almost every day's the same. Except for the rainy days."

Manny wondered if there was a hidden meaning behind that. "And today's a rainy day— for me?"

"I guess you could look at it that way, yes sir." He was dabbing at his forehead with a Kleenex. "You see, when I said not to worry, I didn't have any evidence. And now things have changed."

Manny laughed, held out his gloved hands. "Go ahead, arrest me, Lieutenant."

"I got somebody else to do that," Columbo said, looking back toward the street. A uniformed police officer stood there, watching them.

Manny felt more sweat breaking out on his face, but not from the heat. He stripped off his gardener's gloves, started to stuff them in his jacket pocket.

"Don't do that," Columbo commanded. "You see, it's the gloves, Mr. Paz, that are going to put you away."

"What are you talking about?"

Columbo snapped the gloves from his hands. This was the quickest thing he had seen the cop do, usually the guy seemed a little slow and indecisive.

"There's an old saying—revenge is a dish best served cold. But you didn't wait that long after you two got back to what-do-you-call-it, CONUS? You planned the murder very carefully, Mr. Paz, I guess like a general figures out a battle plan. You drugged Captain Lamont and then you put on gloves so you wouldn't leave any fingerprints. It had to look like he was alone when he took his life. But your carefulness did you in. You took the new bottle—"

"You're fixated on that goddamn bottle!"

"Yeah, I guess I am. You were wearing the gloves when you brought the bottle over to the table and poured some into the Captain's glass. Right? Well, the Captain's fingerprints should have been on the bottle, but there were no fingerprints on the bottle and that got me thinking." He paused. "Could we maybe get into the shade over there?"

"No! We're staying right where we are. *What about the gloves?*"

"You shot him wearing the gloves. You had to because you couldn't have your prints on the weapon when you put it in his hand. But a .45, like most guns, leaves residue on the hand of whoever fires it...."

Now Manny understood. He had a quick, sickening sensation that the bottom of his stomach was about to fall out.

Columbo gestured with the gloves, then secured them in an evidence bag he took from his raincoat. "And if the person is wearing gloves—it leaves a residue on them too. These are going right to the lab."

Columbo waved to the policeman who came quickly toward them. "I'm placing you under arrest, Mr. Paz, for the murder of Captain Lawrence Lamont."

"The gloves... " Manny muttered.

"Sometimes you can be *too* careful when you plan and carry out a murder," Columbo said. "But I really don't think, Mr. Paz, you'll have the opportunity to make that mistake again."

RICOCHET

HIGH NOON AT WONDER WORLD. It was a scorching August and there were swarming crowds of parents with their out-of-school children, long lines at all of the attractions. He had followed Hammershield to the Spine-Chiller, one of the most popular rides, and now he was right behind him, only a few feet away. His .38, equipped with silencer, cracked only once and Hammershield couldn't really fall since he was packed so tightly in the moving crowd. By the time he did, his assailant was on his way, walking casually toward one of the exits.

The police chief was not in the business of displeasing Lieutenant Columbo, but the man had to get over his silly fear of flying.

"When will I leave?" Columbo asked with an expression of just having whiffed a carton of rotten eggs.

"ASAP. You and I both know he's our prime suspect and we've got to move on this as soon as possible."

"Yes, sir, I'm aware of that. But you know how I feel about planes—"

"For God's sake, Columbo, I can't send you back on a Greyhound bus, can I?"

"No, sir, you can't."

"Have a drink before you board. Two drinks." A grin: "I'm authorizing that, okay?"

Columbo looked as if he had just lost his dog. "Okay." He moved uneasily toward the door.

"Your contact in Manhattan is Lieutenant A1 Dempsey. He's a good man and he'll help you in every possible way."

Columbo went to the door. He stopped, turned back. "Just one more thing, sir."

"What's that?"

"Would you maybe authorize three drinks?"

Columbo slept for most of the flight. The three drinks had at first settled him into a mellow mood, but then acted like the blow of a crowbar to the base of his skull. He missed lunch, which was probably lucky, and woke up over socked-in Baltimore or somewhere.

"What's the weather in New York?" he groggily asked the flight attendant after he woke.

"Fifty-five degrees, rainy."

Hmmm. Figures.

It was rainy, all right. He thought of using his badge to get a cab quickly, but lost his nerve when he saw a group of rain-soaked old ladies and a priest waiting dejectedly in the long line for cabs.

He went right to the precinct house in mid-Manhattan. Lieutenant Dempsey, a buff, middle-aged man with graying hair, almost broke his fingers shaking hands. "Welcome, Lieutenant. I see you were smart to bring your raincoat. How was the flight?"

"Pretty uneventful. I slept most of the way."

"Amazing. My wife's so afraid of flying she sits bolt-up, wide-eyed, the whole trip. What's your secret?"

"Booze," Columbo grinned.

They briefly discussed the case and Dempsey jotted down something on a slip, handed it to Columbo. "I gave you the fiancée's name and phone number," he said, getting up from his chair. Briefing session terminated.

"You said she gave him an airtight," Columbo said.

"Yes. But there are air-tights and then there are air-tights. I'd suggest you see the suspect first. . . . You come with quite a rep, Columbo, so we're all counting on you to break this damn thing."

They exchanged another bone-crushing handshake and a few minutes later Columbo unbelievingly caught a cab right outside the precinct house. The driver wore a towering turban and had mutton-chop whiskers that almost disappeared into his leather jacket. Columbo inadvertently caught the man's narrow suspicious eyes in the rear-view, and quickly looked away through the rain-smeared window. He was going to have to get used to this town!

The address was on the Upper East Side. Columbo gave the driver a good tip (the department was paying), and ducked out of the rain into an empty lobby. The slow, wood-paneled elevator took him to the twenty-third floor, and he knocked on the door of apartment 2310.

Taylor Ashe opened the door almost immediately. He was six-foot, a good-looking mid-forties, wearing an open collared white dress shirt, blue blazer, and flannel slacks. Behind the bright surface sheen of his manner, there was something measured and withholding.

"So you're the hotshot cop from L.A.," he said as Columbo came in. The living room was extremely well-furnished, and Ashe's persona and upscale attitude matched the neighborhood.

"You mind if we sit?" Columbo asked.

"No. But I had assumed we'd cab somewhere and have a nice, lavish dinner on you folks."

Columbo gave him a vague smile. "Never assume anything with a cop on a low expense account, Mr. Ashe." He sank down into a well-upholstered couch, shifted over to an even more comfortable cushion.

Ashe sat in a leather wing chair opposite him. "I've already been through the mill," Ashe said. "So don't tell me you're going to ask me the same boring cop questions."

"I hope not." He took out a cigar, but didn't light it.

"Why the hell are all you people on my derriere?"

"Isn't it obvious, sir? Twenty years ago Kenneth Hammershield tried to kill the president. The bullet ricocheted and killed your fiancée. Hammershield gets out of prison and *wham!* somebody suddenly kills *him* at Wonder World of all places."

Ashe sighed. "Lieutenant, Hammershield's leaving prison made every newspaper and TV news show in the country. *And* Europe. You don't think there were a hundred other people, nut cases, who wanted to kill this guy because he tried to kill the president ... If you want to light that thing, light it already. You're driving me crazy fondling it like it's a woman!"

"Sorry." He put the cigar back in his coat. "The attempt on the president's life made this guy a target."

"So why center on me?"

"You're on record saying you wanted to kill him. You can't deny that, sir."

"Sure, twenty years ago, back when it happened, I said some stupid things. I admit I hated him for killing my girl, but to think I would kill him? I mean he paid for it. He served twenty years."

Ashe, agitated, rose up from the chair. "I'm not going to argue with you. Pretend you're a tourist—go to Coney Island, eat at a Nathan's hotdog, take a Circle Line Cruise, gawk at the Statue of Liberty, but leave me the hell alone, okay? Some people might say the man who killed Kenneth Hammershield performed a valuable public service."

"And some might say the crime was an unjustifiable homicide."

Ashe said, not unpleasantly, "Am I going to get a lecture on law and order now?"

"Oh no, sir. I do lousy lectures." He pulled out a notebook, found a page. "Kenneth Hammershield was murdered last Tuesday, August 22nd. Could I ask where you were that day?"

"The same old questions. Didn't I warn you about that?"

"Just doing my job."

Ashe paced around the living room, looking out the window at the East River. "I was here. New York City, New York, the United States of America. Three thousand miles away from LaLaLand. Hard to kill someone at that distance, wouldn't you say?"

"And your proof of that?"

"My fiancée, Alex Fairchild. Your colleagues already talked to her and she confirmed I was here that day."

"Can anybody else confirm that?"

"Who knows? I really think you should get a better compass. You're in the wrong time zone with the wrong man. Now you'll have to excuse me, I have an important call to make."

"To your lawyer?"

Ashe glared at him, then broke into harsh laughter. "You're really something, Columbo. It must be some toxins in the smog out there. Sometime we must have drinks at the club. You can regale me with all your stories of how you've sent up innocent people."

Columbo rose from the sofa, tucked the notebook back in his coat. He gave Ashe a card. "Call me on my cellphone. I'd really like to have that drink with you, Mr. Ashe."

The next day, the precinct lent him a car and he somehow found his way out to Southampton. The rain had subsided but the windshield wipers were still wildly semaphoring because he couldn't figure out how to turn them off.

Alex Fairchild's mansion loomed palatially behind iron gates, which were fortunately open.

A manservant directed him into the study, a rosewood paneled room, four times the size of Ashe's apartment. He could see a tennis court outside and a smattering of woods behind it. Alex Fairchild greeted him with a confident handshake. She was a stunning blonde of a certain age, probably late fifties. She was very tan, wearing a blouse and tailored jodhpurs with beautifully polished leather boots in which he could almost see his face.

"I guess you're here about Taylor," she said. He saw her upfront cheerfulness was forced; she was nervous. She gestured him to sit down in an enveloping upholstered chair.

Columbo sat, feeling like he was sitting in the palm of someone's accommodating hand. "I guess you know your fiancé's background," he began.

"Actually no." She smiled. "Taylor has never been very forthcoming about his 'background,' as you put it."

"Nothing about the woman he was going to marry twenty years ago?"

Her elegant high-cheek-boned face, like the sky, clouded over. "Yes. Naturally he told me about that. She was accidentally killed in Los Angeles."

Columbo nodded. "A man tried to shoot the president and the bullet ricocheted, struck the young lady, Terri Townsend, who was near him in the crowd. Awful tragedy."

"Yes, so he told me. Dreadful. I think Taylor's still affected by it, has depressions. How terribly senseless it was."

"You mind if I smoke?"

Pleasantly: "Yes. I mind."

"Oh. Sorry I asked, ma'am." He seemed slightly at a loss, then: "The murderer served twenty years and when he got out last week, somebody killed him."

"Yes, I read about it." She was nervous again, one boot scratching the other. "Can I get you a sherry, Lieutenant, coffee?"

"Oh no, no thanks." He laughed. "I had enough drinks on my flight."

"Surely you don't think Taylor had anything to do with this?" Hesitantly: "Do you?"

"Last Tuesday, you told the police you were with Mr. Ashe that day."

"Yes."

"The whole day, ma'am?"

The boot was scratching again. "Yes."

"Could you describe that day?"

"Well...We—we met for lunch and then we spent the afternoon at Taylor's place. And then that evening.... Oh, we saw this awful comedy off-Broadway. It was so bad I can't even remember the title." She laughed, a bit too heartily. "I think I'm repressing it!"

Columbo was making notes. He looked up from the pad. "That's okay, I don't really need the name. You kept the ticket stubs?"

"I don't keep ticket stubs, Lieutenant." It was as if he had asked her if she kept fingernail clippings. "Why are you asking about that particular—oh, right—that was the day that crazy man was murdered."

"Yes, ma'am."

She stared at him; blue eyes, beautiful blue eyes under real lashes. "Then you really think Taylor is a suspect? But that's ridiculous!"

"It certainly is, seeing how he was with you all day and night."

Her smile was sexually provocative. "Did I say *night*, Lieutenant?"

He didn't return the smile. "No, I guess you didn't."

"Then you can write down—yes, they did spend the *night* together."

"Did Mr. Ashe ever make any remarks about his former fiancée's murderer?"

"No. We've created our own relationship and we try not to bring up any...unpleasant things. Can you understand that, Lieutenant?"

"Oh yes, ma'am." He tried to extricate himself from the voluptuous grip of the chair. "I'm a married man."

Columbo felt somewhat out of place in Taylor Ashe's exclusive men's club. It was very quiet and the members were all in expensive-looking suits and many spoke as if it hurt them to move their lips. He unconsciously imitated them when he ordered coffee and the waiter asked him, politely, to speak up please, sir.

Ashe appeared, looking more Californian today, wearing a beautiful sports coat and razor-pressed jeans. "So you talked to Alex," he said, after he glanced at the menu.

"Airtight alibi, sir."

"You don't seem happy about that," Ashe smiled.

Columbo said, "I try not to be judgmental this early in a case."

Ashe was skeptical. "Do you *really* think that's possible?"

"Oh yes, sir. Sometimes it's hard, but you do your best."

"What do you say we order?"

They gave the waiter their orders and Ashe leaned forward in his chair, his eyes level with Columbo's. "If I've got an airtight you might as well get back to L.A., shouldn't you? Not that we're chasing you out of town."

Columbo drank some of his coffee.

"Well don't you have any other suspects, Lieutenant? Or was I luckily the only one on your list?"

Columbo shrugged. "Hammershield was in prison a long time. His wife divorced him and he had no other family as far as we know. What about you, Mr. Ashe? You ever married?"

"Three times. Bad choices. They all got rid of me, but it cost them."

"And what's been your principal means of support?"

"I've kicked around, not doing anything special." He smiled a cynical smile. "The three ladies I married were wealthy. Get the picture?"

Columbo got the picture. With his charm and good looks he lived off the rich. Now with the older Alex on the hook, she was probably even paying the bills for this expensive club. Male gold digger, par excellence.

The meal came and Columbo ate quickly while Ashe poked at his food, talked about a stock he had just bought. "Am I boring you, Lieutenant?" he asked suddenly. "You've been very quiet."

Columbo looked at his watch. "No, not at all. But I've got to get back to the precinct."

Ashe laughed. "From your grilled tuna to a *real* grilling? What a life you people lead!"

Columbo gulped down the rest of his coffee and got up. "I'm sorry to be rushing out, sir, but I'm late now."

As Columbo headed for the check room, Ashe called after him: "Keep in touch!"

On the street, Columbo ducked into the doorway of a building next to the entrance to the club. He knew he was flying blind, but sometimes it paid big dividends.

It wasn't more than a ten-minute wait before Ashe emerged from the club and sauntered at his leisure down Fifth Avenue, Columbo following. He remembered his early cop's training, looked in shop windows in case the subject peered back over his shoulder. But he knew Airtight Alibi Ashe had no reason to believe he was being followed.

Ashe suddenly cut down west on Forty-Sixth street, going only a few feet before he ducked into a restaurant.

Columbo hung back for a while before he quickly moved up and glanced through the window to see Ashe sitting at the bar up front next to a sleek brunette who looked half his age. He was leaning close, talking intimately, lighting her cigarette.

This could be a long wait. After ten minutes, Columbo took a chance, hurried into a tobacco store across the street where he could still see the entrance to the restaurant. The clerk condescendingly informed him that they didn't carry his brand of cigar—try a drugstore. Columbo loitered a minute or two, partly to watch the building, and partly to annoy the snotty clerk.

He returned to his vigil across the street and it was only a few minutes before Ashe and the brunette left. Columbo turned quickly away while Ashe leaned over to light another cigarette for his companion.

He waited until they had gone safely far enough down the street before he went into the restaurant, sidling up to the bar.

There were no other patrons there at this pre-happy hour. The barman, a bulky African-American, took his time coming over to take Columbo's drink order.

Columbo showed him the badge in his wallet. "Like some information."

"Sure," the big man sighed. "Lot better than some drunk telling me his life story."

"The gentleman just here?"

"Mr. Ashe. Regular customer. He stick up a bank or something?"

Columbo's corns were killing him: he hopped up on one of the red plastic stools. "That young lady he was with? Has he been in here with her before?"

"I really shouldn't talk about a customer."

"I assure you, sir," Columbo said, "this will all be kept confidential."

"Well, they know each other pretty good. They meet here often, they're friends." He winked at Columbo. "Maybe bosom buddies?"

"You happen to hear her name?"

"Cindy used to be a waitress here, Cindy Fortunato. That's how Mr. Ashe met her. She left, works in a store now over on West Sixty-Third. You want something to drink?"

"Club soda would be fine, thanks."

The bartender filled a glass with his soda-water gun. "I take it you're interested in Mr. Ashe."

"You could say that, yeah."

"You got an L.A. license, but you sound New York to me."

"Born and bred."

"The best people. Well, Mr. Ashe has been coming in here for a while. But I don't know very much about him."

"How's he pay for his drinks?"

"That I don't know. But he worked for a charter plane company in Florida a few years back. They let him go." He laughed. "And he wasn't even black!"

"Worked for them. You mean a pilot?"

"Yeah. Probably flew some of those Cessna Citation C-525 jets. I'm ex-Air Force, I know a little bit about planes."

Columbo was more thirsty than he thought. He drained his glass of soda water. "You think he doesn't fly anymore?"

"Ask him. Guess he gets his bread someplace else these days."

"He ever come in here with an attractive, older blonde lady, very elegant, blue eyes?"

The barman refilled his glass. "Hell no, that'd screw him up big time with Cindy. You don't mix your drinks and you don't mix your women. Don't'cha know that, you a New Yorker?"

Columbo smiled. "I mentioned this is confidential police business so I know you won't repeat our conversation to Mr. Ashe or his girlfriend."

"Hell no." He watched Columbo get up. "You sure I can't give you a *real* drink—on me?"

"Only if I'm going to fly," Columbo said. He reached over and shook hands with the bartender. "Take care of yourself."

Lieutenant Dempsey and Columbo were having coffee that night at the precinct house. "You've had yourself quite a New York adventure, Columbo."

"It's still not over. I gotta make a few phone calls."

"The pilot thing is interesting. Very interesting."

"From what I found out, he could've chartered one of these light jets at a private airfield around here or New Jersey, fly out to L.A., do his thing with Hammershield, and fly back. But I checked with the charter companies. No record of him doing that."

"But he could've flown commercially."

Columbo was thumbing through his notebook. "That's what I thought too. I'll check. He could've used fake documentation with an assumed name. You can get most any kind of documentation made up these days. What's the world coming to?"

Dempsey's frown cut deeper lines into his already lined face. "Why'd he leave his job in Florida?"

"He didn't. They got rid of him. Guy on the phone said they thought he was a little reckless, 'unstable.'"

Dempsey broke a packet of sugar into his coffee. "The Fairchild woman says she was with him all day and all night."

Columbo linked his hands behind his head and stretched. "I think maybe we've got our wedge."

"How do you mean?"

"One of our best secret weapons—jealousy." He fought a yawn back with the palm of his hand.

They were in her study again, this time drinking tea from a beautiful silver service in which Columbo could see his face. First the boots, he thought, and now I see my face in her silver. Boy, am I going up in the world. Alex wore a lace dressing gown and a slightly pained expression. "I welcome you back, Lieutenant, but must you come so early in the day?"

Columbo removed a cellphone from his pocket and let her see a photo on the screen. It showed Ashe and Cindy caught emerging from the restaurant. It wasn't a crisp shot, but the two faces were perfectly legible.

Frowning, Alex studied the cellphone, then looked up at him with a puzzled expression. "I see it's Taylor but who's the young woman with him?"

"His girlfriend, Miss Fairchild. Her name's Cindy Fortunato. He met her at that restaurant they're coming out of."

A smile slid slowly over her lips. "I know all about her, Lieutenant. She *used* to be Taylor's girlfriend, but I never met her. So what are you trying to prove here?"

Columbo was surprised, thrown off stride. He stalled, thinking, and then picked up the cellphone, but missing it, tried again.

Alex's smile had disappeared as quickly as it had appeared. "You're embarrassed and I think you should be. You came all the way over here to show me that photo, thinking I'd get angry at Taylor and tell you something that would involve him in that murder." The smile again, like the sun playing hide and seek on a cloudy day. "But it didn't work, did it? I have nothing to fear from Taylor's occasional infidelity. He's got a good thing going with me, a damn good thing, and I assure you he's not dumb enough to blow it."

Another late coffee session with Dempsey, this time at a Greek coffee shop on Sixth Avenue. A definite dispirited mood hung over them. Columbo looked around, but he couldn't see his face in anything.

"Tough luck," Dempsey said. "It was a good plan, but sometimes it's just not your day. I hope you're not going to give up on this thing."

"No way," Columbo said. He laughed. "I gotta tell you, I dread that return trip on a plane even worse than if I failed here!"

"Now you don't really mean that, do you, Lieutenant?"

"I don't know. The Fairchild woman is lying, I can feel that deep in my bones. My wife says she's tired of hearing stuff like that, that it's really arthritis. But I really thought Ashe cheating on her would get her all riled up and we could break his alibi."

They sat there in silence for a minute, Columbo staring up at the painted tin ceiling. He suddenly whacked his hand on his thigh. "Why didn't I think of this before!"

"What?"

"This Cindy. Maybe it'll work on *her*."

Lieutenant Dempsey had to admit, only to himself, that he was totally perplexed. "What do you mean?"

"The jealousy angle."

Columbo, a newspaper under his arm, found the young woman in a haberdashery store on West Sixty-Third like the barman had told him. Close up, she was a little cheap, overly made-up, a bit sexually forthcoming, which probably hyped her sales with the male clientele.

Columbo flashed his badge and asked if there was someplace private where they could talk. She told him to follow her, and he did—trailing in the wake of her inexpensive perfume into the stock room in back.

"You know a Mr. Taylor Ashe?" Columbo asked, and couldn't help noticing a whole rack of stylish raincoats behind the young woman.

Cindy's smile narrowed, but stayed pat. "What about him?"

"We think he's involved in a murder in Los Angeles."

The smile vanished, as did most of her pert composure. "Murder?"

"We think he shot a man to death at Wonder World. You might have seen the story in the papers."

"I don't read the papers." She took a deep breath. "Jesus Christ," she murmured, almost losing her balance, sinking back against the raincoats.

He caught her, steadied her. "Miss?"

"I'm okay, I'm okay. Why'd you come to *me*?"

Columbo tried to lock into her evasive eyes. "You in love with the man?"

"That's—no damn business of yours, cop or no cop."

"You'll have to excuse me, miss, but I'm going to take that as a yes."

"Take it any goddamn way you please. For your information, Taylor's talking marriage."

"Really." Columbo unfurled his newspaper, found an earmarked page, and held it out to her. There was a photograph in the Sunday Styles section of a smiling Taylor Ashe and a smiling Alex Fairchild at a charity function.

Cindy grabbed the paper from him, stared at the photograph, then crumpled it and threw it violently to the floor. "I knew it from the start—it was about the sex, all about the sex and nothing else. He would've told me anything I wanted to hear if I gave him what he wanted. And like an idiot I did! Still am!"

Columbo said nothing, looked at the price tag on a raincoat. "What do you want?" she said finally. "And don't say my body!"

"Oh no, no, nothing like that, miss. I said we're investigating this murder in Los Angeles."

Her mouth gaped open. "Oh my God! I should've known!"

"Known what?"

"Two weeks ago. He asked me for a gun my father had left me among some other crap when he died. Stupidly I had told him about that."

"A gun. And you gave it to him?"

Her hand nervously groped a sleeve on a raincoat. "Like a love-sick bimbo, yeah. He took it and I never got it back, the son-of-a-bitch!"

"Did he tell you why he wanted it?"

"Oh, something about robberies in his neighborhood." Columbo watched her twist the sleeve. "Did you ask him why he never returned it?"

"Once. I don't remember what he said. I didn't much care, I hate guns. Wait a minute! You think he really killed the guy in L.A.? *With my father's gun?!* Is that what you think?!"

"Would you mind coming down to the precinct after work, make a statement?"

"Wait a minute. How could he kill a guy in L.A. when he's here in New York?"

"There're airplanes, miss. Did he ever tell you he used to be a commercial pilot?"

"No. And he never told me he was going to marry that socialite bitch either!"

Columbo handed her a card, after scribbling down the precinct's address. "I'll be waiting for you downtown." He started out, but turned back. "You think maybe you could give a *paisano* a nice deal on a raincoat?"

Taylor was slapping on shaving lotion, preparing to go out for the evening when the doorbell rang. He had an uneasy premonition who it probably was, and to his chagrin he was right. "Back again, Columbo?"

A sheepish smile. "I've only seen you twice before, Mr. Ashe."

"Well, hurry it up, I've got a date."

"Which one? Miss Fairchild? Or Miss Fortunato?"

Ashe slipped into his jacket, shaking his head. "You're priceless, Columbo, you know that? Both of them told me you've been annoying them too. And boy did I catch hell from Cindy because you told her about Alex. Why the hell don't you get back on a plane and leave me and my women alone?"

"Funny you mention it. It was planes I wanted to talk to you about, sir."

Taylor flicked lint off his jacket with a thumbnail. "I'm miles ahead of you, Lieutenant, but I suspect most of your suspects are too. You think I flew back and forth to L.A., murdering poor Hammershield before he could get his spine chilled? Incredible. You get paid for these wild speculations?"

"You have to admit it would be one way of you working it."

Ashe checked himself from stem to stern in the full-length mirror. Maybe the tie was a bit too somber, but he didn't have time to change it. "Any proof I flew a plane?"

"Not yet. But somebody could've rented one for you…Maybe another one of your girlfriends. But then there's the gun."

Ashe grinned at him in the mirror. "Where did that come from—the gun? You've always got something up your sleeve, don't you, Columbo? What about the gun? Beats me why Cindy even told you about it."

"If you're in a rush, we could share a cab to wherever you're going."

Ashe had to laugh in spite of himself. "These days I wouldn't even share a pizza with you. Columbo, I *needed* a weapon, there'd been a series of holdups and robberies around here. You can look it up in the police reports."

Columbo made a note in his notebook. "I'll do that. Thanks for telling me, sir."

Ashe turned away from the mirror. "I wanted to buy one but it's a big-deal waiting process, lots of red tape, et cetera." He smiled ironically: "Even murderers can be paranoid, Columbo."

The cop was studying his attire. "I gotta tell you, you really look swell, Mr. Ashe. Sharp. You buy all your clothes here in New York?"

What he *wasn't* buying was all this guy's bullshit: "Now why aren't you asking me why I didn't give Cindy the gun back?"

"Yeah, I was getting around to that. How come?"

"I tested it a few times, thought something was wrong. Showed it to a gun expert and he said the firing pin was damaged. Hell, I knew she wouldn't want a screwed-up, maybe dangerous weapon so I got rid of it."

Columbo nodded slowly, very slowly. "How'd you dispose of it? Threw it in a dumpster somewhere?"

"How'd you guess?"

Columbo put his notebook away. "Well, enjoy yourself on your date, sir. You sure you won't share a cab?"

"You just want to see where I'm going. Sorry, Columbo, you'll have to get back on your lonesome."

The big news at the precinct was that Dempsey had become a grandfather. There was a small celebration in the squad room and Dempsey motioned to Columbo, signaling him that he would appreciate it if he would kindly drag him away.

"Albert Dempsey the Third," he announced when they were safely ensconced in his office. "He'll probably be a cop like everybody else in the family since the turn of the century. *Last* century! Next time, goddamnit, I want a poet! You have kids, Columbo?"

"Nah. Unfortunately it didn't work out that way." He lit a cigar. "Ashe knows we don't have a shred of proof."

"We don't, we can't even prove he took a trip to L.A. So how are we going to ring the D.A.'s chimes? And you know we'll *never* find that .38 he used."

Columbo had his hands laced over his forehead, leaning back in the chair like he was suffering a headache. "There's one thing we *can* prove, though."

"What's that?"

"The Fairchild woman gave him a false alibi. She's looking at a pretty good stretch there if we can nail her."

"But that's still not enough to nail Ashe, and frankly we don't have any proof that Fairchild lied."

Now Columbo was hit with a new thought. He got up, energized. "We're not dead yet, Dempsey."

Columbo sat on the back lawn of the estate, watching Alex Fairchild and a woman friend play tennis. He was sweating profusely and he had forgotten to bring any handkerchiefs from Los Angeles.

The game ended with Alex the winner, and she kissed her opponent, invited her to lunch. The woman begged off, said she had a doctor's appointment in town.

After she left, Alex came over and sat down next to Columbo. She looked dry as toast, her light makeup still incredibly intact.

"You're a terrific tennis player, you know that?" Columbo said.

"Thank you." She looked at him. "Taylor called me," she said, laying her racket across her lap. "He says you're really pestering him and you've got nothing to go on."

A trickle of sweat ran down his face and he brushed it away. "Oh, I've got a little, ma'am. Concerns you, actually."

"In what way?" She called her housekeeper on her cellphone, told her not to make lunch for her friend. After she hung up: "Lieutenant? I asked you a question."

"Well, we do have some proof. Taylor Ashe wasn't where you claimed he was."

"If that was true — and it's not — what does that prove?"

"That you gave him a false alibi. That makes you what we call an accessory after the fact. Very serious crime, ma'am."

A thin bead of sweat ran down from Alex's hairline. "I did no such thing."

"You know I could put you under arrest right now."

She moved slightly away from him and her tone was defiant: "Why haven't you?"

"Why? Because I think you're basically a pretty decent lady who lied because you fell in love with the man."

Her smile didn't reach her eyes. "My, what a wonderful romantic you are, Lieutenant. Seems I picked the right cop out of the hat."

"Maybe you did. I'm gonna give you a chance."

"I like the sound of that. What kind of a chance?"

"I just want you to tell me some things about Mr. Ashe that only you might know."

"Like what?"

He wiped at another trickle of sweat. "Did you ever see him in possession of a gun?"

She hesitated, drummed her fingers over the strings of the racket, a nervous gesture not escaping Columbo. "He brought a gun over here one or two afternoons. Wanted to practice his marksmanship."

"The reason?"

"Said there were robberies in his neighborhood and since he wanted to protect himself and he had never owned a gun before."

"He wanted to learn how to use one. Gotcha, ma'am."

Alex had a feeling that this was exactly what he wanted to hear. "There's nothing criminal about that, is there, Lieutenant?"

"No. Oh no, nothing. So—so where did he practice?"

She pointed over her shoulder to the fringe of woods that bordered the rear of the estate. "He hung a little bull's-eye target on a tree and fired at that."

Columbo was up out of his chair in a flash, the blistering heat forgotten. "Could you show me, ma'am? The tree?"

"Of course. He wasn't very good. That poor tree was full of holes and gashes."

She led him quickly along a narrow dirt path through a patchwork of broken sunlight, a few branches snapping peevishly at the Lieutenant. There was a small clearing right ahead of them, a circle of yellow sunburnt grass in the thick surrounding brush.

Columbo stopped, a little short of breath. He saw the tattered target pinned to the thick trunk of a tree. There were charring and holes in the bark.

"Is this what you wanted to see?" Alex asked.

"Oh yes, ma'am. This is *exactly* what I wanted to see."

Taylor Ashe sat in the interrogation room with Columbo and a scowling Dempsey beside him. He was still his nonchalant self, almost bored, sleepy-eyed, relaxed.

"Our forensic team swept the area, found the slugs in the tree," Columbo said. "It didn't take us long, Mr. Ashe, for ballistics to match them with the bullet that killed Kenneth Hammershield."

Ashe said nothing, looking down at his spread fingers on his trousers, his manicured nails. "You did a great job, Columbo," he decided to say. "I don't know how really smart you are, but you're plodding and determined, I'll give you that. But you never understood me."

"How so, sir? Are you really so hard to figure out? Seems

to me you're a man who lives off women. But once, twenty years ago, you fell in love with someone special. *Really* fell in love, probably for the first and only time in your life. And Hammershield's bullet killed her. It was an accident, but it didn't matter — he robbed you of the woman you probably would've been with forever. Sad, really sad." He touched him on the sleeve. "They say obsessions die only with your own death, Mr. Ashe."

Ashe looked at him with a surprising, newfound respect. "I underestimated you, Columbo. You really do understand ... love."

Columbo smiled. "Thirty years of it. I think by this time I maybe got an inkling."

The barman was surprised to see him. "Back so soon?"

"Last time you promised me a *real* drink. Two of them, really stiff."

He was delighted, plucking a bottle from the shelf. "On me. But why no club soda this time?"

Columbo jerked his head at the door. "Got a cab waiting, I'm going to the airport. I'm terrified of flying."

He poured a stiff double, a very stiff double. "You're a dyed-in-the-wool New Yorker, my friend. You gonna come back and see us again some time?"

Columbo downed the drink, coughing. "I'll give it some thought, but don't count on it!"

GRIEF

AS COLUMBO ARRIVED AT a faux-English Tudor mansion in the flats of Beverly Hills, two Mexican gardeners were riding power lawnmowers like stallions across the lawn. There was a dove-gray Cadillac parked in the drive.

At ten in the morning the neighborhood seemed tomb-silent except for the usual far-off barking of dogs. It was amazing how the rich preferred silence at home, but didn't mind the noise in their overly loud restaurants.

He was less than warmly greeted by a severe, almost militant woman in her early seventies. She introduced herself as Mary Tomlinson, the deceased's sister, and she looked like she wanted him to wipe his feet on the doormat even though it was a beautiful, clear day.

She conducted him into the study and failed to ask him to take a seat. Nevertheless, Columbo settled himself in an armchair near a wall of books and took out his notebook. The woman remained standing, silent.

Columbo cleared his throat. "Miss Tomlinson ..." he began awkwardly, "you told the police you thought maybe your brother was deliberately hit by a car last night. Why?"

"George had told me that he believed his life might be in danger."

"Did he give you any reason why he thought that? Or if someone might be after him?"

"No. Perhaps he was a little paranoid. My brother was a very private man, more so since he retired. Some might say secretive."

"What had been his business, ma'am?"

She almost glared at him. "*Profession.* He was a physician who practiced almost fifty years here in Beverly Hills."

Columbo was about to jot this in his notebook when a dog came barking into the room, straight to this alien intruder. It took one look at him and emitted a theatrical two-note shriek.

"He doesn't like you," the woman said. "Did you carry any dog dirt with you into the house?"

He looked down guiltily at his shoes. "No, ma'am, not that I noticed."

Now the dog parked itself at Columbo's feet, a suspicious sentinel. He did his best to ignore it. "Did—did your brother have any enemies, Miss Tomlinson?"

"No!" She seemed upset that he would even ask the question. "George was a brilliant internist, he prevented many deaths through his diagnoses and his care. He gave thousands every year to charities. He remained a consultant at the Parkman Hospital even in his retirement."

"Was he married?"

"Yes. Grace died a few years ago and my brother was devastated, never quite the same."

There was now a low growl in the dog's throat. "Ah—what's the name of the dog, ma'am?"

"Skipper. You certainly don't seem to have made a new friend."

Columbo shifted his feet, avoiding Skipper's beady eyes. "No ... I don't think so. He doesn't bite, does he?"

"Only tree-climbing rodents. I would imagine that would exclude you, Lieutenant." It was a small attempt at humor and she seemed to have surprised even herself.

"Let me go over what you said in the report." Columbo was looking in his notebook.

"Your brother went out at ten to walk the dog. Fifteen minutes later, neighbors down the block called and told you there had been what they thought was a hit-and-run accident — one that involved your brother."

"Yes. He was killed instantly. They heard the impact and then the murderer's car speeding off."

"No offense, ma'am, but maybe it was an accident. The driver panicked and drove away. A hit-and-run."

"No! It was what you people call vehicular homicide. I think someone deliberately struck my brother and left the scene."

"Hmm. When the neighbors came out they found Skipper at your brother's body."

She pressed the bridge of her nose—maybe to avert tears, maybe the hostility and anger were fading. "There are no more loyal animals than dogs. Do you own a dog, Lieutenant?"

"I did. Basset hound. He passed on and I'm sorry we never got another one."

He looked down at Skipper—it seemed his words had somehow tempered the dog's suspiciousness. But that was crazy. He closed his notebook, got up, making sure he didn't disturb the creature.

"So what is your course of action?" the woman wanted to know.

"Have to find that hit-and-run driver. But I gotta admit, it's not going to be easy. Check the auto body shops if a car came in to be repaired. If the driver's smart he'll wait awhile until he has the damage fixed."

"And what are the odds you'll catch him?"

He walked gingerly to the door, Skipper hot on his trail. "Not too good, ma'am. But I promise you we'll do everything we can on this."

It turned out to be a lot easier than he had predicted. There was a report waiting for him at the station of a stolen car that had been recovered with a smashed headlight, some body damage, and traces of blood on the front fender. It had been found only a few blocks from the Tomlinson mansion, and forensics was going over it.

The car's registration was in the name of Felix Younger with an address on Elm Drive in the flats. He had phoned early that morning to report that his car had been stolen.

Columbo grabbed a bite at his chili joint and drove over to Elm. This was decidedly a more modest mansion with no gardeners on the lawn, just a few argumentative birds and a slightly lopsided For Sale sign.

The man who opened the door might have been a year or two older than Tomlinson's sister. He had coarse, uncombed gray hair, and an old-fashioned, prominent hearing aid. His eyes had red rims as if he was a man who had been crying. Columbo showed him his badge.

"Oh," Younger said. "Yes. Come in."

The Spanish-tiled hallway was dim and bare, and Columbo cooled his heels until Younger decided to take him into the living room. He walked a bit awkwardly as if he needed a cane but his vanity prevented him from using one.

The living room was old—old everything and musty-smelling. Columbo sneezed. Twice. There were dust motes dancing in the columns of light that escaped through corners of the old velvet drapes that were still closed against the bright, inviting day.

"Please sit down," Younger said. At least he had none of the Tomlinson woman's discourtesy.

Columbo sat. "You reported your car was stolen, Mr. Younger. When exactly were you aware of that?"

"Well, I haven't been parking it in the garage as of late because I've been clearing some things out of the house and storing them in there."

"So you parked it in the driveway or the street?"

Hand to his ear: "What was that?"

Louder: "Where'd you park the car, sir?"

"In the driveway. I got up this morning and noticed the car was gone. That's when I called you people."

"Are you married, Mr. Younger?"

There was a frown in the already age-creased forehead. "Never married. Why do you ask that?"

"Only if someone else had a set of your car keys. Anyone work here, might've had access to them?"

"No. Day worker comes to clean on Thursdays, but she wouldn't take them. They're always in my pocket."

"How do you think somebody managed to take off in your car?"

"You people should know that. What do they call it, hot something?"

Columbo stifled a burp—almost—knowing the chili was the culprit. "Hot-wiring. So you think the car was stolen sometime last night? When was the last time you drove it?"

"Late yesterday afternoon. Left it in the driveway, came in to make dinner. Watched TV and went to bed at nine, my regular time. Never heard anything. 'Course I don't hear much anyway!" His first attempt at humor, but unlike the Tomlinson woman he wasn't surprised by it.

"A man was killed last night by someone driving your car."

"Say again?"

Columbo repeated what he said and Younger's mouth jerked open, frozen in disbelief. "No! You can't be serious."

"Very serious, sir. The victim's sister believes it was vehicular homicide."

"Who was the victim?"

"A Doctor George Tomlinson. Did you know him?"

"Tom what?"

Louder: "Tomlinson. Doctor George Tomlinson."

Younger pondered the name. "Never heard of him. He practice here in Beverly Hills?"

"Yes, sir. But he was retired."

"Been going to the same internist for forty-three years. Walter Rothstein. Lovely man, died last month, got to get somebody new. Ironic. Could've maybe gone to this Tomlinson when he was still alive." A veil of sadness came slowly down over his eyes. "Did Tomlinson have a wife?"

"Widower. He lived with his sister."

He squeezed the bridge of his nose, much like Mary Tomlinson had. "Lucky."

Columbo nodded. The man was going to be stranded now

without his car until it was repaired. "You have friends, someone who can help you shop, get around for a while?"

"Not many friends. Some have died, good friends, some have moved away, some in rest homes."

"Well, you'll have to get your car towed to a body shop. We can handle that for you. You can always rent one while they do the work."

Hand to ear: "Rent what?" He adjusted the hearing aid.

"Rent a car. So you can get around."

His smile was sad around the edges. "Not too many places I want to go to anymore," he said. "Times have changed. The whole city now. Went to my old shoemaker last week, no longer there. Some kind of cellphone store took its place."

Columbo got up, handed Younger his card. "You can always phone me there, sir, leave a message."

Younger rose too, a little shakily. An idle ray of sunlight from the window was not kind to his face. He stared up at the diffused light seeping around the drapes. "The sister thought it was murder....That means someone wanted to kill the poor man and didn't want to use his own car so he wouldn't get caught...."

He wanted to walk with him to the door, but Columbo motioned he could make it on his own.

He walked slowly to his car, the sun blinding now, his instincts pushing his thoughts around. Yeah, the murderer didn't want to use his own c a r.... Maybe, he did. Oh, come on now, that's really reaching.

Well, gotta puzzle that one out, he thought. He usually trusted his instincts. Unless he had an instinct not to.

When he got to the abandoned Buick sedan, a tow truck was about to haul it away. The tech team had gone, but Sergeant Pagano was still there, talking on his cellphone.

He hung up just as Columbo came up. "It'll hold, they're going to call me right back."

"So what's going on here?" Columbo asked. He felt like a cigar but he had left his day's supply at home.

"I talked to the neighbors. It looks like the perp, if this was a planned killing, struck the doctor and left the damaged car here."

"How fast did the neighbors get out here?"

"Not too fast. By that time they saw just the car, the dog, and his body. Nobody else around."

Columbo looked down near the curb where yellow tape

marked where the body had fallen. "Yeah, they were probably too distracted to see somebody getting away."

He looked off under the heavy summer foliage of the elms that lined each side of the street. "Y'know, this is not far from Tomlinson's house."

"He walked his dog every night. The sister said this was his regular route."

"Hmmm." Columbo swiveled slightly in another direction. "Funny. Younger, the guy whose car was stolen? He's only four blocks away."

Pagano looked at him as his cellphone rang. "What are you getting at?" He answered the phone. "Pagano.... You're sure of that? ... Yeah, that's something Columbo will want to know. Thanks, Sal." He hung up.

Columbo smiled. "What should I know?"

"There's a big malpractice lawsuit against Doctor Tomlinson. You think maybe the litigant's grudge was so bad that the litigant—?"

"The sister mentioned Tomlinson was connected with Parkman Hospital. I know one of the lawyers on their board, and I can talk to him."

"Y'know," Pagano said, "if they got a good case they can probably get at the estate. I hear the sister's going to inherit a hell of a lot of that smooth green stuff."

Columbo started crossing the street to his car. "That's interesting, Sergeant," he called back. "I'll have to keep that in mind."

He sat with Larry Saltzman, his attorney contact at Parkman, in his sun-splashed office. Saltzman was late forties with salt-and-pepper curly hair and an ingratiating manner. He was squeezing a tennis ball.

"A patient, Samuel Stebbins, brought a lawsuit against Doctor Tomlinson. The suit alleges that when Tomlinson was practicing, he prescribed an experimental cancer medication that only aggravated his condition."

"You think Stebbins might've been angry enough to go after the doctor? I'm talking about a hit-and-run last night."

There was a wry smile in Saltzman's sun-wrinkled eyes. "No way, Lieutenant."

"Why do you say that? You know the man?"

The smile held. "No. Trouble is, he died last week."

Columbo almost smiled himself. "Yeah, I guess that pretty

much precludes Stebbins from attacking Doctor Tomlinson."
But he wasn't deterred. "Do you know any of Stebbins' family?"

Saltzman stashed the tennis ball in his desk drawer. "Never
had the pleasure. Why do you ask?"

"Maybe one of them wanted to get revenge for Stebbins'
death."

"You got time for me to make a call?"

"Yeah, go ahead."

Saltzman had his secretary get someone. "Roberta?" he said
to the phone. "Sam Stebbins? He had a wife, family?" He waited,
tapping an impatient foot on the floor.

"Who's Roberta?" Columbo asked.

"Records. She went to look up the file—" He kept waiting, then: "I'm here, babe, shoot....Uh-huh. Uh-huh. Just what
I wanted to know, thanks." He hung up, looked at Columbo.
"Divorced. Two sons, one in Florida, the other in Seattle. That
answer your question?"

"Yeah. Dead end. But I appreciate the help, Larry."

He returned to the Tomlinson mansion, found Mary planting seeds in the small backyard. Some of these incredible Beverly
Hills mansions, Columbo thought, had backyards no bigger than
the one he had played in behind his house when he was a kid.

"Did you find the driver?" she asked accusingly before he
could even say hello. She was wearing a large floppy hat that protected her from the hostile sun and a long-sleeved T-shirt over
immaculate, tailored jeans.

"No, not yet, ma'am."

"Then what are you doing back here? Get on it, man, time
is precious."

She stood up, brushed the clinging grass from her knees.

"I wanted to ask you whether your brother took the same
route every night when he walked Skipper."

He looked warily around—where was that dog? Hopefully
locked safe and sound in the house.

"My brother was very methodical," the woman said. "He
was like a clock with legs. I am a very methodical person myself,
but George was extraordinary. He had been that way since we
were children."

"So he always left at the same time very night? Ten o'clock
with Skipper? Always walked the same route?"

She pulled the brim further down to defeat the glare of the

sun. "Every night, same time. Same route. For years." Her eyes pounced on him. "Why do you keep harping on this?"

"Well, I'm sort of following your theory, ma'am. If somebody was out to get your brother, he had to know his routine so he could follow him when he took his walk with the dog."

"That sounds like simple-minded logic. So how is that going to help you?"

Columbo was about to answer when his cellphone rang. He always put it in his raincoat's right pocket, but it wasn't there. Ring, ring! He finally located it in his inside jacket pocket where he had never placed it before.

Very annoying. "Columbo," he answered.

Mary Tomlinson watched him as he turned slightly away.

"....Yes, I'm over here at the Tomlinson house right now... Uh-uh. Really. Okay, thanks for letting me know."

He clicked the phone off, made sure he put it back in the raincoat pocket where it belonged.

"Who was that?" she asked.

"The medical examiner. He told me something from his report on your brother."

"Yes, I gave him permission to conduct an autopsy. Something that will help you?"

Columbo stroked his chin. "I don't know. Told me your brother wasn't legally blind, but he had awful bad cataracts, both eyes. Did you know that, ma'am?"

"Of course I knew it. We were going to schedule a cataract operation in the fall. What does that have to do with anything?"

Columbo was still stroking his chin. "So if his eyes were bad I guess you drove him around when he had to do errands and things?"

"Of course. He had trouble driving during the day and it was impossible for him at night. Why is this important?"

"I don't know if it is, ma'am. Just one of those little things you file away."

"Well file it. Anything else?"

"I don't think so, no." He heard barking from the house. "I'll be on my way."

"To where, may I ask?"

Columbo smiled. "Maybe to see a person of interest."

"I don't have a lot of time," Younger said the next day. They were in the living room of his house again, with the same columns of light filtering in from the curtain-draped window. "A taxi's coming to pick me up."

"When do you think you'll get your car back?" Columbo asked. Hand to ear: "What was that?"

Louder: "When will you get your car back?"

He fiddled with his hearing aid. "The shop says next Monday. But I'm not holding my breath." He coughed. "Dry throat. Will you excuse me if I get some water?"

"I could use some myself, sir. Lotta smog out there today."

Younger led him back through the dim, narrow hall to the kitchen. "How about some iced tea instead?"

"That would be great."

While Younger went to the refrigerator, Columbo's eyes wandered around the kitchen. It was pretty old, thirties probably, cooking-discolored tiles on the walls. The only bright patch was a bright red doggie bowl near the door.

Younger brought a pitcher of tea to the counter with two glasses. He poured them both some. "Sugar?"

"Nah, I'm fine."

Younger drank off half of his glass, his old Adam's Apple bobbing. "What did you want to see me about?"

"I just wanted to know if you belonged to any clubs, went to any social events where you might have met Doctor Tomlinson?"

"No, I don't think so."

"And your health, sir. Has it been good?"

Younger finished the rest of the tea. "Excellent, thank you. Why do you ask?"

"You never had cause to go to the Parkman Hospital? Doctor Tomlinson was a consultant there."

A car honked from the street.

"No, never been to the Parkman. That must be my taxi."

"Okay, sir, I won't hold you."

They went out the front door, Younger careful to lock up. He crossed to where a Beverly

Hills Cab was parked at the curb and got into the back seat while Columbo walked to his own car nearby.

Once in the car, Columbo started the engine but waited until the taxi drove off. He watched until it rounded the corner and then took off following. Instinct again.

The taxi shot up west on Wilshire, Columbo discreetly behind. He followed until it took a left at 26th Street. It went straight to Olympic, then took a turn and parked in the little lot behind a veterinary establishment on the corner. Columbo parked on the side street, watching Younger get out, pay the taxi driver, and hurry toward the building in the back, entering a door.

Columbo left his car. The red doggie bowl in the kitchen and now a veterinary place— things were beginning to link up.

He slipped through the same door where Younger had disappeared. It was a medium-sized room filled with a group of men and women sitting in folding chairs. There was a woman addressing them, talking emotionally, it seemed, about her cat.

Columbo took a seat in the rear, peering around for Younger— who had found a seat upfront. He nudged an attractive young woman who sat next to him.

"Miss—what kind of a meeting is this?"

She stared at him. "Haven't you lost a pet?"

"Uh—no, no. Not recently I mean. I—just sort of wandered in here."

"Well, it's a pet loss support group."

Now it was Columbo's turn to stare at her. "You mean these are all people who've lost their pets? Like some kind of group therapy session or something?"

She smiled a lovely smile. "Yes."

The woman finished her talk, went to her seat, while an elegant elderly woman rose and faced the group. "My name is Harriet Perlmutter," she said in a quiet voice. "I lost my beloved Rosie last week and luckily a neighbor told me about this wonderful group." She fought to hold back tears. "My darling Rosie, a gorgeous light brown poodle, developed heart trouble and I had to put her down...."

Columbo touched the young woman on the arm. "Thank you, Miss. I don't really belong here."

And he got up, lowered his head, and ducked out the door.

That evening, Mary Tomlinson's door chimes rang and she was annoyed to find that that cop had come back. He must have had dinner since there was a tiny speck of what looked like catsup on the edge of his lip.

"I'm sorry to disturb you, Miss Tomlinson," he said in his usual apologetic manner. "Maybe I should have called ahead."

"Maybe you should have. Why are you here again?"

"Can I come in?"

Exasperated, she opened the door wider so he could enter. He went ahead into the study before she could stop him. When she joined him, he remained standing.

"You still haven't answered me," she said. "Why are you here again?"

"I invited somebody over."

"Without my permission?"

Columbo shifted his feet, pushed his hands deep down in his raincoat pockets. "It's the person I believe deliberately hit and killed your brother, ma'am."

"Good Lord . . . ," she said as she met his eyes. They held. "Is that smart? Is it safe?"

"Oh, don't worry, ma'am. Everything is under control."

She was suddenly aware that she had seriously misjudged this man: even with his laid-back, self-deprecating manner, he was no pushover. She was the one who finally looked away— just as the door chimes sounded.

"That must be—?" she said, flustered now.

Columbo was looking at his watch. "Just on time."

"Why—why don't you get the door?" she asked him.

"Oh sure, no problem."

He left the room and she clasped her hands, looking nervously, aimlessly, around at the shelves of books.

Columbo returned with Younger, who wore a navy-blue windbreaker and had neatly combed his unruly gray hair.

"I guess you're wondering why you're here, Mr. Younger. I guess you're wondering too, Miss Tomlinson. Oh—Mr. Younger is sort of a neighbor, lives only a couple of blocks away."

She gathered her strength. "But you said this man—?"

"Was responsible for killing your brother, yes."

Younger jerked back toward the door. "I might be hard of hearing, but I heard that! I killed Doctor Tomlinson? That's crazy."

"I don't think so, sir."

"You have proof of this?" the woman asked. For some reason she felt sympathetic toward Younger, who seemed vulnerable, his anger fading.

"I believe so, ma'am. You see, Mr. Younger here was a very lonely man, even more lonely when he lost his dog. Where's Skipper, by the way?"

"In the basement."

Columbo seemed relieved. "Good ... Mr. Younger's dog was killed in a hit-and-run. He isn't admitting to this yet, and I'm surmising. He was walking his dog at the time it was hit, and he managed to get the make, color, and license plate of the car. I think that probably on one of his walks in the neighborhood, he recognized the car and saw the license plate—the car that's parked on the drive outside. And that's when I believe Mr. Younger began tracking your brother and learning his route."

She nodded, giving him nothing more.

"And then Mr. Younger ran down the man who had killed his beloved dog."

Now she spoke out in anger: "Why didn't he kill Skipper instead?"

"Because he deeply loves dogs—am I right, sir?"

Younger was silent, his eyes fastened on the carpet. There was a very faint twitch in his cheek.

"The next morning he reported his car had been stolen—making it look like somebody else had killed your brother. That was taking a chance, but there was no connection between the Doctor and him. None—so he figured he was safe."

"This is incredible," she said. "He values an animal's life more than a human being's? I don't care what you say, this man is deeply disturbed. Unless you've got this all wrong."

Columbo shrugged. "He believed your brother killed his only companion, a companion I think he loved more than anything else in this world."

Now Younger looked up slowly from the carpet. "You said you're surmising." His small voice strengthened. "You have no proof."

"You made one big mistake, sir. When you had to leave your car after the murder, you didn't wipe your prints off the wheel. If the 'real' murderer had been driving, his prints might've been there. Or if he wore gloves, most of the prints, your prints, would've been smudged when he drove. But no—just your prints, crystal-clear, sir."

The doorbell rang.

"That's my man, ma'am," Columbo said. "He's here to put Mr. Younger under arrest."

The procedure took only a few minutes: the Sergeant took charge of Younger, monotonously read him his rights. The woman watched this with dry, unblinking eyes, the lines of her face rigid as always.

On the way to the door, Younger looked back at Columbo: "How—how did you know I had a dog?"

"The doggie bowl in your kitchen. Got me thinking. And then on an instinct I followed you to that support group." Younger nodded, turned away, and the officer led him out.

It was only after Columbo heard the front door close that he said, "Just one more thing, ma'am."

Her anger returned, but it was weak, diminished. "Tell you what?"

"The night Younger's dog was killed. The Doctor wasn't driving, was he?"

She took a long time to answer. And then a deep breath: "... No."

"You were driving, ma'am. The man had enough eyesight to walk Skipper every night, but you wouldn't trust him behind the wheel. You were the one who killed Younger's dog."

She nodded, her lips tightly compressed.

"If maybe you had stopped, commiserated with Mr. Younger, he might have forgiven you—and your brother might still be alive."

She was undaunted. "Do you want to put me under arrest too?"

"No, ma'am. But you accidentally killed a dog and set this whole thing in motion."

"So what am I supposed to do?"

Columbo went to the door. For some reason he suddenly flicked the speck of catsup from his lip. "I guess all you can do is live with it. And if you're a religious person, well, you might do some serious praying that you can someday forgive Mr. Younger."

SCOUT'S HONOR

ARTHUR MALVERN LOOKED OVER at the young blonde woman seated beside him on the passenger seat. He had told her that he wanted to get to know her better since she was seriously dating his son Neal.

Malvern was a striking presence: a strong, powerful face, flecks of "snow" in the coal-black hair, brawny, authoritative hands gripping the steering wheel. He saw that she had moved slightly toward the window as if her radar was picking up little warning blips.

"You've never been to Neal's cabin before?" he asked her.

"No. I never knew he had one."

"Ah, he probably wanted to surprise you. Sometimes we stay there overnight, get some fishing done. There's a beautiful little stream nearby," he lied. She really had no reason to fear him: he was a well-known real estate developer in the city, a rock-solid citizen, friend of the mayor's and on the county board of public works. But Neal had probably told her his father thought he could do better—much better—in the marriage department.

The headlights cut a wide white tunnel through the darkness, the road bordered on both sides by a dense mass of eucalyptus and pine. He slowly braked, bringing the car over to the edge of the road. "Here we are," he announced in his hearty, confident, radio announcer's voice.

"But—but how can you tell?" she asked.

He laughed. "Neal and I have been here so many times, we could probably find it blindfolded."

He got a flashlight from the glove compartment before he got out of the car. He walked around across the headlights, opened the passenger door, and graciously helped her out. She was as light as a bag of feathers. A thousand bags of feathers. All those expensive dinners Neal had treated her to, why hadn't they put a little meat on her bones? Stringy blonde hair, too much lipstick and eye shadow, forgettable good looks, and only a high school education. What the hell did Neal see in her?

He took her arm and guided her into a small opening in the dark vegetation. He was surprised to see a narrow, almost overgrown path a few feet away, and he gently guided her over to it.

"Why didn't Neal come with us?" she said.

"He got tied up at the office. He's going to meet us here shortly." Malvern made a show of pulling back his sleeve, looking at his massive gold watch. "And he'll be bringing a bottle of champagne when he comes."

"What for?"

"What for?" he laughed. "Your engagement, of course." Now he moved in front, leading her along the path.

"Where's this cabin?" she asked, her radar antenna picking up signals again.

He had already slipped his hand into his pocket, slipped on a glove. "Good God—look over there!" While she was misdirected, he brought the knife out in his gloved hand.

It was over in a microsecond.

He had nothing to wipe off the knife. He left her lying on the ground, moved further along the path and then veered off into the underbrush. He quickly dug a little grave with a gloved hand and buried the knife, pushing lots of dirt and leaves on top of it.

As he headed back to the car, he looked at his watch again. Eight forty-five. Neal would be still establishing his alibi. Even though he didn't know it.

The Boy Scout troop entered the forest the following afternoon, planning on an overnight camping trip. Thirteen-year-old Robbie Dobson found the body a short way from where his buddies were setting up camp. His father, Wayne, the Scoutmaster, immediately called 911 on his cellphone.

Columbo and his tech team arrived a short time later as the setting sun was casting a lengthening, almost sinister red glow over the campsite and the frightened youngsters.

Wayne Dobson immediately introduced himself. He was an athletic-looking man in his mid-thirties, wearing an immaculate uniform, his hair getting a little thin at the crown. "You got here really fast," he said. "Much appreciated."

"We weren't that far away," Columbo said. "Where's the body, Mr. Dobson?"

"My son Robbie will show you. He discovered it."

Robbie came over. The red glow did not disguise the freckles on his round, intelligent face. "You're a police sergeant?" he asked Columbo.

"Lieutenant. Boy, that's a lotta merit badges you got there." He inspected them, impressed. He said, "Suppose you show me where you found the body."

Robbie went off into the clustered pines, Columbo motioning the tech team to follow them.

The young woman lay face down, the wound visible between her prominent, bony shoulder blades. Again, the sun's red glow failed to mask the blood on her blouse.

The tech team gathered around the body as Columbo touched the boy on his

shoulder. "Robbie, why don't we go back to your dad."

"I'd like to get the boys out of here," Dobson said when they had returned. Most of the group was still standing around, some sitting on their rolled sleeping bags. "This has been pretty horrendous for all of us."

"We have a terrific police psychiatrist, Mr. Dobson," Columbo said. "If any of your boys needs counseling...."

"Thank you, Lieutenant, I just might take you up on that. I'll let you know."

Columbo nodded. He had been a Boy Scout himself, many moons ago. He thought maybe he still had his old uniform somewhere in one of the boxes in the garage where his wife seemed to store everything from his past. He would have to ask her. She had this file index in her head that listed where most things were, including his old National Guard stuff in its duffle bag.

Arthur Malvern brusquely opened the door. There was a short man outside in a raincoat, holding an unlit cigar. "Yes?"

Columbo opened his wallet like a book, showing Malvern the gold and silver badge. "Lieutenant Columbo, sir. Homicide. Can I come in?"

"Yes ... yes, of course." He opened the door wider, stepping back. My God, how did they trace the body back to him? Cool it, he told himself—there was no conceivable way he could be connected to the crime.

He led Columbo into the vast living room, a huge, brocaded tapestry on one wall, paintings lining the others. The sun leaked in around the damask drapes on the street-side window. "May I have the housekeeper bring you some coffee, Lieutenant?"

Columbo was admiring one of the paintings, a dark abstract. "No thanks, sir." He flung out a hand at it. "I guess that's some kinda nightclub with sort of a neon sign over the front door?"

Malvern smiled. "Very good. Very good indeed." He sat down, adjusting his trousers so as not to mar the razor-sharp creases. "What can I do for you this morning?"

Columbo took a photo from his raincoat pocket. Still standing, he handed it to the older man.

Malvern studied it, an insistent pulse starting to beat in his temple.

"Do you know that young man?" Columbo asked.

His smile was not as bright as he would have liked. "Well yes, of course. It's my son Neal." An impetuous laugh. "Was he caught spitting on the sidewalk or something?"

"You mind if I smoke?"

"I do, yes. My late wife killed my own smoking habit. You really should give it up yourself." Why had he used the word 'killed'?

"I've been trying, sir, I've really been trying."

"And I would cut out the 'sir,' Lieutenant. We're all on a level playing field here. So what about Neal?"

"A young woman was murdered two days ago. A Nancy Cook. We went over everything in her apartment and we found that picture."

"But how did you know it was my son?"

"Piece of cake. You see he signed it, 'Neal'?"

Malvern handed him the photo back. "Well there're a lot of Neals in this world. How did you know to come here?"

"We found her phone book on the night table. There was only one Neal—Neal Malvern."

"Brilliant deduction," he said, his words had only a slight coat of sarcasm. "Why don't you sit down, Lieutenant. You'd be a lot more comfortable."

"Thank you, Mr. Malvern, but my wife thinks I sit too much as it is. You have no idea of all the paperwork we have to do. She's always after me to start exercising."

"Good idea." He paused, smiling. "So I guess you want to know Neal's relationship with Nancy—?

Columbo was studying another painting, his head tilted to one side. "Is your son here?"

"I believe he is." Neal had been beside himself; he couldn't find Nancy for the past two days. Then he read the news of her murder in the paper, and had been deeply shocked, shattered. Malvern had ordered the boy to get control of himself, take no phone calls, isolate himself. He also told him perhaps it was best all around that she was no longer in his life.

"Could I talk to him?" Columbo said, turning away from the painting.

"Of course." He got up, looking down at his still beautifully pressed trousers, and went out into the hallway. "Neal?" he called. No answer. Louder, a command: "Neal!"

A few moments later a handsome blond young man came down the stairs. Columbo watched Malvern look him up and down as if he was checking for minute particles of dirt on his son's apparel. Neal looked dolefully from his father to Columbo.

"This is homicide detective Columbo. He's investigating Nancy's murder."

"She was a friend?" Columbo asked Neal after they had gone into the living room. He noted that the word "murder" had etched an even sadder look on the young man's face. His eyes flew back to his father's. Malvern's face had hardened, his eyes seeming to signal a cautionary "buck up."

"She ... she was my girlfriend. We were going to be engaged to be married."

"Uh-huh." Columbo's pad and pencil were out. "And when was the last time you saw her?"

"We talked on the phone two days ago."

Another "Uh-huh." Jottings in notebook. "And where were you two nights ago, Neal? Let's say between the hours of seven and midnight?"

Malvern stepped between them. "Now wait a minute, Lieutenant. Are you insinuating that my son had something to do with that woman's death?"

"Oh no, sir. Not at all. But you understand I have to talk to everybody who really knew the victim. And, I mean, your son had to know her if he was planning to marry her. I mean, that would be a no-brainer, wouldn't it?"

Malvern seemed immutably planted now between Columbo and his son. "Neal unfortunately lost his mother at an early age. I brought him up, instilled in him rules of decency and civilized behavior. Right, Neal?"

Neal nodded emphatically, but looked as if he wanted to be somewhere else.

"So where were you that night?" Columbo asked him again.

"I was at a party at a friend's house."

Columbo wet his thumb, used it to turn to another page in the notebook. "What's your friend's name?"

"Jim Davies. You want to know where he lives?"

"That would be very helpful, yes."

Neal looked at his father for no apparent reason. "818 Meadowbrook Road in Glendale."

This was jotted down—after Columbo had wet the tip of his pencil. "Very good. Thank you." He looked up at Malvern. "I'm sorry I had to disturb you, sir. But you and your son have been very cooperative."

Malvern only nodded.

Columbo nodded too, then walked into the hallway and went to the door.

Malvern waited until he heard the door open and close before he went over to the curtained window. He drew aside the drape just a bit and peered out into the street. He watched Columbo go to his car. Satisfied, he let the drape fall back.

Neal was still standing where he had been, silent, his face devoid of expression. He was waiting on his father.

"You shouldn't have been nervous in front of that man," Malvern said. "It appears to be a routine investigation. Why were you so nervous?"

Neal shrugged, laced and unlaced his fingers.

Malvern peered down at Neal's hands, which were now locked in an almost prayerful grip. "You're nervous because he was a cop or was it something else? *Neal!*"

"Something else, sir. When I told him I was at the party? I—I really wasn't there very long."

Columbo rang the doorbell at 818 Meadowbrook. It was answered by a short, rotund young man, Neal's age, with tousled red hair and bloodshot eyes. He was wearing a pajama top over rumpled jeans. "If you're selling something I'm not interested."

Columbo flashed him his badge. "I'd like to come in."

"Sure. But don't expect the Waldorf."

Columbo entered a bright, sun-scrubbed living room. There was a desert waste of glasses, coffee cups, paper cups with remnants of liquor, wine, ashtrays heaped with cigarette butts spilling over onto the ash-strewn coffee table.

"Boy oh boy," Columbo said. "This must've been some long party." Eyeing the butts, he said optimistically, "You mind?"

"Not gonna be good for my hangover headache. But you got the badge. Be my guest."

Columbo found a butt in his pocket, took his time lighting it. "You're Jim Davies?"

"That's what it says on the lease. Why's the law here? Neighbors complained we were too damn loud two nights ago?"

"No." The stub was going good now. "Neal Malvern a friend of yours?"

"Since high school. Why?"

"Was he here at your party?"

"For a while, yeah."

Columbo hid his surprise. "For a while," he repeated, as if he was ruminating on it, puffing on the stub. "And what time did he leave?"

Davies found a glass without a cigarette butt floating in it. He gulped down the little that was left. "Hard to say. I think he got here around six, six-thirty. Maybe ducked out around an hour later. Really can't say for sure." A thought suddenly penetrated the muzzy wall of his hangover. "Wait a minute—somebody called this morning, said Neal's girlfriend had been murdered. Is that why you're here?"

"Did you know the woman, Nancy Cook?"

"Sure. Neal had been going with her for over a year. Trashy little bottle blonde. I could never figure out why Neal wanted to marry her."

"How'd that go down with his father?"

"The murder?"

"The relationship."

Jim's smile was really a hangover grimace. "You know that guy? He's got poor Neal on a leash. I'm surprised he lets him go to the bathroom. Neal's mother was probably so fed up with him, she croaked. If I had a dad like that I'd join the Army."

More puffs. "Interesting. Jim—can I call you Jim?"

"You got the badge."

"Jim, after Neal split your party, any idea where he might've gone?"

Davies found another glass with a scant inch of booze. "The Foreign Legion maybe?"

Columbo went to the Cook apartment in Studio City. There was still a member of the tech team, Sergeant Dave Daniels, cleaning up details in the living room.

"Anything interesting?" Columbo asked, still puffing on what was left of the stub.

"Not really, no. The boys picked up a lotta prints. This was sure some 'social' lady."

Columbo took a trip around the small, unkempt room, looking at some rock posters tacked on the walls.

"Oh, Lieutenant," Daniels said, "there's a tenant in 102, says she knows something about a car...."

Columbo stopped, looked around for an ashtray. "What about a car?"

"I don't know. She'll have to tell you herself."

The young woman in 102 looked around Nancy's age, another Hollywood blonde with severely plucked eyebrows and a surfeit of makeup on a pale facsimile of a face.

Columbo had noticed, when he first walked into the apartment, that her only window looked down on the street. "Did you know Miss Cook?" he asked.

"No. Not well. Sometimes we helped each other find parking spaces on the street. Was she an actress or something?"

"I don't believe so."

"How did she make a living?"

Columbo shrugged. "We're checking on all that, Miss ...?"

"Chambers."

"Miss Chambers, you told one of the investigating officers something about a car?"

She nodded, went over to the window. "Two nights ago? I saw a car double-parked on the street, right in front of our apartment house."

Columbo didn't bother with his notebook. "And what time would that be? Do you remember?"

"Around seven or so. I was waiting for my date and I

kept looking out the window to see if he had driven up. You know how nervous women can get about dates, Lieutenant. I should know better after all these years."

Columbo nodded sympathetically. "My own experience was a while ago, Miss. My girlfriend's father was always suspicious of me. I had an old Ford with a door that was roped to the frame. And he didn't like the idea that she might marry a poor guy who wanted to be a cop."

She smiled. "And what did *he* do for a living?"

His smile was a carbon copy of hers, only a sliver more serious. "He was a cop."

She laughed and pointed down at the street. "The car was right there, but I knew it wasn't my date's car. This was one of those nifty new Jaguar convertibles."

Columbo came over to join her at the window. "You remember what color?"

"It was very dark, probably black. You know the light is still pretty good at seven. I would definitely say a black Jaguar."

"Sure about the make?"

Her smile was back with a vengeance. "I was born in L.A., Lieutenant. Cars are in our genes."

"And did you see Miss Cook come out to get in the car? Or the driver who maybe went in to pick her up?"

"I don't know. I went back in the bathroom to check myself out for my date."

"Wow," Columbo said. "You must really be interested in this guy."

"Not really," she admitted. "He says he's thinking of joining the F.B.I."

When Columbo returned to the cop shop, he found himself engulfed in a flurry of activity: a fugitive who had escaped from an upstate penitentiary was reported in the area and all available personnel were being sent out on a manhunt.

Partly seeking relief, he returned to the Malvern mansion in the waning afternoon. He thought how the sun was particularly kind in Beverly Hills: it seemed to show more aging on its houses than on its women. Did houses get face-lifts?

Luckily the garage door was open, and he saw a Bentley and a black convertible Jaguar. He walked over closer to take a better look at the Jaguar. It looked polished and new even in the growing dimness of the garage.

Malvern senior was not overjoyed to see him. "What now?" he asked in his usual radio announcer's voice.

"Some questions to ask Neal," Columbo said, not interested in looking at any of the art this time.

"Concerning what?" His voice had sharpened.

"Is he here?"

Malvern frowned, shaking his head in puzzlement and irritation. He went to the bottom of the stairs and called, "Neal!"

No answer.

He called again, "Neal!" his voice more forceful this time and colored by his growing vexation.

Finally a distant voice responded, and a few moments later Neal came cautiously down the stairs.

"Why were you so engrossed that you couldn't hear me?" Malvern asked, looking him over with his usual scalding, miss-nothing scrutiny.

"Just reading the paper."

"Well the Lieutenant here has some questions to ask you."

They were standing in the hallway and Malvern had noticeably failed to invite Columbo into the living room.

He redirected his hard focus on the cop, who seemed as usual — wearing that useless raincoat and looking as if he still had a crust of sleep in his eyes.

"Well go ahead, what're your questions?" he asked. But maybe he was lucky so far that the cop hadn't steered his investigation toward *him*.

"Neal," Columbo began, "you said you were at your friend's party. But he said you left after you had been there an hour or so. Any truth to that?"

Malvern stiffened. He had set up his son with an alibi and he knew that stupidly, unconsciously, Neal had blown it.

"Yes ... yes I did leave." He gave his father a quick, questioning glance. A not very subtle one.

"So where did you go?" Columbo said, picking up on it.

"Just ... drove around, I guess." He made an effort to meet Columbo's eyes.

"Just drove around. Uh-uh. A young woman in your girlfriend's apartment building said she saw a black Jaguar convertible double-parked on the street around seven that night. Was that you?"

"...Yes. Now I remember, Lieutenant — I drove up to her place. I called Nancy on my cellphone, but she didn't answer so I left."

Columbo was quick to follow up: "Did you leave a message on her message machine?"

Malvern was even quicker to follow up: "I'm sure you checked that machine at her apartment. I hope you're not playing 'gotcha,' Lieutenant."

"Oh no, not at all, sir. I never play 'gotcha.' We did check her machine. There were a few messages from friends, but not any from Neal. It was an old machine and sometimes they lose messages."

"Then what's this all about?" Malvern's tone had turned cold now, rapidly approaching sub-zero.

"Well I have to find out where he went after he left the party. That's my job, sir." He took a few slow steps toward the door, suddenly turned around: "Just one more thing, Neal. You told me you were at the party—but you didn't tell me you left. How come?"

Malvern stared at his son: his answer better be good. Damn good. Would he have to bail out the frightened fool again?

"I—I guess I forgot. I haven't been thinking too clearly after Nancy's death." He blinked back a sudden rush of tears.

Pleased, Malvern took over: "I think you're intruding, Lieutenant, at a very sad time for my son. For both of us. I hope you're trying to find out who would want to do this terrible thing. Can I trust you on that?"

"Oh yes sir," Columbo said. "You certainly can." Now he actually went to the door, nodded at both of them, and left.

"If he'd been bald he'd have his father's fingerprints all over the top of his head. Indelibly."

Columbo was at the Sherman Oaks apartment of Trina Knowles, Nancy Cook's best friend. She was a diminutive brunette with a lithe, probably gym-molded, physique.

"Do you know the father?"

Trina looked at an unopened pack of cigarettes on the coffee table, as if they were there to test her. "Luckily, no.

Neal's father hated Nancy, thought she was some kind of ex-hooker slut. This was probably the first time, Nancy told me, that Neal had ever defied his father."

"Hmmm." Columbo prowled the small living room. "Do you think Arthur Malvern hated Nancy so much he might have killed her?"

Trina jerked back on the couch, surprised by Columbo's question. "That's— that's a pretty heavy-duty thing to lay on me, Lieutenant. There's hatred and there's hatred. I really don't have a clue as to how deeply Neal's father hated her."

"I take it you know Neal?"

"Yes. A very nice guy. I think he and Nancy would've had a great marriage."

Columbo's aimless prowling suddenly stopped at the couch.

He looked at her. "Once again you didn't answer my question, Miss Knowles. Do you think Arthur Malvern murdered your friend?"

"I really wouldn't know. If he thought Neal's marrying her would destroy Neal's life, he was probably capable of it. Sometimes these very macho businessmen have no checks and balances. You get what I'm saying?"

Columbo looked like he was ready to sit down beside her. "Yeah, yeah, I get what you're saying." He paused, still standing, looking over at some doodads on a table. "Neal ..." he said, stretching out the name.

"What about him?"

"He was at a party—at his friend Jim Davies' house— and he left early. He says he was just driving around. That was about the time Nancy was killed."

Trina sighed, nervously re-crossed her legs. She suddenly got to her feet, went over and grabbed the cigarette pack. "Are you telling me you think Neal killed her?"

"I don't remember saying that."

Long pause while she contemplated lighting the cigarette, but didn't. "Neal came over here."

Columbo paused again. "Why?"

"We—we were having an affair." Her eyes were lowered, still considering the cigarette.

"And Nancy had no idea?"

"Right." She looked up at him, her eyes clouding over.

Columbo nodded, bent over slightly, his hands linked

behind his back. "Interesting, very interesting. How long did he stay?"

"Not long. But doesn't that give him an alibi?"

"Not really. He still could have killed the girl and used you as an alibi. The murder site isn't very far from here."

He stalked off again, back on his journey around the room. He stopped, looked at her. "He was still committed to Miss Cook even though he was fooling around with you?"

"That's the way it happened, Lieutenant. I guess it might have been different in your time."

Columbo's smile was wry. "I'm not exactly a dinosaur, Miss Knowles."

"I didn't say you were." She looked over at a clock on the mantel. "I've got an appointment at the gym."

"Did Neal ever show any anger toward your friend?"

"None. I think he was in love with both of us. As I said, he's a lovely guy. I wish him the best."

"Do you think you two will get back together—I mean after what happened to Nancy?"

"Who knows. Your guess is as good as mine."

Columbo nodded, thought for a long minute, then went to the door. "I thank you for your time, Miss Knowles. You've been very helpful."

She frowned. "Nothing I told you will get in the media, will it?"

"None of it will get in the media." He went out.

Malvern came into Neal's room just as he was hanging up the phone. "Who was that?" he asked.

"Lieutenant Columbo. He wants me to come see him at the police station."

"Alone?" His pulse had quickened again. Was Columbo bearing down on Neal because he had fudged having an alibi? Or was it something else, something more dangerous?

"Yes, Dad, he made that very clear. Just me."

"I want our lawyer to go with you."

Neal backed away slightly, but he held his father's eyes. "No ... I don't think that's a good idea. I think it makes me look suspicious."

Malvern was surprised: his son never resisted his suggestions before. What had happened to him ever since he had defied him with that girl? Didn't he realize everything his father insisted upon was for his own good? Was he losing control over his own son?

"Well I'm going to go with you," he said in a voice that told Neal he would definitely brook no disagreement.

"No, Dad. I don't need a shepherd with me when I meet with Columbo."

"Did you just hear what I said? *I'm going with you!*"

Now Neal stepped away, but his eyes didn't falter or leave his father's. "I'm going alone."

"The hell you are!" his father yelled.

"Get off my back! I'm going by myself."

Columbo was in his usual friendly mode. "This is kinda a personal question, Neal, but I have to ask it."

Neal sat in Columbo's office, facing the cop who was standing, an unlit cigar in his hand. The police station had seemed very quiet this morning, almost empty. "Go ahead, Lieutenant, feel free to ask anything you want."

"A friend of Nancy's told me you had an affair with her. Any truth to that?"

"—Yes. That's true." Neal buckled. He knew Columbo was aware of his nervousness.

"So you talked to Trina."

Columbo tried to take a long drag on his unlit cigar. He didn't answer.

"Trina was always jealous that Nancy had so many boyfriends."

"So you didn't mind having an affair with somebody like that?" Columbo's eyes, regarding him over the cigar, were gently amused.

Neal shrugged. He didn't like the question and he decided not to answer.

"And if you were going to marry Nancy," Columbo continued, "why mess around with this other girl?"

Another shrug, this one more listless. "You know how guys like to have a last fling before they settle down? Like they have a stripper at their bachelor party?"

"Yeah ... I've heard that." He got up, went over to a small fridge in the corner. "You want a soda?"

"No thanks."

"It's funny—when it's hot I like hot coffee and when it's

cold I like a cold soda. My wife says even a dog has a better metabolic system than that."

"Whatever." He had a disdain, just below the surface, for those he considered his inferiors. God, he hoped he wasn't turning into his father!

Columbo went over and opened the door. "Well, that'll be all for today, Neal. I thank you for coming over."

He had been right when he resisted his father accompanying him. Maybe he was learning a lesson: he had to respond to most of his father's unreasonable demands with a defiant no. Drawing that line in the sand was the only thing his father understood.

"You mean I can go, Lieutenant?"

"Oh yeah, you can go."

Five minutes later, Columbo received an urgent phone call from Sergeant Rodriguez whom he had assigned to the murder site to make sure no trespassers violated the crime scene. Columbo and his tech team had been about to search the area after the body was discovered when his men were immediately pulled away to spearhead the manhunt for the fugitive.

"Lieutenant," Rodriguez said, "there's a bunch of young boys, come outta nowhere."

"What're they doing there?" He could hear the voices of the kids in the background.

"I don't know. But they're looking all over the place."

"Are they in Boy Scout uniforms?" Columbo asked.

"No."

"See if there's a boy named Robbie Dobson with them."

"Will do."

A moment later Rodriguez was back on the phone: "I got 'im. He's right here."

Columbo sighed. "Put him on, Sergeant."

"Lieutenant?" Robbie said, just on the verge of being out of breath.

"What are you and your friends doing there?" Columbo asked in a calm voice.

"Looking for the knife. We heard a report on a news show that the murder weapon hadn't been found yet. So— so we were trying to help."

"Does your dad know you're out there?"

He hesitated, and when he finally spoke his voice was quaking a little with guilt. "Ah ... well ... no." Quickly: "Are you going to tell him?"

Columbo was about to speak when there were shouts and cries of triumph from the near background. "Robbie," he said louder. "Robbie?"

Robbie was suddenly back on, his voice a trumpet of jubilation. "Billy Rhodes found it!"

"Don't touch it," Columbo said.

"Don't worry, Lieutenant, I warned them to be careful not to touch any evidence."

Columbo smiled. "Scout's honor?"

"Scout's honor."

Later that evening Columbo and his fingerprint man came to the Malvern mansion. Malvern was in the living room, dressed to the nines, annoyed that they had walked in unannounced just as he was preparing to leave.

He hung up the phone and glared at Columbo. "*Now* what do you want?"

"We have to take some fingerprints, sir."

"My son's?"

"Yes sir. And yours."

Malvern ignored this. "I hope you have a court order."

"We do." He took a folded document from his pocket, gave it to Malvern. "Is Neal here?"

"He's on his way home from the club. I wanted him to get out, play a little golf, have some drinks with friends. Anything to forget this terrible tragedy with Nancy."

"I understand, sir. My man can get your prints while we wait for him."

Malvern decided not to sit down, circled the chair. Why was he so uptight, exhibiting his anxiety to this cop? He had worn a glove, there was no chance his fingerprints could be on the knife. Besides, he had buried the damn thing. Why the hell had he buried it so close to the body? Was he *crazy?* What was he thinking? He could have buried it miles away. Screw it. Even if they found it, there was no way it could be traced to him—or to Neal. Just what kind of ploy was Columbo trying to pull?

Neal returned a few minutes later. He seemed in a dizzy, almost slap-happy mood, a strong smell of liquor on his breath. He shook hands with Columbo. Malvern quickly interceded.

"I'm glad you enjoyed yourself at the club, Neal, but perhaps you'd better settle down. The Lieutenant and his man came here to take our fingerprints." His voice was iron and his son made a conscious effort to control himself.

"Fingerprints?" Neal asked Columbo.

"Just part of the investigation," Columbo tried to reassure him.

"So you think we had something to do with the murder?"

"I didn't say that."

Malvern sat down, watching his son. Neal was looking nervously at his hands, obviously sobering up quickly.

Columbo motioned to the fingerprint man who was standing in the doorway. "Sid —you can do your thing."

Sid took brushes, vials, ink pad, and other items from his black kit. He took a full set of prints from father and son with a minimum of effort and packed his accoutrements back where they came from. "I'll be going," he said to Columbo. "I'm sure I'll have a comparison by the time you get back."

Malvern felt a sudden tightening in his diaphragm. If they were going to make a comparison, they must certainly have some prints from the crime scene. But he had purposely worn a single glove and had hidden the gloved hand with the knife behind his back so as not to alarm Nancy. And why Neal's prints too? Neal hadn't been anywhere near the crime site. Or was this just Columbo twisting a tourniquet on both of them, waiting for him to make a slip?

He decided to voice his concern: "Why do you want our prints? You must have a reason. Did the murderer leave prints at the crime scene?"

"Not that I know of, sir." His face was as guileless as an infant's. "I should be heading back now."

"You'll let me know what your 'findings' are?"

Columbo didn't smile, but he said, "I promise you, you'll be the first to know, Mr. Malvern."

Malvern took his time driving to the police headquarters a little after eight that evening. The acidic constriction in his stomach had prevented him from eating even a light dinner. And Columbo's phone call request to come in had pressured him even more. Should he bring Neal? Columbo had given him a firm no. Surprisingly firm for such a laid-back cop. What kind of trap was he setting?

Columbo was in his office in shirtsleeves. He looked amazingly fresh, as if he had just had a battery-charging nap. The only illumination came from a goose-neck lamp on the desk.

"The department's saving money on their electricity bill?" Malvern asked with a smiling wryness.

"Nah. I don't like a lotta lights blazing in my face. Stops me from thinking clearly."

"So why am I here?"

"It's about your son."

Malvern dropped heavily down in a chair across from the desk. He wasn't worried about his trouser crease. "What about him?"

"We think he murdered Nancy Cook. In fact we know he did."

"That's crazy, that's impossible! How dare you even suggest something so stupid."

"I didn't suggest it, sir, I affirmed it. We have proof. Very solid proof." Columbo studied him for his reaction.

Malvern's tone lost its belligerence. "What proof? And don't say you can't tell me because it's police business."

"We found the murder weapon, a knife. The blood on the blade matches Miss Cook's. Neal's partial prints were on the handle of that knife."

"That's impossible." He had found the knife in a box in the attic, knowing there was no way it could be traced to him. But wait—wait a minute ... if Neal had placed the knife there (and who else could have?) yes, his prints would be on it. My God! Now it became clear: he had worn a glove so his prints weren't on the weapon. *But he had inadvertently preserved some of Neal's!*

"This is evidence that will hold up in any court of law, Mr. Malvern. You can hire the best defense attorney in the county, but it's irrefutable. I'm very sad to tell you this, but your son is a murderer. A cold-blooded one at that." He leaned back in his swivel chair, looking depleted now, his job accomplished.

Malvern slipped a hand inside his shirt, rubbed his sore stomach. Stupid, stupid. Trying to protect himself, he had hung a noose around Neal's neck. "I—I still don't believe it," he managed to get out.

Columbo reached over to the phone. "I'm going to call your son. I want him to come in under his own steam. I don't want to send out my men to arrest him."

Malvern paused, stood up, shaky on both legs. He put out a hand to steady himself on the desk. "Lieutenant, you don't have to call," he said, his voice weak, strangely unfamiliar to him. He paused again, trying to summon up what was left of his strength. "I'm the one who did it." It was another few seconds before he said, "I killed Nancy."

"You?" Now Columbo rose to his feet, his swivel chair bumping into the wall behind him.

"You trapped me, Lieutenant. I think you knew damn well Neal hadn't killed her even though his prints were on the knife. You—you knew I controlled him. You knew I wouldn't permit Neal to marry such an inappropriate woman and ruin his life. Admit it—you knew everything."

Columbo was silent for a long moment, horns honking on Santa Monica Boulevard. "I suspected. And I also suspected something more important — you loved your son. When the chips were down, you could never let him go up for a capital crime he didn't commit. . . . You turned out, sir, to be a good father after all."

Malvern sank back down in the chair. "But not a good man, Lieutenant... not a very good man."

SUCKER PUNCH

HE WAS WAITING IN the thick autumnal clump of woods, the pungent smell of evergreens in his nostrils. The woods edged the path on both sides where Washburn took his usual morning and afternoon runs. He would have preferred a thicker density of underbrush, but it really didn't matter since by the time he made his sudden appearance, it would be too late—for Washburn, that is.

He hated waiting, especially when he faced his opponent while the ref gave them instructions and he could feel the deep bass rumble of the fight crowd hot in his gut.

But now there was no heavy surf sound of the fight fans, just the mindless twitter of birds around him somewhere in the trees.

He looked at the dial of his watch—seven-fourteen. He should be coming right about now. Time to ease the 9mm Cobra handgun from his jacket pocket, realizing he had suddenly become calmer now, like when he heard the opening bell in the ring.

There were footfalls pounding on gravel, but it sounded like more than two feet coming down the path.

He was right! It was not only Washburn but one of his sparring partners, Billy Henderson, running right behind him.

As they came closer, he gripped the handgun tight as a lover and emerged quickly from his cover. They both saw him simultaneously, but they had no time to duck away. He shot Washburn through the head and Henderson once in the chest, aiming for the heart. He heard the birds thrashing, frightened in the underbrush, tearing their way up to freedom in the bright sky.

As he jogged the three miles back, he brooded over his only piece of bad luck. Who knew that Henderson would accompany Washburn on his morning run? He was positive he had killed his enemy but he wasn't sure if Henderson had met the same fate.

Sheriff Atkins, a gray man—gray uniform, gray hair— looked with skepticism at the creature in the raincoat. The detective, Columbo, had come up here to Santa Clara from

L.A., even though this was a few hundred miles from his proper jurisdiction. Washburn's body was now resting in the morgue and they were sitting in Atkins' little office in the little town, a tired fan beating dispiritedly at the lingering summer heat.

"I guess you know this guy was a bigshot boxer," Atkins said. "He has his training camp up here. Was he a champion or something?"

"Yeah. Welterweight. He just beat one of my favorites, Eddie Glasso."

Atkins decided to ask the Sixty-Four Dollar Question: "So what brings you here, Lieutenant?"

"After Mr. Washburn beat him, Glasso vowed to kill him."

The Sheriff nodded, for some reason not really surprised. He was drinking diet Pepsi and he finished what was left in his glass. "Would this Glasso be crazy enough to do something like this? I mean after he made a threat?"

Columbo shrugged, moving closer to the fan. "Anger, Sheriff. I don't have to tell you some people say a lot they shouldn't say when they're angry. Besides, Mr. Washburn was the second guy who ever beat him."

"Have you talked to this Glasso?"

"Not yet ... Was there anything interesting you found at the murder scene? Anything I should take a look at?"

Atkins listened to the ice crackling in his glass. "Nothing so far. It's about three miles from here, wooded area off Chalmers Road. You can send your men up, double check us. Now about the other guy—"

"Yeah," Columbo said. "Billy Henderson. I was just gonna ask you about him—"

Eddie Glasso decided to treat it as a joke. "Sure I said I'd kill Chuck Washburn, Lieutenant. *In the ring*. The clause in the contract says I was entitled to a rematch."

They were in the small, rough-hewn structure behind the Brentwood house, a mini-gym office with desk, mat, punching bag, sets of maroon boxing gloves on the desk, and a row of worn sport shoes on the floor. They were drinking coffee, Glasso sprawled in a chair, perfectly relaxed, a smile that seemed painted on his rugged face. There was still a fading, purplish bruise on his forehead, a souvenir from his fight with Washburn.

"You know I'm one of your biggest fans," Columbo said. "I even saw you take out Torey Cooper at the Staples Center. I was way up in the nosebleed seats, but I saw it."

Now Glasso's smile transmogrified into a genuine laugh. "I killed Cooper, *in the ring*! Didn't I?"

"Yeah, you sure did." He picked up a set of boxing gloves. "Can I ask you, Eddie, where you were two days ago, Tuesday morning?"

"That's when Washburn bought it?"

Columbo nodded. He tried slipping on one of the gloves. "I was with my wife. Right here."

Another nod. "Is your wife home?"

"Yeah, you want to talk to her?" He picked up a phone, punched on the intercom. "Honey? You around? Yeah, could you come back to the office? There's a cop here, wants to ask you something."

"Boy," Columbo said, "this glove's a little heavier than I thought."

"How long you been interested in boxing?"

Columbo, his hand in the glove now, gave himself a semi-hard rap on the cheek. "Since I was a kid. My father and I used to watch the fights on television every Friday night. You know, when they were free?"

"In those days everything was free." He grew serious. "It hasn't been all wine and roses, Lieutenant. You remember I had that little drug and alcohol problem."

Columbo nodded. "So did Mando Ramos. He won a title at twenty and the drug abuse wrecked his career. You were lucky." Glasso's wife came in with a hesitant smile. She was a dark-eyed lovely, wearing a bright yellow short skirt and tight yellow T-shirt.

"Caitlin, this is Lieutenant Columbo. He's investigating the Washburn murder."

Columbo rose slightly from his chair. "Pleased to meet-cha, ma'am." He clumped back down. "I wanted to ask you—your husband—was he here at the house two days ago, the morning of the 23rd?"

She darted a look at Glasso. "Was that when—?"

"Washburn was killed, yeah."

"Was he, ma'am?" Columbo asked. He was awkwardly trying on the second glove.

"Yes." She volunteered nothing more. "I have to get

back in the house, Lieutenant. Our daughter's not feeling well this morning."

"You go ahead. I just wanted your confirmation."

She nodded, relieved, and left.

"How's Washburn's sparring partner doing?" Glasso asked. "I hope he's okay."

"Did you know Mr. Henderson?"

"Not really. He's been with a lot of the guys. Before Washburn I think he worked with Oscar Diaz among others."

"He's still in a coma at Parkman General. They brought him down from Santa Clara."

Glasso began slipping on another pair of gloves. Casually: "So he hasn't been able to tell you anything?"

"Not yet. He was following Washburn on his run so he must have seen the assailant. I mean, it seems likely the shooter must've shot him because he didn't want to be identified."

Glasso pretended to be thinking this over. "Yeah. That would figure." He began to box Columbo playfully with the gloves. Better not harp on this identification thing. But then he had another idea, a diversionary tactic: "You think the would-be killer maybe had a grudge against Henderson too? Wanted to take them both out?"

"Could be. I'll be talking to Washburn's manager later this afternoon. Do you know if Washburn had any enemies?"

Now Glasso gave Columbo a soft rap on his cheek. He laughed. "You mean besides me, 'cause he beat me? No, I don't know much about Washburn. I watched tapes to learn his style before I fought him. I'm sure his manager can help you out in that regard."

"Wow," Columbo smiled, feeling his cheek. "That's the first time I've been hit by a world champion!"

Glasso was practiced at keeping any meanness from his voice. "Ex-world champion."

Glasso was doing some relaxed sparring in an old South Central gym when he noticed the cop had drifted in from the street. Columbo took a seat a few rows back, watching Glasso deliver a hard hook to the side of his opponent's head. They mixed it up for another minute and then Glasso called a halt. "We'll pick this up tomorrow, Antonio. I want to work more on that hook. And don't make it easy for me!"

He came down from the ring, toweling off the glistening sweat, and walked a few feet up the aisle to Columbo. "We charge in here for outsiders."

"Oh," Columbo said, taking him seriously. "How much would that be?"

"You here on the investigation?"

"Yeah, yeah, I am."

He laughed. "Then no charge. If you want to talk, come with me."

Columbo followed him into a back area of the gym. They wound up in a changing room with sinks, latrine, and two shower stalls. Glasso stripped off his shoes and shorts and preened naked, flexing his biceps in a mirror. "Think I'm in good shape, Lieutenant?"

"Great shape. Wish I had a body like that." He removed a cigar from his pocket. "You mind?"

"Not allowed. You'll just have to suffer without your fix." He went into one of the shower stalls, leaving the door ajar. "Now what do you want to talk about?"

Regretfully, Columbo put the cigar away. "We're going to have to look at your car, Eddie."

Glasso had turned on the shower, was adjusting the spray. "My car? Why?"

"I'm gonna be very honest with you. We want to check if there's any soil evidence that you've been in Santa Clara."

Another laugh as he lathered soap all over his chest and groin. "You still harping on me doing Washburn in? You could tell from my tires that I was up there?"

"Maybe. It's amazing what the lab can do these days."

"What about the body of the car itself?"

"They take samples from that too."

Harder lathering: "Suppose I've washed the car?"

Columbo came over closer to the shower. "Did you? Wash the car?"

"Not in the past two weeks. I'm sure your little elves in the lab can check that out too."

"Yes, sir, they can. So there's no problem if we go ahead and take samples from your car? And your wife's?"

Now he was shampooing his hair. "No. Go right ahead." A gurgling laugh. "Aren't I turning out to be the most cooperative murderer you've ever known?"

Five days later Columbo returned to the gym. This time Glasso made him wait while he completed his sparring session. They went back to the changing room, but Glasso delayed taking his shower. "So you checked out the two cars?"

Columbo didn't answer right away. "Got the lab report early this morning."

"And?" Goddamn, he thought, this was the kind of guy you probably had to prod to find out the time!

"Clean. The cars have been driven around town here, but never to Santa Clara."

"What I tell you?" He dropped down on the semi-clean tile floor, eased into some calisthenics.

Columbo had the cigar out again, but only just to look at it. "I have another request, Eddie."

Now he was doing pushups like a steel pneumatic machine. "Whatever," he breathed.

"Those shoes I saw in your little gym back of the house? There was a whole row of them."

He stopped, peering up at the cop standing over him. He had his mental guard up, typical of a fighter. And a murderer, he thought with an inner smirk. "What about the shoes?"

Columbo seemed almost apologetic. "I need to check those out like we did your cars."

"Now wait a minute, Columbo. Just what are you saying here?"

Now there was a definite apologetic note in his voice. "You didn't drive up there, Eddie. But if there's soil trace evidence on one of the pairs of shoes...." He didn't bother to finish the sentence.

"Boy, you are something. I thought you were a big fan of mine."

"I am. Ask Mrs. Columbo. She's heard me rave about you plenty of times. She's seen me watching all your fights on TV."

Glasso sprang to his feet. Now he was practically in Columbo's face. "You really think I hated Washburn so much 'cause he beat me that I took a big fat chance putting him away? Is that what you think?"

"You mind if I wash my hands? My wife says I should wash them as much as I can like the people do in the hospitals. You know, bacteria? Didja know there's millions of germs all over my hands right now?"

"Wash your goddamn hands. And answer my goddamn question. *Do you think I killed Chuck Washburn?*"

The question was practically shouted, and Columbo jerked away from the sink before he could wash, his hands still extended. "This is all routine, Eddie. Just routine." He turned back, began lathering his hands.

"Well if you're a fan, get off my back, okay? I don't want to see you again. If you want to see me, turn on your goddamn television set!"

Now Columbo smiled, pulling a paper towel from the machine, tearing it off. "I thought your sparring session was over."

Glasso's smile was as mechanical as his pushups. "Hey, Columbo, we're Italian, right? We get angry, we show it. We're, what's the word? Volatile. But you don't seem that way, you're cool. Where your folks from? Northern Italy, I'll bet."

"Nah, nah. Palermo."

Glasso studied him. "You know, you look like the kinda cop can slip a few punches."

Columbo was still smiling. "You're famous for that yourself." Still drying off his hands: "So my men can pick up the shoes?"

"Suppose right after you leave I call my wife, tell her to get rid of the shoes?"

"My men are sitting right now in front of your house. I told them where the office is out back."

"Boy oh boy," Glasso marveled. "For a murderer I really gotta watch my step with you."

The smile stayed put on Columbo's face. "You wanna come into the station, Eddie, give us a signed confession?"

"Nah, I just wanna make you earn your money the hard way. More fun that way."

It was only after Columbo left that Glasso realized he hadn't answered his question: did the cop really think he killed Washburn? He'd better be very, very careful with this Italiano.

Columbo went into the Neutral Corner bar on Western, a small, ill-kept, well-irrigated hole-in-the-wall with only the bar, a Bud sign, and a single pool table, no players at the moment.

He found Moses Shorter by himself at the far end of the bar, nursing a single shot.

Shorter was a trim African-American in his late sixties with a full head of gray-black hair.

Columbo sidled up to the stool next to him, proffering his open wallet with the shield. "Lieutenant Columbo, Homicide."

Shorter sized him up with an offhand, sideways glance. "You're investigating Chuck's murder, right?"

"Right."

The African-American bartender came over. Raised his eyebrows at Columbo.

"Ah—just a ginger ale, please."

The bartender gave Shorter a quizzical glance, then went down to talk to some men at the other end of the bar.

"I know you trained and managed him a long time," Columbo said. "I've been a fight fan a long time myself."

Shorter emitted a mild grunt, stirred the single cube of ice in his shot glass with a finger.

"Can you give me some help?" Columbo asked. "Like who'd do such a terrible thing?"

"He was a white boy, but Chuck was still like a son to me." He slurred the last two words and Columbo realized he had probably been drinking single shots since the place opened. "Came up through the foster homes, never had a mother or father. But he was as clean as this bar counter when I found him doing some amateur boxing in Sacramento."

"Love at first sight."

Now Shorter shifted over on his stool, suddenly gave him his full attention. "Yeah, you can say that. You seen Chuck fight?"

"Many times, sir. On TV, unfortunately. Never had the pleasure of seeing him live." The bartender padded over with his ginger ale. "Thank you."

"I can smell the Law from here to Oakland," the bartender said, not unpleasantly. "The plainclothes don't fool me." He gave Shorter another quizzical look, longer this time, padded off.

"Who had it in for your boy?" Columbo asked. "And I don't just mean in the ring."

Shorter downed the rest of his drink, looking at his face in the dark mirror.

"Try Eddie Glasso."

"Why do you say that?"

"Chuck beat him plenty good. You see Glasso bounces a lot when he throws, and a fight fan know that. And that boy's got an ego too big for his britches. It was only the second loss in his career."

Columbo sipped his ginger ale. "You really think that loss would make him do something as awful as this?"

"I don't know. But sometimes an ego's got just as much control as a cancer cell." He slurred the word "control" and the word "cell."

Who else?" Columbo prodded.

"Louie Savage. You know him, light heavyweight?"

"Big bruiser, tattoo?"

"Yeah. Heart that has a snake coiled around it on his left bicep." He signaled the bartender for another. "I'm getting a little juiced here, you mind?"

Columbo smiled "Not if you don't. Why was Louie an enemy?"

"Don't know. Louie had some kinda hard feelings against my boy Chuck."

The bartender brought Shorter his shot. He carefully polished off just half of it. "You gotta cut me some slack," he said to Columbo. "I'm not a big drinker, but this week..." His eyes drifted back to the mirror again, his anchor to his grieving reality. "I—I loved that boy. He told me once I was the only—only father he ever had...."

He slowly slumped forward over the counter. Columbo got up, laid bills in front of both their glasses. He gently patted Shorter on his shoulder and quietly left the bar.

They were at it again, this time in Glasso's sunken living room in the main house.

"Okay, I killed him," Glasso joked. "What do you want to know? You come here one more time, Columbo, without an arrest warrant I'm gonna get you a cot in my kids' room! You'll like all the colored giraffes on the wallpaper."

"Just trying to do my job, Eddie."

Glasso lit a cigarette. "I'm not supposed to smoke while I'm in training, but I cheat. Use these cancer sticks mostly when I'm under pressure. But I guess you know how us murderers act." He blew out the match, dropped it in an ashtray. "So you checked out the shoes. Whatja find?"

"Soil evidence that they've been in the Santa Clara region. How do you explain that, Eddie?"

Glasso shrugged. "I was up there early last year, wanted to see Ivan Kazakian's training camp. You know he owned it before Washburn bought it."

Columbo looked put out. "Why didn't you tell me that before?"

Glasso grinned at him. "As a good citizen who pays his taxes, I want you to earn your money the hard way. Didn't I tell you that before?"

Columbo had no comment. He sank down in a plush, overstuffed chair, felt the cushion under him. "Boy, really comfortable. I gotta tell my wife we need at least *one* comfortable chair in the living room."

"You do that, Lieutenant. Now I gotta go to a meeting." Columbo got up, made a motion like he was going to leave. "Don't you have any other suspects, for Chrissake?"

"Working on it, Eddie, working on it."

Columbo found Louie Savage in a tattoo parlor on downtown Main Street.

Savage scrutinized Columbo's ID while the tattoo artist worked on the clean arm. He had his T-shirt off and Columbo was surprised that he had relatively thin arms for a knockout expert.

"This about Chuck Washburn or Eddie Glasso?" Savage asked in a hoarse baritone voice. "Or both?"

"Why do you mention Glasso?"

Savage shrugged. "I bumped into him last week. He'd grown a full beard so he must be really cooling it between fights. You can only have a very short, trimmed one in the ring."

"I just saw him. He's clean-shaven."

Savage sighed. "So he figured he didn't like it. Or his wife didn't. You here about the Washburn killing?"

"Yeah, 'fraid I'm investigating it. I hear you had a grudge against him."

Savage was watching the artist doing his quiet, meticulous work on the arm. "Yeah. Past tense. That was a while ago." He turned his heavy head on its thickly corded neck, frowned at Columbo. "You're not thinking I killed him, are you?"

"No. But I have to check out the people who might've had grudges against him."

"Look, he stole my girl from me, married her. But I found another woman and we've had a very happy marriage for a long time now. Tough New York broad with a heart of gold."

"I'm glad to hear that," Columbo said.

"Let bygones be bygones I always say." He thought about something, hesitated, then decided to let it out. "There's been a rumor floating around...."

"Really? What about?"

"That Washburn had been playing around with a married babe."

Columbo's eyes lost their sleepy look. "What married babe, Louie?"

Savage looked away from the growing tattoo. "Babe by the name of Caitlin. Caitlin Glasso."

Columbo looked sharply at him. "Made-up rumor, or one that had some credibility?"

"I'd say it rings pretty true. Washburn was a player, didn't care if a babe was married or single." Smirking: "Sorta like my own attitude."

"And you think Glasso might've found out?"

Savage's instinct was to shrug, but with the needle working on his arm he luckily thought better of it. "Who knows." He laughed. "Go ahead and ask the man. But watch out for a quick sucker punch."

More mulling. Then: "I will, Louie, I will."

"Or better yet," Savage smiled. "Bring a bodyguard."

That night Eddie Glasso waited until his wife had gone to bed before he drove over to Parkman General. He knew the hospital's layout because he had been there a few times to have some injuries taken care of after a particularly tough fight.

He rode the empty service elevator to the fourth floor and took advantage of the nurses' new shift coming on to move past their station and down the corridor. He was in dark wraparounds, old clothes, a Lakers cap pulled down low over his eyes and forehead. There was a police guard posted in a chair outside the room, but luckily he was dozing. Boy, there was nothing like your luck holding good when you really needed it!

He found Billy Henderson asleep, the respirator slightly humming.

Tough luck, he thought as he leaned over and pulled the plug on the respirator. The cord obviously wouldn't take prints. He planted a quick kiss on the man's forehead before he left the room. The kiss of death, he thought.

Columbo heard the news at five the next morning, a call from Supervising Sergeant Pagano who was at the hospital.

"The respirator plug was pulled from the wall?" he asked Pagano.

"Yep. I don't think it just fell out of the socket, Lieutenant."

"And nobody saw anybody near the room?"

"Nope. Visiting hours were over at nine when a nurse checked on him. That was the last time anybody saw him alive."

Columbo made a call to the lab before he went back to the Glasso house. Glasso was teaching his children a complicated game on the back lawn when Columbo came up.

"Didn't I warn you about coming back here?" Glass said. "Even a murderer can get impatient with the boys in blue, can't he?"

"I'm sorry to interrupt you, Eddie, but can we go in your office?"

Glasso patted his small son on the shoulder. "Play with your sister, I'll be back in a few minutes. Isn't that true, Lieutenant?"

"Maybe a little longer than that."

"Boy, that sounds ominous."

They went into the little gym-office. "Sit right there," he ordered.

Columbo sat down, realized Glasso had put him in a chair where the sun struck directly in his eyes from the open, blindless window. He moved the chair over.

Glasso yawned. He faked it, but he knew it looked real. "What can I do for you? I gotta get downtown to the gym pretty soon."

"I got some bad news this morning."

"What's that?"

"Billy Henderson's respirator was shut off during the night."

Glasso feigned surprise and concern. It was a hell of a lot easier than feigning a punch. He came over, looked down at Columbo in the chair. "That's terrible. How did it happen?"

"It was murder," Columbo said. "Pure and simple. Somebody wanted to shut him up."

"Really," Glasso said with an edge of sarcasm. "Who could that possibly be?"

"Didn't you keep telling me you were the murderer?"

He leaned closer. "I was ribbing you, Columbo. I thought you slipped those kinda punches."

"Before Henderson died he managed to grab something from the little table next to him."

Glasso laughed in Columbo's face. "Was it a slate? He wrote my name in chalk?"

"It was a glass. Glasso? A dying message."

Another laugh, bigger than before, leaving some spittle on Columbo's cheek. "You gotta be kidding. What're you, lying? Trying to set me up? You'd bring something as bullshit as that into court? I thought you were a smart guy, Columbo."

Columbo got up slowly from the chair, a hand shielding his eyes from the sun. "You killed Chuck Washburn too. You probably took a train up there so there'd be no evidence on your car or your wife's. To play it safe you grew a beard, wore sunglasses, work clothes so it'd be hard for any boxing fan to recognize you on the train."

Glasso's smile was back. "I disguised myself? This is screwy Sherlock Holmes stuff. How'd you know I supposedly grew a beard?"

"Louie Savage told me. He bumped into you last week."

"Louie's been full of crap since the cradle."

Columbo nodded at the door. "Should I get your wife in here? Ask her if you sported a beard last week?"

Glasso was silent. He had taken out a cigarette but hadn't lit it. "Although she'd probably lie again for you," Columbo said. "She lied about you being here all morning when Washburn was murdered."

Glasso snarled, "You can insult *me*, but you *can't* insult my wife. Got that?" He brought his face close again to Columbo's.

Columbo held his ground. "You knew Washburn's route when he took a training run every morning. You hid in the woods near the path."

"Prove it. And get ready for a major lawsuit, my fumbling friend."

"You didn't know he was taking his run that morning with Henderson. So you were forced to shoot him too."

"What am I, some kind of maniac?"

"No. Just a very well-motivated killer. Like in the ring, Eddie. Only there you don't have a 9mm Cobra."

"You say well-motivated. I killed a guy because he beat me in a fight?"

"Not only that. I think your real motivation was that he had your wife on occasion. Am I right?"

Glasso looked away, silent.

"You knew if Henderson ever regained consciousness he would identify you as the shooter. So last night you made sure that would never happen."

"Suck it up, Columbo," Glasso said, finally lighting the cigarette. "You've got nothing you can prove on your plate and you know it."

"You were waiting a while before Washburn showed up and you shot him. The criminalists found some cigarette butts on the ground near the path. They checked DNA through the FBI's national DNA database, but there was no match with anybody."

Glasso glared at him. "You bet there wasn't." Why did he say something so stupid?

"You see, I knew most dedicated good fighters don't smoke. So I put that on the back shelf in my mind because I wasn't really sold that you killed him. But then yesterday you lit up, said when you were nervous you had to smoke. Like now. And you had to have been really nervous while you waited for Washburn. I'm afraid your smoking raised a red flag, Eddie."

Glasso stubbed the cigarette out in the ashtray. His hand was shaking and he wondered if Columbo had noticed.

"I'm taking you in now for a mouth swab," Columbo continued. "I'll bet you anything you want we'll get a match with the butts."

Glasso was silent again, watching the blue spiral of smoke twisting up from his semi-dead cigarette in the sunlight. He had thought it was perfect, really perfect. But he should have known there's nothing perfect on this planet—except maybe his left hook.

The only sounds now were the happy, innocent voices of his children playing outside.

"Can I tell my kids I'll be back later to teach them the rest of the game?"

Columbo looked troubled. "No, I wouldn't do that. Give them both a kiss, Eddie. Caitlin too. You might not be back for quite a while...."

THE CRIMINAL
CRIMINAL ATTORNEY

THEY HAD MUCH to celebrate.

They went back immediately to Sandford Buckman's office, straight from the courtroom, fighting off the tiger-ravenous media crowd. Building security stopped *them* in the lobby while Buckman and his client went upstairs. Anticipating the verdict, Buckman already had a bottle of vintage champagne on ice in his secretary's reception area. He was a knife-slim, handsome man in his early fifties, impeccably dressed. "No visitors," he warned his secretary.

"You won!" she said, staring at the young man, Kenny Santoro, at Buckman's side. She was a stout Latina, always stylishly coiffed and dressed.

"Never bet against your boss, my dear," Buckman said, guiding Kenny into his office. "And Luvia—bring us the champagne with two flute glasses. Pour yourself some too. Today *everybody* celebrates!"

In the office, Kenny collapsed into a chair, thrusting hands through his shiny dark hair with a pomaded hint of a pompadour. His grin seemed sutured on his face.

"My Dad's going to top off your fee, Sandy," he said. "You were talking about that new Alfa Romeo, weren't you?"

"That would be a very nice bonus indeed." He took off his dark blue suit jacket, draped it over a chair as he went behind his desk. Kenny made no motion to remove his.

Luvia came in with the champagne and the glasses. Placed them on the desk, began opening the bottle, while Buckman called his wife's cellphone. She went out as he pressed the speaker button so Kenny could hear.

"Hi, dear."

"My God, you got him off!" his wife cried. "I just saw it on the TV! Give Kenny my congratulations."

"You just did—he's right here."

"Thanks, Mrs. Buckman," Kenny called through the rictus of his grin.

"Don't have time to talk," Buckman said into the speaker. "See you tonight!"

They both hung up simultaneously.

Kenny got up, came over to the desk to get a glass of bubbly. Buckman rose and clinked his glass to Kenny's in a toast. "To the future," he intoned. "And you promise me, son, you'll never do anything like that again."

The grin was still in place, solid as his biceps. "If I do, I know where to come."

Now Buckman was smiling, a man who maybe smiled only when greeted with lavish gifts on his birthday. "You're incorrigible, my boy." But there was something behind the smile.

They both sat down, sipping their champagne.

"So what's on the agenda?" Buckman asked.

"I'm not going back to college, if that's what you mean. I'm this notorious celebrity, wouldn't you say?"

Another rarified smile. "Sometimes beautiful young women don't find that very radioactive."

Kenny's smile was a mirror. "Let's hope you're right."

"I'd stay out of trouble, Kenny. Just some fatherly advice."

"I get enough of that from my real father. I tell him that goes for him too. How many times have you represented *him*?"

Buckman poured himself more champagne. "Three. All successful." He looked casually at the digital clock on his desk. It was about that time. He opened his desk drawer, looked down at the knife.

He really didn't think he would be representing Kenny Santoro again.

He came out of his office, suit coat back on, looking over his shoulder "Stay as long as you like, Kenny," he called back. "Finish the bottle."

Buckman closed the door, went to Luvia at her desk. "Kenny's going to stay a bit, make some phone calls. Don't disturb him. If he wants something, he'll tell you."

Luvia nodded, turning away from the little television near her desk. "It's no longer breaking news, Mr. Buckman, but it's a big, big story."

"I guess. Listen, I have a better idea—why don't you close up here and I'll give you a lift home."

She was delighted. "Oh would you? Luis has a tough test coming up and I need all the time I can get to help him study for it."

They went down to Buckman's car in the underground garage.

"That's one happy fella back there," Luvia said while he drove.

"Well, he's really putting away the champagne and I don't blame him. He's got to put all this behind him, a bad dream."

He dropped her off at her home and then made one more stop at a gas station before he joined his wife at Armand's.

It was a very quiet, discreet restaurant, and the maitre d' shook hands after they were seated. "We're honored, counselor," he said. "What a victory you've had today."

But Buckman questioned his sincerity—getting off the scumbag son of a major Mafia don?

They had champagne cocktails to celebrate. His wife Michelle, a lovely stylish brunette in her early forties, had a lustrous shine in her eyes tonight as if they were suddenly time-machined back to their honeymoon. He had shut off his cellphone so their dinner was romantically intimate and uninterrupted.

"Kenny must be on cloud nine," Michelle said.

"Floating." He sighed. "It's been quite a day."

Arriving home at their mansion in Brentwood, he was suddenly aware of an old car parked at the curb. It was only after they had almost reached the front door that he saw a small man standing a little hunched in the shadows.

"Lieutenant Columbo," the man said in a slightly gravelly voice, extending his wallet with ID and shield. "I'm terribly sorry to surprise you out here, but the maid said it would be better if I waited outside."

"We're the ones to be sorry, Lieutenant," Michelle said.

"We apologize," Buckman said. "We're going to have to have a talk with Marta about that. Please come in."

The whole house seemed lit like a great ocean liner at night—crystal chandeliers, sconces, all blazing like bonfires. Buckman led Columbo into the huge living room, nodded toward an upholstered chair.

Columbo planted himself, awkwardly crossed his feet, said, "I guess you heard the news, Mr. Buckman."

"News? I never listen to the radio in the car. What news?"

"Well ... your client Kenny Santoro was murdered in your office."

Buckman was about to sit down, but he staggered, gripped the chair for support. "No. No, that's—that's—" He was unable to finish.

"It would seem it happened late this afternoon after you and your secretary had left." He paused. "I take it he was okay, when you left?"

Buckman was groping around the chair. "He was ecstatic.

We had been drinking celebratory champagne and I must admit I was ecstatic too. My God, Lieutenant, this ... this ... I have a—very hard time assimilating this."

"Did anyone come into your office while you were there with him?"

He brought his hands to his eyes. "No, no one. They have extra security in the lobby today, and they never let anyone come up without checking with us. They always have very tight security down there, keep the media out." He brought his hands down, stared at Columbo. "Was he shot? Did anyone hear a gunshot from my office?"

"No. He was stabbed, sir. Through the heart. The death was probably instantaneous."

The hands were back at the eyes. "Poor Kenny. Poor, poor Kenny." He reared away from the chair.

"There wasn't much blood. The young man still had his suit coat on, so a lot of it was absorbed by the jacket."

Buckman remembered he was still wearing his own suit coat, took it off, tossed it away on a chair.

"Boy, your white shirt, sir," Columbo said.

"What about it?"

"The collar is really sharp. My wife can never iron my collars to look anything like that."

Buckman's mouth twisted. "Is this any time to be talking about shirt collars?"

Columbo raised apologetic hands. "No, sir, it's not. I get distracted sometimes, I gotta admit, and it's not right."

Buckman was silent, thinking. "His father, Joe. You've called his parents?"

"That's all been taken care of, yes sir." He went on a different tack: "So you left Kenny in your office and went home?"

"I left him and went to a restaurant where I met my wife for dinner—after I dropped my secretary off at her house."

"Got it." He placed a flat hand alongside his cheek. "Do you have any idea who would do a thing like this?"

Buckman finally slumped down in the chair. He massaged his eyes. "Come on, Lieutenant, use your head. Half the world thought Kenny Santoro raped that girl. When I got him off today you can be sure there were plenty of angry psychos out there who wanted to reverse the jury's verdict in their own sick way. I think you've got your work cut out for you."

Columbo nodded gravely. "Lots of suspects, right, right." He slowly extricated himself from the chair. Seemed at a loss for a moment, then touched Buckman's tan suit coat where it lay. "Beautiful fabric, sir. Got a little wrinkled."

Buckman shook his head, more amused now than consternated. "When I'm in court I perspire." He studied the cop's attire. "You don't look like much of a clotheshorse, Lieutenant."

An embarrassed smile. "I try, Mr. Buckman, I try. My nephew keeps wanting to take me to one of those pricey places in Beverly Hills—Rodeo Drive, is it?—and get myself all fitted out." The thought was suddenly dropped, and he ruffled the hair on the back of his head. "Something bothers me."

Still somewhat amused: "What's that?"

"If you were scared about all those psychos out there, why'd you leave Kenny alone in your office?"

He realized this guy had the potential of becoming tiresome, really tiresome. "I mentioned the good security in the lobby, didn't I?"

"Yeah, you did. But somebody might've got through there. I'll be talking to that security person, take my word."

He watched Columbo circle his chair and then list slightly in the direction of the door.

"Anything else?" Buckman said. "It's been a long hard day that's ended with a tragedy. I could really use some sleep."

"I realize that, sir, and I'm sorry to be keeping you up." Another thought: "How come your phones here haven't been ringing like crazy?"

"I have a rule: they've been turned off ever since the trial began. After this horrible thing I don't think we'll be turning them on for a good long while yet."

Now, thank God, he had reached the door.

"I don't blame you, Mr. Buckman. I'll be on my way."

"Drive safely."

An hour later, Buckman told his wife he just wanted to drive around for a bit, clear his head. She told him she understood perfectly as he stroked her face and kissed her.

He drove through the main shopping area of Beverly Hills, practically deserted at this hour, no black-and-whites in sight.

He thought it funny, and now ironic, that Columbo had mentioned the "pricey" clothing stores on Rodeo because he was now moving slowly along the alley behind some of them. He braked abruptly, left the car carrying a sealed manila envelope which contained the knife newly cleaned of its blood and his fingerprints. He buried the envelope under a little mountain of refuse in one of the dumpsters, and feeling strangely rejuvenated, returned to his Mercedes and drove off.

Late the following morning, Luvia was stacking mail after the crime crew had done their mopping up and had clattered out. Security called asking if they could let an LAPD lieutenant up to see her boss. She was watching the TV when she looked up and saw a short man in a raincoat smiling at her and proffering his ID and shield. "Lieutenant Columbo, and your name, ma'am?"

"Luvia ... Ortega." She quickly muted the sound on the set, but left the picture on.

"I really don't have much to ask you, Mrs. Ortega. You and Mr. Buckman left Mr. Santoro in the office late yesterday. Around five, five-thirty?"

She quickly sipped from her coffee mug. "Yes."

"And Mr. Buckman drove you home?"

"Yes, he did, yes." She wished she had a window in her reception room—was it raining? The paper said clear. Strange, there were no drops on the detective's coat.

"And during the drive, Mr. Buckman didn't call Mr. Santoro to check if he was all right or anything?"

"No."

"They had been drinking champagne, ma'am?"

"Yes. Mr. Buckman said Kenny had been 'putting away the champagne.' Who could blame them?"

"Did Mr. Buckman say why Kenny didn't come with you?" She thought for a moment. "I believe he said Kenny wanted to make some phone calls."

The cop seemed a little sleepy-eyed, looking past her at the muted screen of the TV. "Anything else that you remember, ma'am?"

Gee, she really hoped it wasn't raining, she had to meet Juanita for lunch across town. "No, I don't think so."

"Did you see Mr. Santoro before you and Mr. Buckman left the office?"

"No, I didn't. Mr. Buckman came out of his office and we left for the garage."

Now the man was poring over a page in his notebook. "Left for the garage, right. . . ." Still looking down: "You liked Mr. Santoro—Kenny?"

Her lips tightened. She looked at the closed door to Buckman's office. "No—not really," she said, her voice lowered.

Now he looked up, interested. "Why do you say that? You thought he really raped that young woman?"

She nodded, lips still zipped.

"But your boss represents plenty of criminal people. Mafia people too. That's his job. Is that why you suspected this young man?"

Voice still lowered: "This is all none of my business. I respect Mr. Buckman, he's a wonderful employer, every Christmas and every birthday he gives me a thousand dollars. I couldn't work for a finer gentleman."

Columbo nodded. He had taken the stub of a cigar from his pocket, but he knew not to light it. Weren't cops excused from rules? "Very fine gentleman. Gives you a terrific Christmas and birthday bonus every year. But what about young Santoro?"

Another look at the closed door. "He—he made advances one day—when Mr. Buckman wasn't here. I don't put up with things like that. I'm a married woman, two children. Do you understand, Lieutenant?"

The stub went back in the pocket. "Oh I do, I surely do. I'm sorry that happened, ma'am. ... So how did you feel when you learned that somebody stabbed him in that office right in there?"

"I felt nothing. Nothing at all. Can you blame me?"

"No. No, I guess I can't." He closed his notebook, put it in the same pocket with the cigar. "But do you want us to catch the perp who did it?"

She turned the sound back up on the set. "What kind of a question is that? Of course I do!" She took a deep breath, regained control of herself. "Is it raining out there?"

"No, ma'am."

"Then why are you wearing that raincoat?"

He smiled at her. "Like to be on the safe side."

Luvia picked up the phone to announce that Lieutenant Columbo was here to see him. He told her to buzz him in.

Buckman was on the phone when Columbo entered. He noted the cop was in practically the same attire as the night before. Raincoat, wilted green suit—it even looked like the same white shirt

Hanging up, he buzzed Luvia. "Hold my calls, dear. We've got the law on our trail."

He stood up, appraised his guest. "Good morning, Lieutenant. May we get you some coffee?"

"No thanks, I'm already coffeed out. This is sure some kind of beautiful office."

"After your men made it spick-and-span again before they left. Just how can I help you today?"

The notebook was out again. "Well ... I was wondering where you went last night after you dropped Mrs. Ortega off at her home. Did you go straight to the restaurant?"

"I got some gas on the way. Is this really important?"

"Just tying up some loose ends, sir. Always like to get a timetable." He smiled deferentially. "What was the service station where you got the gas?"

"It's that one on Wilshire near La Cienega, a Crown, I think. You know how you can go to a service station for years and not even know its name?"

"Yeah, I do. Sometimes I go to my wife's cousin's in the Valley and I don't know its name to this day. How do you like that?! Never thought of that before."

"My point exactly. Anything else? It's building into a very busy morning."

"Did you ever come in contact with any of the victim's friends?"

Buckman carefully adjusted the Venetian blinds, the sun climbing high over the serrated skyline of Century City. "Just one, a girl named Joey. Very pretty. They weren't dating, just friends. The family might have more information on her."

"No males?"

"I'm sure he had male friends, I just wasn't introduced to any. Why do you ask?"

Now Columbo got up, scratching the back of his head in that way he had. "Well, the victim was sitting right there it would seem and the assailant must've been very close to him to deliver that kind of deep wound. Very accurate too."

"So what does that mean?"

"Well you're a brilliant criminal attorney, sir, you must deal in cases like this. For someone to get that close, he had to be someone Kenny knew, maybe even a friend."

"*Au contraire*, Lieutenant. The killer might have threatened him with the knife, gesturing at him with it. That would have allowed him to get close and plunge it in."

"Most victims, at least in my experience, once they see the knife they usually try to fend it off. Flail their arms, back away. It gets a lot more difficult for the killer to strike—especially when the heart's the target."

Buckman sat down behind his desk. "I'll bow to your expertise, Lieutenant. But did Kenny have knife cuts or tears in the sleeves of his coat?"

"None, sir. I'm still wondering...."

"Wondering about what?"

More head-scratching. "We just got the preliminary autopsy report on Kenny. Your secretary said you told her he had been 'putting away the champagne.' But there was very little in his body."

"That's just an expression. I hadn't any idea how much he put away. I certainly put my share away." He looked down at his morning's phone list. "Now if you could bother me some other time—"

"Something else, sir. You told Mrs. Ortega he was staying in your office to make some phone calls."

What the hell could he be getting at? "What about it?"

"Well we checked the phone records. There were no calls made from your number after approximately four forty-five, after you called your wife's cellphone."

"I know. So, what the hell are you getting at?"

Columbo raised his hands in a not quite supplicating gesture. "Well *you* said he wanted to make some phone calls after you left him."

"That's what he told me. I guess he must have changed his mind."

The buzzer sounded on Buckman's desk—and then Luvia's voice said, "Sorry to disturb you, but Mr. Bernstein is on the line—says it's an emergency."

Buckman looked at Columbo. "I have to take this and I'm afraid it's confidential."

Columbo was already at the door. "Gotcha, sir. I'm on my way."

Buckman's smile was wryly insinuating. "And will I have the great pleasure of seeing you again?"

"Could be, sir."

Outside the building, Columbo stopped to light his cigar. There was a clever little wind blowing from between the monoliths that deftly managed to extinguish his match. He shook his head in frustration, tried again—just as a sleek black limo with smoked windows coursed along the curb and braked almost alongside of him.

Two tall, well-dressed men emerged from the car.

"Lieutenant Columbo? Joseph Santoro would like you as his guest at lunch."

Columbo blinked, more from the sun than the invitation. "Well ... ah, fine. As long as I can make a three o'clock appointment?"

"No problem." The taller one held open the rear door. "Please."

Columbo got in, the taller one sliding in next to him, his twin up front next to the visored driver. The limo moved smoothly off.

On their way to somewhere, Columbo studied his companion's suit. His wife had read somewhere that the good ones were probably Zegna or maybe Brioni, but always Italian. Italian tailors were the best, too. This guy wore a beautifully tailored, lightweight job with peaked lapels. What's got into me? he thought. I gotta get off this clothing thing, I'm only a working stiff.

Joseph Santoro was at his exclusive club in Beverly Hills, old-fashioned in its decor, a brass rail running along the almost deserted length of the bar.

Santoro was more casually dressed than his boys, a solid, still-muscular man in his early sixties with a rich crop of white hair and big white caterpillar eyebrows half-hidden by a pair of aviators with extra-dark lenses. Columbo never trusted men who wore sunglasses indoors. He sat down across from him and the two tall men went off somewhere.

"Pleased to meet you, Columbo," Santoro said. "Can I buy you a drink? This here's a vodka martini."

"Glass of wine maybe? Red?"

"A man after my own taste." He signaled a waiter. "One of the Antinori Super Tuscans." His hands cupped his glass, rolled it between blunt fingers. "I talked to my lawyer, Sandy Buckman, this morning. Wanted to discuss what happened to my son."

Columbo nodded.

"I notice cops don't offer any condolences when a man has a death in his family. Is that the rule or are you just naturally impolite?"

Columbo was unfazed by the man's insult. "Usually not from the investigating officer, sir."

The waiter brought a bottle, poured Columbo his wine and waited while he took the first sip.

"Very good," Columbo told him. "Thank you."

The waiter went off and Santoro regarded Columbo over a steeple of fingers, his powerful arms resting like anchors on the table. "Sandy tells me you're really badgering him."

"He said that?"

"No, Popeye said it. *Are you?*"

Columbo let the wine sit. "Your son was killed in his office—

probably not long after Mr. Buckman left. Wouldn't you say, sir, that Mr. Buckman might be the logical place to start?"

"Yeah, but Sandy left—and he can prove it—wouldn't that rule him out?"

"Something bugs me, sir."

Santoro lowered his hands to the table. "I asked you a question."

"It was a starting place, as I said. I was also questioning him about people your son knew. He mentioned a Joey."

"Yeah. Joey Pritchard. Works down at the King's Row Cocktail Lounge." Santoro took a generous swallow of his vodka martini. "You said something's bugging you."

"Just little things. That your son was killed in the office of the man who got him off. That it happened right after the trial. That there was good security in the building to prevent an outside killer from coming in."

"Columbo, there's a rumor around that you're not stupid, and you're Italian. I like that. But why would a murderer kill a man *in his own office*? A man who just broke his ass in court getting his client off?"

"Some people might say that would be very audacious. A murderer would *never* kill a man in his own office. You see what I mean?"

"I see, but I'm not buying. You want lunch?"

"Maybe just an appetizer. My wife says I'm putting on weight, wants me to join one of those health clubs. You look pretty trim, sir, what's your secret?"

Santoro smiled his shark's smile. "Shedding pounds fencing with guys like you." He broke a roll with two fists but didn't butter it. "I want you to find my son's killer, Columbo."

"That's my job, sir."

"I'm not going to push you around. I'm not in the pushing-around-cops business. But you better bust your butt on this, know what I'm saying?"

Columbo nodded. He had picked up the menu.

"I don't know what you thought about the trial, but my son didn't rape that woman. You know how the young babes are today, they ask for it. Kenny was tried because he made the mistake of being my son. He was a good boy, a damn good boy, and I was glad as hell that Sandy got him off."

Columbo was studying the menu.

Santoro finished his drink, got up, pushed away from the

table. "Enjoy yourself. They got a great *bistecca fiorentina*. It's a lot of meat for a little man, but I'm sure you can handle it."

"I really shouldn't eat that much, sir."

"Then you want the *carne cruda* with another glass of red. Everything on the house. I'm counting on you, Columbo. I want my boy's killer."

Columbo found the Crown station, told the attendant he wanted to talk to the service manager. The man pointed to the office.

The manager was tilted back in his chair, his feet up on the desk. When Columbo showed him his ID and badge, his feet came down with a thud.

"You know one of your customers, a Mr. Sandford Buckman?"

"Sure." Nervous. "Getting his gas here for years. Just won that big case."

Columbo was eyeing a rack of chocolate bars just outside the office. After that meat, better not! "He got some gas in here last night?"

"Yep. I congratulated him for his win. Acted like it was just another day in court. Modest guy, Mr. Buckman."

"And that was it? He was in and out?"

The manager frowned. "Ah—no, he had to go to the restroom."

"Just a quick trip?"

More frowning, thinking. "No, he was in there a while, if I remember."

Columbo turned away from the candy bar rack. "People have to have a key to get in your restroom?"

He nodded. "I don't want any punks off the street going in there. I've had trouble in the past, writing filth on my walls and stuff. Broke a window."

"Mr. Buckman ever use your restroom on other occasions?"

"Not that I remember." A memory suddenly jabbed him. "Something funny, though. Most people go in there in a hurry. Mr. Buckman, when he came in to get the key—he had one of those—whatdyacallem—?"

Columbo knuckled his forehead. "Try to remember, sir. It would be helpful."

The manager was stumped.

"An attaché case? Sort of square, leather?"

The manager snapped his fingers. "Yeah! Took it right into the restroom with him."

Columbo's hand slid slowly to his chin, cupping it. "And when he came out, he went right to his car?"

"Right. With that attaché case."

Columbo nodded. "You've been very helpful, sir. Appreciate it."

Early the next morning, Buckman was jogging around the edge of the UCLA campus off Sunset when he noticed an old, dingy, foreign-looking car was following him at approximately his same speed. It seemed very familiar.

He came indignantly to a halt just as the car swung over and parked at the curb behind him. A beat later the driver, Columbo, got out and ambled over to him.

"Gee, I'm sorry to interrupt your run, Mr. Buckman, but I have a few questions—"

"They couldn't wait till I got to the office?" Buckman said, running in place to maintain his rhythm.

"I didn't want to interrupt you there. I know you're a pretty busy guy, got a lot on your mind."

Buckman palmed sweat from his brow. "What do you want to know?" Cars were streaking by both ways on Sunset, and young joggers were racing past.

"Well, you know where you get your gas, that place on Wilshire?"

Buckman was trying to tamp down his irritation. "Yeah?"

"Well the manager said there was something a little funny—you took your attaché case into the restroom."

Buckman had to laugh. "And *that's* why you've interrupted my run? For something as stupid as that?"

Columbo shrugged, seemed to shrink a bit in his raincoat.

"Lieutenant, do you ever read when you're on the pot?"

Columbo smiled, a little embarrassed. "Uh—yeah. My wife puts the morning paper in there if I haven't read it yet."

"Well, I keep my business papers in my attaché case. I didn't know how long I was going to be, so why not get a little work done in the john? We were going to be early anyway for our restaurant reservation." Still running in place: "Any more *crucial* questions?"

"I don't think so, no. I'm really sorry I interrupted you. I really am."

Buckman took off, called back: "So am I. Don't let it happen again! I'd *love* to get you on the witness stand, Columbo. I'd tear you to ribbons!"

Columbo smiled, held up his hands defensively. He called something back, but Buckman was already a hundred feet away.

Columbo came in to the cocktail lounge, took a seat at a little table illuminated with a tiny spray of light from a red-shaded lamp. A waitress came over almost immediately for his order. "Does a young woman named Joey work here?" he asked.

"Yeah." Giving him a calculating look: "You want her to serve you?"

"If it wouldn't be too much trouble, Miss."

Columbo sat still, staring around in the semi-dark room, the little lamps like motionless fireflies on the tables. A few minutes later, a cute young woman came over to his table. She was dressed like the first waitress, very short skirt, dipping neckline. "Can I help you, sir?"

"I think so, yeah. You were a friend of Kenny Santoro's?" Even in the dimness he could tell her expression had darkened.

"I was. I still can't believe—" She put a hand to her face. "I just heard the funeral's on Friday."

"I'm very sorry," Columbo said. "Were you close to Kenny?"

Now she stiffened. "Who are you?"

He showed his ID badge. She drew back a little. "Relax," Columbo said. "I'm investigating Kenny's death, trying to find his killer."

She took a deep breath. Another. "Oh. Okay."

Columbo smiled at her. "How close were you to him?"

"Friends. We weren't romantic or anything. What do you want to know?"

"I guess you followed his trial and everything. Am I right?"

She nodded.

"Had Kenny ever before been involved in anything like that?"

She was silent. The barman was looking over at her, probably wondering why she hadn't gotten a drink order yet. "I'm not asking you to malign his character, Joey. But I'd like to know anything that might lead us to his murderer."

"Yes," she said finally. "There was a girl—two-three years ago—who said Kenny had done something like that."

"Was it ever reported?"

"You sure I can't get you a drink?"

"No, but I'm gonna leave you a nice big tip. Why didn't the young lady report it?"

"We—we thought Kenny's father might've paid her off. We all knew he's this mob guy."

Now Columbo was silent. Then: "You think, maybe, Kenny had a history of stuff like that?"

"You mean something before what happened to that girl we heard about?"

"Uh-huh."

"Maybe. But I'd hate to think that about Kenny. He was a swell guy."

Columbo leaned toward her. "You and he were just friends, but did any of *your* friends date him? I mean romantically."

"No."

"How come?"

She drew away a little farther. "They were—sort of—afraid."

His voice was very quiet: "Because of what the girl said?"

"I—don't know."

"Probably?" He was laying out a bill on the little table as he rose.

Long pause. "Probably."

The dentist's office was in a pristine building on Spalding Drive. He sat in the waiting room, looking over the display of high-end magazines and selected *The duPont Registry of Fine Automobiles* because it looked like the closest one to *Sports Illustrated*. He paged through it until the receptionist said he could go in.

The dentist, Ruth Buckman, was an attractive woman in her early forties, dark-haired, pale makeup, relatively sexless in a white coat and colorless slacks.

He showed her his ID and remained standing, not wanting to occupy the dentist's chair, the only available seat in the room. "I want to ask you about your ex-husband," he said, still eyeing the dentist's chair.

"What about him?" Not angry, just disinterested.

"You read or heard about what happened in his office?"

Humorless smile: "Who could avoid it? He got a kid off who was obviously guilty as sin. But Sandy has a habit of doing little things like that."

"Are you still friendly with him?"

"We rarely see each other. If we had had kids, it would probably be a different story. I like it just the way it is."

"Could you tell me something about his background? Something that people might not know?"

Now the smile turned genuine. "Aren't you warm in that coat?"

He shuffled. "No, no, ma'am. I'm fine."

She mused. "Something the public might not know.... Not what he was like between the sheets, I hope?"

"Oh no, ma'am. Nothing like that."

She gave it some thought, looked at her watch. "I have another patient in five minutes."

It was as if Columbo hadn't heard her. "Anything interesting, something about his life he might have told you that was out of the ordinary...."

"There was one thing ... something awful, actually. His mother had been attacked, raped, when he was only seven or eight. He's kept that pretty hidden, at least away from the papers, the media."

"Mmmm. Did they catch the guy?"

"I don't think so. Sandy said he was some kind of serial rapist who always got away."

"Always got away." He ruminated over this. "You think it really affected him—as a child?"

She looked at her watch again. "Absolutely. Maybe it was one of the reasons he went into the law."

"Why do you say that?"

"I don't know. Wanted to see justice done in cases like that. Although I can't figure out why he kept defending that Mafia family."

Columbo went to the door, turned back to her. "I have to thank you, ma'am. Both for your time and your information."

"You think that's pertinent? I mean about what happened to his mother?"

Columbo opened the door. "Oh yes, ma'am. *Very* pertinent."

Sandy Buckman had been in his office no longer than five minutes the next morning when Luvia announced that Lieutenant Columbo was there to see him.

"Well, at least you didn't interrupt my jogging again," he said after the detective had come in.

Columbo seemed taken with his clothing. "That's another of your beautiful suits, Mr. Buckman. Excuse me for asking, but where'd you get it?"

"Brioni, Lieutenant. Please don't get one. We can't have the cop sartorially equal to the suspect, now can we?"

Columbo bypassed the humor: "It was the suit that gave you away, sir."

"You want to decode that for me? Maybe I haven't had enough coffee this morning."

"You stabbed Kenny Santoro and you put the knife in the pocket of your suit jacket."

Buckman leaned back in his chair, hands linked behind his head, perfectly at ease. "That's quite a jump—suits to murder weapons."

"You haven't asked me the real question—why would you kill the man you just got off for rape?"

"Damn good question, I'm holding my breath—why?"

"This is one of the strangest motivations I've ever run across, Mr. Buckman. The terrible incident in your childhood compelled you to seek revenge on Kenny. He was the first serial rapist you had ever represented. You got him off so you could kill him. Who would expect a brilliant lawyer to murder a client he had gotten off?" He paused. "Perverse."

"Very perverse." Buckman was still leaning back, loose-limbed, casual. "I'm still waiting to hear about my suit."

"You left here, stopped at the gas station. You had another suit, the tan one, in your attaché case. You went to the restroom, put on the clean one, and stashed the blue suit with the knife in the case."

"And why would I do that?"

"Because you didn't want to go to the restaurant with that incriminating knife in your pocket. There were stains. Make sense?"

Buckman gave him a half-smile. "Fabrications rarely make sense."

His phone rang. He picked it up, listened. "Thank you, Luvia." He hung up, his stomach tightening. "It seems your men have just entered my home with a search warrant."

"Something didn't compute," Columbo said. "When I questioned you at your house that night you were wearing a beautiful tan suit. But in the color footage of you and Kenny leaving the court on TV, you were wearing a dark blue suit. I noticed all you defense attorneys usually wear blue suits in court. And you remember I remarked on the wrinkles in the tan one. That was because it had got a little crumpled in your attaché case. It all comes back to why you changed suits before you went to the restaurant if you didn't stop at home."

"You're getting hung up on trivial details, Columbo."

"I've had a man watching your house and tailing you to make sure you didn't take that blue suit to the cleaners."

Buckman laughed. "A smart murderer would have gotten rid of that knife before your man was put on the case." Then he stopped, realizing that there *was* a noose around his neck — and that it had suddenly started to choke him! "That's what they're doing in my house right now! Searching my clothes closet for the blue suit!"

Columbo didn't nod. "Your blue suit that had the murder knife in its pocket. I'll bet you got rid of the knife, but there are sure to be blood stains in the lining. Blood stains that the lab will match to Kenny Santoro's blood."

Buckman slowly slid his chair away from the desk and nearer to the window, the sun a warm, welcome compress on his shoulders. "You're good, Columbo," he finally said. "I really underestimated you."

Columbo shrugged, turned over his hands, palms up.

"Did you ever get those white shirts I sent?" Buckman wanted to know.

"Oh, yes sir. I can't accept them, but I'm really sorry I never got around to thanking you. You got to understand, I've been really busy these days."

Almost despite himself, Buckman was forced to smile. "Yeah, I know—trying to nail me."

Columbo shrugged again.

"But you know I'll be defending myself. So I'm warning you— watch out. Don't get too cocky, Columbo."

"No way. I just told my wife this morning—you're one of the very best. Not so careful 'sartorially,' though...."

THE BLACKEST MAIL

AS USUAL ON THE FIRST MONDAY of the month, Cathy went to his house with the five thousand dollars sealed in a large envelope. She repeatedly rang the bell but there was no one home. As per his instructions, she slid the envelope under the door and returned to her car.

On the first Monday of the following month she called him, said she was tied up, could he come to her home that night and pick up the money.

"Get real," he said. "Why should I come over there?"

"It's only a short distance. The money will be here. I'll place it in your hands myself. You can't drive over here?"

He grunted. Then, grudgingly: "Okay. When?"

"Tonight at eight. I'll be reading the script for my new film with the director, but that's no problem. Come up and honk and I'll be out with the money in a jif."

"You're breaking our routine."

"For Godsake, you can't afford the gasoline? I've already paid you almost sixty thousand dollars."

"I'll be there. With my hot little hands palms up."

Cathy was in her garage, a few minutes before eight. Wearing latex gloves, she held the remote that worked the garage door, the driver's door to her new Mercedes SUV wide open. She had left a fully loaded .45 automatic, also new, resting on the hood. The naked overhead bulb gleamed on a sharp-bladed kitchen knife next to the gun.

Almost at eight on the button, his car pulled up on the deserted road. There was usually little traffic, the large houses few and far between. It was a new BMW M3 and she knew the blackmail money had financed it. He honked. It was a full minute before he honked again and then impatiently got out of the car. Almost immediately he saw her waving to him from the garage.

She went back near her car, waiting for him to appear. Now she took the gun from on top of the hood, held it down at her side.

He came up, stopped, finally came a few feet into the

garage, blinking at her in the weak light. "You said you'd come out and meet me. What's the deal? Where's the money?"

She pressed the remote and the motorized door slid down, trapping him in the garage. He jerked around, confused, realizing in a panic that he was suddenly under her control.

"What the hell are you—?" he started to say, before he saw she was pointing the gun directly at him.

She fired, missed. He moved quickly toward her and she fired again, this time hitting him. He sank down without a whimper to the concrete.

She took the kitchen knife from the hood, gripping it by its knobby handle. He was no longer breathing. She placed the knife in his jacket pocket and dug around in his trousers to find his house and car keys. Looked at her watch.

She went to his car on the road, opening the driver's door with his key and placed it in the ignition. She removed a pair of lacy black panties from her pocket and flung them across to the passenger's seat. She slammed the door and leaned against it, thinking. No one around on the tree-shadowed road, no cars passing by. Sometimes she was lucky, all her stars in perfect alignment.

Within fifteen minutes, she had jogged to his house on a secluded, backwater little street, the only brightness a patch of hibiscus near the front door. She let herself in, searched around for a lamp in the dark living room. Found it, lit it.

Now she removed some eight-by-ten publicity photos from the little portfolio she carried, and, still wearing the latex gloves, left one in the living room, and then went into the bedroom, hanging two more with Scotch tape on the walls among his film posters. Not through yet, she remembered to autograph one of the photos with a grease pencil.

She saw some one-hundred-dollar bills on the dresser, obviously the blackmail money. She snatched them up, stashed them in her coat pocket.

She checked her watch again: time to leave, looking around to see if she had forgotten anything. Oh yes, the light in the living room, but he could have left it on.

Back home, she deposited the bills in the top drawer of her bureau in the bedroom. Then she rehearsed her hysterics before she picked up the phone and called 911.

Columbo wasn't used to dealing with movie stars. He knew they were just people like everybody else, but they weren't neighbors or somebody you'd see walking down the street or buying a toothbrush at Rite Aid. He remembered he once saw Sidney Poitier getting a prescription filled and he felt guilty because he had been too shy to ask him for an autograph for his wife.

And this one was really beautiful, natural blonde hair, big hazel eyes that swallowed you up. His wife probably knew who she was, she followed the show business stuff on the tube, but he didn't have a clue.

Cathy Cole. Sergeant Pagano had told him she wasn't a big star yet, but another popular picture and she'd probably be near the top of the heap. Even Pagano knew these things.

They were in the garage of her home, the tech team going through their drill. The body was covered now with a sheet, but there was still blood leaking out on the concrete. Cathy stood near the entrance, pressing a Kleenex to her reddening eyes. There were curious neighbors lining the road, held at bay by a uniform. Media uplink vans were trying to find parking spaces near the house.

"You wanna go inside?" Columbo asked her as gently as possible.

"Y-yes."

On the way to the connecting door to the house, Columbo stopped to get an evidence bag from one of the techs. He followed her in.

They went through an immaculate kitchen, down a short hall, to a lavish well-lit living room. Columbo nodded to a plainclothesman who was speaking on his phone.

"Why don't you sit down, Miss Cole," Columbo said.

She sunk into a chair, still wiping her eyes with the Kleenex. "I hope you won't mind, but I have to ask you some questions," Columbo said, his voice very modulated.

She nodded, she didn't mind. The plainclothesman hung up the phone and left the room.

"The victim? The driver's license in his wallet states that his name was Ray Matos. Did you know the man?"

"Yes. He—he's been stalking me for the past few weeks."

"Stalking you. Did you report this to us?"

"No." She moved the Kleenex aside and looked at him

with angry eyes. "I was stupid. I told my agent and we both agreed it would be bad publicity. That maybe these kind of freaks got frustrated and just—just move on to somebody else."

"That's usually not the case."

"I know, I know. I was stupid."

"Had he approached you before?"

She was slowly regaining her composure. "The first time when I was coming out of a restaurant. Another time in an underground parking lot in my lawyer's building. That really scared me, Mr.?—I'm sorry, I didn't catch your name."

"Columbo. Lieutenant Columbo. Did he verbally threaten you on either of those two occasions?"

"Nothing—nothing verbal. But he looked *strange*. He was unshaven, looked like he had slept in his clothes, hadn't had a bath since Lent."

"Ummm." He nodded meditatively, as if he was listening to a radio program playing somewhere in his head. "So tonight, you came home and got out of your car in the garage. And that's when you saw him again, he was suddenly standing at the entrance to your garage?"

"And he was taking an object out of his pocket—I suddenly saw it was a knife—!"

Columbo showed her the transparent evidence bag, the kitchen knife visible inside. "Something like this?"

"Yes! And that's when I shot him."

Columbo placed the bag on a table. "How come, Miss Cole, you had a gun so handy?"

"Whenever I come home by myself at night I have it next to me on the passenger seat. I've been chased sometimes by the paparazzi, but I never really worried about them. But this stalker—what was his name, Matos?"

"Matos."

"This man really frightened me."

The phone rang—and a plainclothesman came quickly in and took it.

"Taking that horrible knife from his pocket wasn't enough provocation?"

A moment later, the plainclothesman turned from the phone—"Ms. Cole," he said, "your agent, Ms. Kramer, would like to talk to you."

"Lieutenant," Cathy said, "I *must* talk to her. All this horribly affects my career."

"Tell her you'll call her back in a few minutes."

The plainclothesman relayed this to the agent, then left. Columbo said, "I know how women can be intimidated. But you have to realize, Miss Cole, you killed a man tonight and we have to get all the details we can."

She had gained the upper hand and she knew exactly how to use it, essential when dealing with the male studio execs—like using a symbolic well-placed knife. They understood symbolic knives, those people. "I would assume you believe in self- defense, Lieutenant."

"You bet I do."

"My gun is registered. I have a permit, you can check." She crumpled the Kleenex in her fist. "How much more do you want to ask me? This has been a horrific experience and I have to make a thousand phone calls before I take a sleeping pill and try to get some sleep. My new picture starts tomorrow morning and I have to look my best."

Columbo seemed impressed, maybe even inhibited by her quietly growing strength. He walked a few feet away from her on the ultra-thick carpet and then suddenly stopped, turned, looked back at her. "Something—something else," he said, scratching his chin.

"What?"

"Just a simple question, Miss. You said you always had the gun beside you on the passenger seat. So how come you had it in your hand when you were out of the car, before you suddenly saw him?"

She sighed, the tears starting to liquefy her eyes again. "I had dinner with a friend at the Hotel Bel-Air tonight. On the way home I thought there was a car following me on Stone Canyon Road. Once I got on Sunset I thought maybe it had turned off somewhere. But I was still very apprehensive on my way here."

More chin-scratching. "And you think this could've been Matos?"

"Probably."

"And what time was it, approximately, when you were driving home?"

"Seven-thirty. I remember exactly."

He looked like he was about to leave again. But then he fooled her—"Funny, something that important you forgot to tell me earlier."

You bet it was, seeing as how she had just made the

goddamn thing up. She knew her studio infighting with the bigwigs was really going to pay off with this slow dude.

"Just one more thing," he said. "How many times did you shoot the man?"

"I shot once, but it missed. The second one killed him." She sniffled. "Anything else, Lieutenant?"

"No. Get some sleep."

"I'll try."

He met with Cathy Cole's agent, Roni Kramer, in her office in a big agency building on Wilshire. There were squiggly abstract paintings in elegant frames on the cork walls and nothing on her desk, like nobody really worked there. Boy, if only he could keep his own desk like that.

Roni was probably edging fifty, trying to look like thirty-five. She had ink-black hair cut close to her skull and wore a black T-shirt under an elegant ivory jacket.

"This is a terrible tragedy, Lieutenant. Cathy is a beautiful person, honest, responsible, a saint-like client. And let me tell you, I don't get many of those in this town."

Columbo nodded. The air conditioning was very cold and he was glad he was in his raincoat. "Miss Cole said she had discussed this Matos stalking her."

"True. She had been bothered before by a paparazzo but Cathy had no crazy love affairs, stayed out of the nightclubs, no DUIs—nothing to exploit."

"And that would keep them away?"

"Cathy is not red meat to that kind of carnivore. They've come at her in the past, but nothing ever paid off. She came out here as just a little lamb from Idaho. A stalker just sniffs out the vulnerable in the evolutionary process like Darwin's natural selection, I guess." She laughed a silvery laugh. "You know I don't know shit what I'm talking about half the time. But Cathy I *do* know."

Columbo seemed to be in agreement. "She said she decided not to report the stalking to us because it might be bad publicity for her."

"My recommendation. I remembered another young actress who was a stalker victim. The tabloids went to town, just about ruined her career. We decided to keep mum until—"

"Until what, ma'am?"

"Until maybe it got a little serious and then we'd come to you people."

Columbo brought his collar up. "Did you know Miss Cole owned a gun?"

"Yes." Motherly: "Are you too cold in here, Lieutenant? I'm afraid I'm one of those people who sleep with all the windows open at night." Laughs. "At least I did when I lived in New York."

"No, no, I'm fine, ma'am. You weren't the one who had dinner last night with your client, were you?"

"No. Why do you ask?"

"Miss Cole says she had dinner and then she suspected she was being followed home."

"I didn't know that. Matos probably knew where she was dining."

Columbo was very interested. "How would he know something like that?"

"They're like the paparazzi. Somehow they know where you hang out, restaurants, gyms, watering holes. The paparazzi are known to pay off hotel clerks, limo services, anybody who can help them get a bead on their prey."

Columbo got up, suddenly energized. "This has been a real education, Miss Kramer. This is a whole kind of world my wife likes to watch on TV."

She smiled indulgently at him. "While you're doing what?"

"Watching sports, the fights." He went to the door, a blast of air following him. "Thanks again."

"It's been my pleasure, Lieutenant."

On a backlot soundstage at Universal, Cathy was holding her own in a frenetic domestic scene with an actress playing her obstreperous daughter. It was only after the director called "cut" that she saw Columbo watching from the periphery of the set.

"That's a print," the director beamed at her. "We'll set up right away for the next scene."

She was lost for a few moments in the hectic ebb and flow of the crew swirling around her until she saw the cop waving.

"How did you know where to find me?" she asked him when they found a safe haven in a corner.

"The gate guard on Lankershim had all the production schedules and locations for the day. He told me this is the soundstage where they shot Bela Lugosi in *Dracula*. Is that true?"

"I really wouldn't know. You've caught me at a very busy time, Lieutenant. This is our first day of shooting on the new picture."

"Yeah, I know, but this won't take long. Is there some-place really quiet where we can go?"

"My trailer. Come with me."

Her Winnebago was parked only a hundred yards away down the main studio street. Cathy's makeup woman had followed them, applying some touch-ups while Columbo sat stuffed in a pull-down chair in the cramped confines.

"Well what is it?" Cathy asked. "I have to study my script before the AD calls me back."

"Nothing really important, Miss Cole, just something I have to clear up. I like to clear things up."

She looked at him in the round makeup mirror. He was such an unpretentious sort, almost humble, hesitant, like he was never quite sure of himself. She had played with plenty of movie cops in her pictures, but they were never anything like him. "Well, fire away," she said. "What do you want cleared up?"

"Correct me if I'm wrong, but didn't you tell me last night you fired one shot that missed and then one more that hit the target?"

"Yes. I did."

"Well, Miss, the medical examiner found a slug in Mr. Matos' heart. But we couldn't find the pellet from the first shot."

She let that sink in. The makeup woman was putting a little under-eye cover on, hiding the damage done from her crying jag the night before. "I told you I fired and I missed. Do you think I'd forget something like that?"

"No, no I don't." He tried to cross his legs, had trouble in the chair, gave up.

"Did you check my gun, Lieutenant? It was fully loaded before I shot—eight bullets. How many were left?"

Columbo looked pained. "Two missing. And we found two cartridge shells on the floor. And that's the mystery: where's that second slug? My men hunted all around and outside the garage. Nothing."

"Who knows, maybe a squirrel went off with it."

She removed the apron of tissue around her neck that protected her blouse. "Are you through, Kitty?"

"All through," the woman said, gathering together her things.

"I never heard of squirrels liking metal," Columbo said. She looked at him again in the mirror: was he playing with her?

"Neither have I. But we're both hardly experts on the dining habits of squirrels, are we, Lieutenant?"

"Guess not." He torturously extricated himself from the chair. "You better get back, Miss Cole."

She rose herself, realized for the first time that she towered over him. "I'm always here to help, Lieutenant. And you certainly know where to find me."

"The man you shot last night?" he said offhandedly. "He was in your business."

She didn't have to feign surprise. "An actor? He was an actor?"

"No. An extra. Maybe he was in one of your pictures. Crowd scene, something like that."

"Maybe he was, but I don't remember him. Anything else?"

"No. That'll do it for today."

She smiled at him. "But what about tomorrow?"

He smiled back. "In my line of work I never try to think too much about tomorrow."

But he was in her face again that night. She had gotten home around eight, exhausted, wanting a drink and her single cigarette of the day. While she was pouring, the doorbell rang. Annoyed, she went to answer it.

"You said tomorrow," she said, as he moved past her into the house. She always studied how people moved, and this guy seemed pretty graceful on his small feet. But those shoes! "I was just having a drink. May I fix you one?"

"No thanks, Miss. I really apologize coming over here this late, especially since you've had such a grueling day, but I got another thing to clear up."

Get used to it, Cathy. He's a nudge, but don't lose your focus with him. "Your mind seems to be a clearinghouse, Lieutenant."

"Yeah, mostly junk."

"But sometimes there's something gold and glittery in the trash?"

"Sometimes."

She lit up, watching him over the flame. "So what's in your trash tonight?"

"The slug I mentioned this morning? You know, you said you fired and you missed but we couldn't find it?"

"Yes, I remember."

He was pacing about and she wished he had sat down where she could concentrate on him. He was making her nervous and maybe that was his intent.

"You know where it was?" he said, like he was still amazed by its discovery. "I didn't find it myself, I gotta give credit to Detective Ruiz, he's a really smart young guy."

"Why don't you tell me?" She involuntarily tensed, like right before a big scene, knowing this might be one of his curveballs.

"It was in the garage door, the inside of the door. Can you believe that?"

Now it hit her, but she kept her face perfectly still. "Yes. But…"

"When he came into the garage, bringing the knife from his pocket—you must've closed the door."

She took a long drag before she answered. "I have no memory of my doing that."

"But who else could have closed the door? Do you have a transponder in your car? Or a remote?"

"A remote."

"And where do you keep that?"

Be careful, very careful. "In my car, clipped on the sun-shade over the driver's seat. Is that important?"

Now Columbo finally settled down in a love seat, looking up at her. "When you said you took the gun, you never mentioned you took the remote too."

"I just didn't remember doing that."

Now Columbo took his own time before he said, "Why would you want to bring down the garage door, trapping yourself in the garage with this threatening guy?"

"I thought—I thought I could bring it down and keep him out. But he came in too fast."

"Hmmm. If you had gotten it down and kept him out he'd probably still be alive today."

She used the sad expression that had worked so well in

her last picture. "How true. . . . Now is there something else, Lieutenant? I have to make myself some soup and start learning my lines for tomorrow."

He brought out her pair of black silk panties in a plastic evidence bag from his raincoat pocket. He looked a little distressed, like he was holding something X-rated. "Do you recognize these, Miss?"

She took the bag from him. "May I take them out?"

He nodded. "The lab has already checked them."

She removed the panties, looked at the label. "Yes, they're mine all right. Where did you get them?"

"They were in Mr. Matos' car. How could he have gotten them?"

"Good God, that slimy pervert must've rummaged through my trash and found them. They developed a little tear so I threw them out. All my trash goes into a dumpster in the alley right behind the house."

"So you think he rooted around in there, found your undergarment?"

She was amused that he couldn't quite bring himself to say the word "panties." "Yes. How disgusting, he was obviously obsessed with me. He must have wanted something very intimate...." (That got an expected wince!) "Oh my God, it's all starting to make sense, isn't it, Lieutenant?"

He nodded, thinking again. He did it just right, she thought, only a tiny wrinkle of concentration showed between his bushy eyebrows. I'll have to try and use that sometime.

She returned the panties to the bag, handed it to him.

"Why would he carry these around with him in his car?" Columbo asked.

"He's crazy. Who knows what went on in that sick mind of his."

He moved toward the door. "Just one more thing, Miss Cole. Mr. Matos didn't follow you from the restaurant."

She looked at him, skeptically.

"His gasoline tank was topped off. We checked with the nearest station in Beverly Hills. They remembered him getting a full tank around seven-thirty. You told me that was the time you were driving home from the restaurant."

"I said he 'probably' had been following me. I had no reason to believe that it was definitely Matos, although I was suspicious of any strange car I thought was tailing me."

Columbo was at the door, and opened it. "You still got some media people out there."

"Ants at a picnic. Have a good evening, Lieutenant."

"I will, Miss." Then wry: "What's left of it."

He started out, then, embarrassed, remembered he still had the evidence bag with the panties in his hand. He quickly stuffed the bag in his raincoat pocket, trudged stolidly to his car, ignoring the media and their shouted questions.

Breathing a vast sigh of relief, she went into the kitchen. If she had even a semblance of appetite before, Columbo had managed to stifle what was left.

She took a can of tomato soup from the cabinet and was staring at it when the phone rang. Probably the production manager with something she should know about tomorrow's shoot.

She took it on the kitchen extension. "Yes?"

It was a low, masculine voice, vaguely familiar. "Miss Cole?"

"Yes. Who is this?"

"One of your fans. One with a camera."

The "camera" gave him away. His name was Pignotti, once her chief nemesis among the hunting hounds of the paparazzi. A painfully thin young man with black spiked hair who had various cameras draped around him like some kind of space-age ornaments. He used to haunt her day and night, a tireless vampire seeking access instead of blood. He still had the liquid remnants of an Italian accent.

"How did you get this number?" she asked sharply.

"We can get anything. I'll make this brief, Miss Cole, I know you're shooting a new picture. When I hang up I want you to go to your computer."

"Why?"

"I've sent you an encrypted file. The password is 'money.' *Capisce?*"

"I don't even know why I'm listening to you," she said in disgust. But a suspicious, protective part of her whispered to do what he said.

"Take a look and we'll talk again." Then he abruptly hung up.

She went into her office, flipped on the light, and booted up her computer. She had been having trouble with it lately, and she hoped to God the damn thing wasn't going to crash at a time like this.

She went immediately to her e-mail, clicked on the file, and put in the password.

It was a dim color night shot of what was no doubt her standing at Matos' front door, her hand inserting a key in the lock. It was a back shot, but she could recognize her blonde hair and the casual black jacket she had worn last night. *Jesus, had he followed me to the house when I planted the photos?*

The phone rang.

She took it on the office extension, feeling the hairs coming to attention on the nape of her neck.

"Recognize the lady?" the smooth, insinuating voice said.

"What do you want, Pignotti?"

"You *remember* me, I'm very flattered," he said.

"What do you want?"

"Thirty thousand dollars. Cash. I'm going back to Italy in two days and . . . " He laughed. "I need some pin money."

"And if I refuse?"

"The District Attorney will get the photo. What do they call it in pornography— the money shot?"

"And how do I know if I give you the money that you'll delete the file and all copies?"

"You've got no choice, baby. You've got to trust me."

"Trust a blackmailer?"

"Honey, you're clean out of options." It sounded like he blew smoke into the mouthpiece. "I'm leaving this country and I'm not coming back. This is a one-shot deal. I'll delete the photo. Believe me, I don't need a blackmail rap. Life is too short."

"Your name suits you," she said, and then wished she hadn't.

"You mean pig. I've been getting that since grade school. I *am* a pig, but you, my dear, are something far worse. Know what I mean?"

There was a long pause while she studied the incriminating photograph. "How will I give you the money?"

"Good girl. Get the money and we'll figure it out. But I must warn you—it *will* be in a public place."

Columbo was looking around the Matos house by himself, smoking, wandering at his ease. He was looking at Cathy Cole's publicity shot on the coffee table in the living room when he heard the sound of a key scraping in the front door lock.

A young woman came in, her head down almost furtively. When she closed the door behind her and looked up, she almost dropped the key. "Who—who are you? How did you get in here?"

"I was gonna ask you those same questions," he said, equably.

"This is my boyfriend's house. He was killed last night." She was no more than twenty, not unattractive, with straight features and smooth black hair.

Columbo nodded, opened his wallet to show her his badge. "Lieutenant Columbo," he said, "I'm the investigating officer." He paused. "Why'd you come over here, Miss—? What was your name again?"

"Janis. Janis Carpenter. Ray's aunt called me from St. Louis. Said she was too ill to come out here to clean up Ray's things and would I check on the house and handle having the body sent back to her."

Another nod. He was looking down at the publicity photo of Cathy Cole on the table. He motioned Janis to take a look at it.

"That's—that's that movie actress." She flared up: "She was the one who shot Ray!"

"Ummm. So how come your boyfriend had a picture of her? He's also got two others on the bedroom wall."

She stared at him, more confused than outraged, a hand pulling at her long dark hair. "This is crazy. Ray never had pictures of that woman *anywhere* in this house. Not even one of me. We slept together two nights ago and there was no picture of her on the wall in the bedroom. And I never saw that one out here either!"

Columbo took a long puff on his cigar, waved some of the smoke away from her. "Did he ever mention her?"

"No. Ray and I hardly ever went to the movies. Ray said he got paid to be in them, not watch them. We both liked television."

"I would think some of her old pictures were probably on cable."

She was making an effort to calm herself down. "I'm telling you, we never saw her in a movie or anyplace else."

More meditative puffs. More waving. "Maybe he had an

obsession with the woman and he didn't tell you. Could I be way off base on that, Miss Carpenter?"

The faint glimmer of a sympathetic smile. "Men hide things from women. Usually things about sex. But I knew Ray, we were planning on getting married. He wasn't obsessed with that woman because he didn't even know her. Am I making my point?"

Columbo's smile was faint, but equally sympathetic. "Yeah, I gotta admit you are. Anything else you can tell me?"

She looked around the relatively neat living room. "I don't think so. Ray was a very nice man. He always dreamt of being an actor, a good actor, but he wound up as only a face in the background. He never had much money."

"This is a nice house, Miss."

"Left to him by his mom."

"And he had a nice car."

She gave that some thought. "Yeah. He had come into some money lately. It was like it came on Mondays, at the beginning of the month. He'd bank some, leave some. I used to see it on the bureau in the bedroom. When I asked him about it, he said something like it was an inheritance from another aunt, but I didn't believe him."

"Why not?"

"I just didn't. Ray's dream was to save some money, good money, and open his own school for young actors." Her face began to fold into a prelude for tears. "The Cole woman blew that away big time."

"Well," Columbo said, "better do what the aunt wants you to do. If I want to talk to you again—?"

"Here's my cell number."

Columbo went to the door, waved, and left.

They had agreed to meet at a popular new restaurant on Maple Drive. Pignotti had told her she could park in the building and that had given her the clue on how to kill him.

She waited in the car on the street until she saw him drive past, pull into the parking entrance to the building that housed the restaurant. She had "borrowed" the car from the studio motor pool and it might be weeks before anyone realized that it had been damaged.

She gave him five minutes to park and take the elevator

to the restaurant. Then she drove into the building, grabbing a parking ticket from the machine.

She took her time moving past the stalls of parked cars until she saw Pignotti's parked on the second tier. She moved past it and slowly took a U, coming to a stop where she could see Pignotti's car.

She waited, waited—saw the time on the dash that she had only a half hour to get back to the studio for the afternoon shoot. She had missed lunch, but she wasn't hungry.

She was lucky—when she was under extreme tension she never wanted to gorge like other actors she knew.

He came out of the elevator, his dark, saturnine face angry, knowing she had stood him up.

He had almost reached his car as she gunned her own, came hurtling down at him—somehow the bastard ducked away—fell, hit the concrete, and sprawled off safely to the side, hitting his head against a car's fender. She realized as she streaked away that she had missed him by only scant inches.

She didn't stop, continued screeching down around to the first level, screaming curses at herself. Idiot! Now she had no way of stopping him from sending that goddamn picture to the D.A.

As she handed her ticket to the attendant in the booth, her mind was scrambling thoughts: how was she going to explain that picture?

Back in her Winnebago, waiting for her call to the set, she studied the screen on the laptop. The more she thought about it, the more she realized that there was something wrong with that shot of her at the door. But what? Suddenly the answer almost slapped her in the face.

She had gone to Matos' house with a portfolio of her publicity photos. The woman in the shot at the door had no portfolio. One hand had fitted the key in the lock, the other was empty at her side. And there were no other keys dangling from the key chain. *The picture was a phony.* Pignotti had set up the shot with someone else, another blonde with a similar jacket. But she couldn't tell Columbo about the portfolio because that was admitting she *had* gone to the house. Damn Pignotti! Damn him to hell! she thought. He really doesn't know I went to the house. He's trying to set me up, bleed me for money and leave the country before the cops figure it out. He must have sniffed something out in the paparazzi gossip as they stalked another celebrity. This was his way of capitalizing on some dirt he suspected Matos had on me.

They were going to shoot late and already the unit manager was handing around dinner chits to the cast and crew. Cathy had been suffering from an adrenaline letdown, digging deep to find the energy for the final scene of the day.

They split for dinner and as she came out into the company street she saw Columbo lighting his cigar in the darkening twilight. "Can I talk to you, Miss Cole?" he said in his usual deferential way.

"How can I stop you?" She started walking along the street, Columbo having to run to catch up with her.

"I know you had a terribly long day, but—"

"But you have to 'clear some things' up again. That's starting to become your mantra."

"Where are we heading?" he asked, as if she was leading him toward the Gates of Hell.

"Nowhere in particular. For some reason walking fast builds my energy level up. It looks like maybe we'll be shooting until midnight tonight."

He was still having trouble keeping up with her. They were passing the looming, barn-like shooting stages, some with red lights on metal stands outside the door. Huff. Puff: "Can I ask you a question?" Columbo said. "What're those red lights?"

"It means pictures are shooting. A warning not to talk too loud or try to enter while the light is on."

"Wow, how do you like that? You live and learn."

She tightened up, knowing what was coming, another rabbit out of his seemingly inexhaustible hat.

Huff. Puff: "We ... we been going over Mr. Matos' house. It's—" breathing harder—"it's fairly close to yours. Did you know that?"

"No, how could I?"

"Well, he had some pictures of you in the living room and the bedroom. I guess you'd call them publicity photos."

"Well, he *was* obsessed with me."

"Funny thing, though." He was almost out of breath with

the rapid walk. "The man's ... girlfriend said she never saw those photos when ... when she was there two nights ago."

"Why would he *ever* want his girlfriend to know about his sick fantasy life?" She was relieved that he hadn't said anything about the other photo, Pignotti's.

Huff. Puff: "Another funny thing—the photos have no fingerprints on them."

She stopped as they approached the front gate of the studio. "Gee, you're really out of breath! You don't seem to be in very good shape, Lieutenant."

"Yeah, I used to walk a lot more. But these days, it's mostly head work."

"Well I'd get more exercise if I were you, it's important. And definitely give up those cigars."

He had forgotten the one he had been smoking. "Oh, I'll try." He squinted at her in the low, fading light. "How could a man leave a photo in his living room and hang one to his bedroom wall without leaving his prints on them?"

He had her there, but she wasn't going to back down. "How would *I* know? I really can't help you, Lieutenant." A beatific smile. "All that is *your* department, isn't it? And I'm sure you're very clever about things like that. But usually when photographers work on my headshots, they wear those thin white gloves."

"You could be right, Miss Cole. You could be right." But those guys are professionals, he thought, and Matos wasn't. He reached into his raincoat pocket.

Oh God, she thought, steeling herself. I need a Xanax for this guy. Here it comes.

He produced the photo, showed it to her.

"What is it?" she asked.

"It was delivered anonymously to the District Attorney's office this morning. We know it came from this guy, Pignotti. Do you know him?"

"The name's familiar, but I just can't place it."

"He's a paparazzo—a real shady individual."

She decided she better divert him. "But how do you know it was Pignotti that sent it?"

"He had a DUI about five years ago. We yanked him in then and fingerprinted him. We matched the prints on the envelope with his in our data base."

"See how clever you are," she said without a trace of sarcasm.

Columbo pointed at the photo. "It's a photo of the front door of Mr. Matos' house. Does the woman remind you of anyone?"

"Are you being disingenuous? It's shot from the back, but it looks like me. And that's impossible, because as I told you I didn't even know where he lived. There's no way this could be me."

Columbo was breathing normally again and he was relighting the cigar. "You got that right," he said. "No way this is you. We believe it's a young woman named Janis Carpenter, Mr. Matos' girlfriend. Why would someone want us to think it was you?"

"I don't know." She was upfront with her puzzlement. That was always important when an emotion was authentic, on-camera or off. "Why would someone do that?"

"Good question. Very good question," Columbo said. They had to move to the side as a stream of cars began to move past them, leaving the lot by the front gate. "Well, you'd better get back, Miss Cole. I'll keep you up on our progress—if there is any."

"Oh I'm sure you will, Lieutenant," she said, trying to strain the sarcasm from her voice. "I'm sure I can count on that. But I'd really start exercising more and cutting down on those cigars."

He had asked Janis to meet him in a coffee shop on Santa Monica near the San Diego freeway on-ramp. She was picking at a hamburger steak when he came in, slid back a chair, and sat down across from her at the table.

"What do you want now?" she said. "You pretty well picked my brains clean yesterday."

Columbo gave a quick smile to a waitress who had come up with a flask of hot coffee. "Something stuck in my head. Keeps buzzing around in there like a mosquito."

"Something I told you?"

He ran a hand through his thick, uncombed hair. "You said he always seemed to have new money lying on the bureau. And you didn't believe where he said it came from."

She had no reason to lie to him. "That's what I said, yes."

He leaned across to her. "Now this is very important, Janis. When you were with Mr. Matos for the last time—

when you stayed overnight—was there any money on the bureau?"

"Yes. Why are you asking me this?" She could see there was something igniting behind his eyes, like he was onto something.

"When we went over Mr. Matos' bedroom," he said, "there was no money on the bureau or anywhere else in the house."

She put down her fork, stared at him. "Are you saying somebody *took* the money? How could that be? Only I had a key to get in." Flash of anger: "You're not accusing *me*, are you?"

"No. No way." He picked up her untouched glass of ice water. "You mind? I'm really thirsty, it's been a hot day."

"No."

He took a long, deep swallow. "Somebody else got in there with a key."

"But—how?"

Columbo wiped his mouth with the back of his hand. "With Ray's key."

She returned from the studio, too tired to even make herself some eggs. She promised herself she had to get a much bigger house, a housekeeper. Here she was making all this money and she was still living like back home in Idaho.

When the doorbell rang, her nerves felt a current tingle through them like an electrical charge. It had to be that cop.

It was. Same apologetic demeanor, same cigar breath. There were two plainclothes people behind him, a man and a woman.

"Good evening, Miss Cole," he said.

"Who are these people?"

"Fingerprint team. Can we come in?"

She half-closed the door. "I don't think so. I'm very tired, I have a headache. I was going right to bed."

"We have a court order, Miss." He unfolded a document, held it up so she could see it.

She was still blocking his entry. "Why are you here?"

"I'll be happy to explain, but you have to let us in. I'm afraid it's the law." He kept the document open in front of her.

She opened the door wider. "Whatever."

They came in, the fingerprint team glancing at Columbo.

His knowing blink signaled something back to them, and they headed down the hall.

"Where are they going?!" she asked angrily. "They have no right—!"

"I'm afraid we do," Columbo said, folding the document closed now. "They have a court order to search the premises."

This sent her in retreat, and her tone conspiratorially softened. "What are they looking for, Lieutenant?"

He didn't mince words: "You shot Ray Matos to death, Miss Cole, and he wasn't a stalker." His once-genial tone had hardened. "That was just a scam you invented to try to fool us."

She turned her face away. "I've been playing a fictional person all day. Now you're telling me I played another one?"

"He was blackmailing you, the payments came every month on the first Monday. We have his bank statements to prove it."

"So? That money could've come from anywhere."

It was as if he hadn't heard her. "I don't know what he had on you, but you both came from the same small town so it was probably something that had happened there that you were trying to hide. Something that could jeopardize, maybe destroy your career."

She sat down, sprawling her legs out, casual, as if she hadn't a care in the world. She said nothing.

"You had it with him milking you, knowing it could go on forever—so you killed him. And then another blackmailer popped up like a jack-in-the-box—this Pignotti fella, only he was clumsy. He took a photo of a woman who looked a little like you from the back. He figured he could put the squeeze on you and flush out the link between you and Mr. Matos."

Now she managed to speak, her voice suddenly hoarse. "You can't prove anything."

"I can prove that when you said you never knew Mr. Matos that that was a lie. And that's all I need."

The male fingerprint man looked at Columbo from the hallway. "We found the money, Lieutenant. Top dresser drawer in the bedroom."

"Run the test, Sergeant. While we're speaking." He went back down the hall.

All the energy, all the resistance, was slowly draining

from her. She wanted to get up, confront him, but it was so much more comfortable in the chair. And she was so very, very tired.

"You don't have to be a genius," Columbo said, "to know that after you killed him you took his keys and went to his house—after you planted your panties in his car. You left your publicity photos around the living room and the bedroom, wearing gloves—which you have to admit wasn't too smart, Miss Cole. I mean leaving the photos clean of any fingerprints at all. After all, Mr. Matos wouldn't have been wearing gloves."

"No. Not very smart."

"And you saw some of the money on the bureau that you had given him."

Now she saw what he had and where this was going. She felt her throat close, didn't know if she could speak any more, or wanted to.

"You saw the blackmail money he had extorted from you. And you grabbed it and took it back here."

She found herself nodding. It was so easy to agree with him, he was still so low-key like the soft lights they used when they shot her close-ups.

The fingerprint man was back in the doorway. "We got a match, Lieutenant."

"I'm sorry, Miss," Columbo said, turning to her. "They found Matos' prints on those bills. I'm going to have to place you under arrest."

She was still nodding, stupidly, as if there was something mechanical in her neck, making her do it. "What gave you your big 'aha' moment?" she asked wearily.

"It really wasn't very big, Miss Cole. I was never really comfortable with you having that .45 so handy. It smelled maybe like an ambush."

He was right, but she would never admit it and give him the satisfaction. She finally rose from the chair, her legs weak, rubbery. She mockingly extended her wrists.

"Do I get handcuffed?"

Columbo's smile was low-key, but a little sad this time. "You've been watching too many movies, Miss Cole."

THE GUN THAT WASN'T

LIEUTENANT COLOMBO ARRIVED at the murder scene in the late afternoon while the hot Santa Ana winds were shrieking like lonesome banshees through the canyons. The winds made his mouth dry.

There had been a homicide at a house in Westlake. The victim, Detective Charlie Bevans, was one of their own. And Detective Mason Kincaid, who had found the body, was also one of their own.

There were silent gawking neighbors in the street and Columbo was sure the blood-lusting media was on their way. What was the slogan he had heard: "If it bleeds, it leads!" Well, there was enough blood here and a cop's murder was always a big, important story.

While the criminalists were doing their job in the house, Columbo accompanied Detective Kincaid over to the sparse shelter of a police van. "Fill me in on what happened, Mace. Can we get some water around here? These dry winds, I always need water."

Kincaid was a career cop who prided himself on his meticulous appearance. Always a dark serge suit, not expensive, with good accoutrements like he was going to get his high school diploma. Even a display hankie in his breast pocket that was coordinated with the colors in his tie. There was an ambitious wind at his back almost as driving as the Santa Anas. "You can get a drink in the fridge."

In the shadow of the van, Columbo sighed—the guy was in a dark suit again. Did he have ten of them in his closet? "What happened here, Mace?"

Kincaid was his usual serious self. "It was Charlie's day off, and I had the night shift, so I figured we'd grab a late lunch."

"And you knew where he lived?"

"Sure. We have poker parties over here twice a month. Even before the wife divorced him."

Columbo tried lighting a cigar, knowing the wind would make it difficult. "So when you got over here?"

"I parked out front, started up the path to the front door when I heard gunshots. From the house. The door was locked so I had to bust it open. I found Charlie dead on the living room floor, two slugs in his head, poor bastard."

"Stupid question: so nobody was there?"

Kincaid shook his head. "I ran through the house, searching, gun in hand. The kitchen door was wide open. I ran outside, checked the yard, then I ran down the alley behind the houses. Reached the end, started back around to the street side, checking. Nobody."

Columbo tried lighting the cigar again. "One of the neighbors heard the shots, called 911. Your call for backup came in about four minutes later. That was sorta late, Mace."

Kincaid said in frustration, "I was chasing Charlie's killer. That was the first thing on my mind."

"Okay," Columbo said. "What happened next?"

"A cruiser pulled up no more than two minutes later; they had been somewhere in the neighborhood when they got the call from the dispatcher. When I told them there was a killer loose they called for back-up."

Columbo looked down the dappled, tree-shaded length of street. There were men canvassing the houses, ringing doorbells, talking to the various neighbors.

"If he's hiding somewhere the boys will smoke him out," Kincaid said. He removed his display hankie, wiped sweat from his forehead. "Poor Charlie," he said. "Most I remember of him now is that he was a lousy poker player. Isn't that ridiculous?"

Columbo was ruminating. "Charlie was a good cop but he had a rep for being a little too law-and-order. Well, maybe we'll get lucky, catch this guy somewhere in the neighborhood."

But he knew that probably the only success he would have that morning was maybe getting his cigar lit. Which he finally did on his third try.

Police Commissioner Howland confirmed Columbo's prediction. "Hate to say we lost the guy. Maybe he had a car waiting for him after he offed Charlie. He was working on some Mafia stuff."

They were in Holland's immaculate office, citations on the walls, awards, family photographs, nothing out of place. Columbo always liked the little snow globe that had a color photo of Holland's grandkids. He wondered if you shook it would they disappear in a miniature blizzard? It was tempting to find out, but he had never tried.

Howland sat down behind his desk and Columbo took the chair in front. There were stacks of loose-leaf binders on the blotter and you had to almost peer through their portals to see the man. "What's your sense, Columbo?" he asked. "You always get these early feelings."

"I'm not sure you want to hear this, sir. But—there's been some scuttlebutt around that Bevans was angling for Kincaid's possible promotion."

Howland's eyes smiled more than his mouth. "Hey, Lieutenant, we've got a kettle of piranha fish around here, if you haven't noticed. You're particularly liked because you're not angling for somebody else's position."

"I'm just passing on what I heard, sir."

Howland moved one of the stacks so he could get a better look at him. "Charlie Bevans was an old-school cop. Down through the years he made more enemies than my mother-in-law. When you think of all the guys he sent away, who knows who came out of prison or the woodwork and pumped two .22 slugs in his head?"

"We've got no killer, no gun," Columbo said. "That's what's weird. I had practically a task force going over that street, house by house, yard by yard. When the perp got away, we figured maybe he hid his piece in the shrubbery or in a dumpster in the alley behind the houses. Or maybe he took it with him if a buddy picked him up."

"What did the neighbors say?" Howland asked.

"They say nobody came into their houses or, as far as they knew, hid in their yards. And remember our boys got there within minutes." He sighed heavily. "The media's going to barbecue us over a very hot flame. Those two new rookie cops Martinez and Carstairs are going through all the vegetation and every dumpster in the neighborhood. I'll tell you, they better take a swim in the Pacific before they go home tonight!" He picked up the snow globe, but knew enough not to shake it. "Did you check Detective Kincaid's gun?"

Howland's eyes narrowed. "Are you telling me you think Kincaid did the job?"

"Oh no, sir. But his was the only gun that was around."

"Put that damn globe down. For your information, Kincaid's service revolver hadn't been fired. We checked it as a matter of course. We checked out his clothing too. Why would Kincaid kill a friend? Kincaid and Charlie go back ten years at least, big poker buddies. Kincaid's a first-class cop. Why would he care if Charlie was looking for his position?"

A violent wind tore at the windows. "Just a thought, sir," Columbo said. "It comes under the heading of a premonition, maybe?" Columbo smiled for the first time. "My wife loves this guy on TV, reads minds, has premonitions, talks to dead people. They even talk back to him, he claims."

"Talk back? Lieutenant, my wife is an expert at that. But does *she* make any of that big television money?"

Columbo visited Charlie's ex-wife at Parkman General Hospital where she was a nurse.

"I got the news about Charlie, Lieutenant." She was a diminutive woman with a wan, faded prettiness.

"Had you been in contact with Charlie recently?"

"Week ago. Luckily we had one of those divorces where everybody stays friendly."

Columbo quickly stepped back as two doctors swept by him in the corridor. "Was Charlie disturbed about anything when you talked with him? Worried?"

"No. Just the opposite. He said he was going to 'blow the whistle' on somebody."

Columbo blinked. "Blow the whistle? Somebody on the force?"

"He wasn't specific."

Columbo half-nodded, musing. "Blow the whistle. You're sure that's what he said?"

"Positive. Does that mean anything to you?"

Columbo shrugged. "Not yet it doesn't." He was still chewing on it, not wanting to let it go. "Did Charlie ever mention Detective Mason Kincaid to you?"

"Sure, I know Mace. He used to come over and play poker with Charlie and the others."

"Yes, ma'am." He glanced around to see if there were any more stampeding doctors coming his way. "I know you're very busy so I won't take up any more of your time."

"You think I've said anything useful, Lieutenant?"

"Oh yes, ma'am. Very useful."

The next morning, Columbo went to Mason Kincaid's

home in Culver City, a modest Cape Cod on a leafy quiet street.

As he approached the front door, it blew open. Two stocky, stone-faced men in pin-stripe suits over white T-shirts came swiftly out, brushing him aside.

Columbo, nonplussed, rang the doorbell.

Mrs. Kincaid opened the door. She was a well-proportioned attractive woman.

"Who were those men?" Columbo asked.

"Some plainclothes pals of Mace from Reno."

She took him into their small, modest living room. Columbo thought it seemed not only modest but a bit under-furnished. Her husband was there reading the paper. He wasn't in his customary blue suit this morning, just an ordinary, tasteful sport shirt and jeans.

Columbo hadn't been invited to sit down, but he decided on an uncomfortable hard-back near the wide-screen television.

"The Commissioner told me he wanted you to take it easy today," he said to Kincaid. "I mean after your shock at finding Charlie yesterday."

"It was very kind of him," Mace said, drinking from a mug of coffee.

His wife said, "Can I get you some coffee, Lieutenant?" She was perfectly made-up at this hour, but her face showed strain around the mouth and eyes.

"Gee, that would be terrific if it's not too much trouble, ma'am. Something happened to our coffee percolator at home. It's almost brand-new, my wife just got it at Walmart, you'd think something German-made would work as good as their cars."

"You can't count on anything, I guess, these days," Mace said laconically "So you want to ask me something more about what happened yesterday?"

"I guess you know they didn't catch anybody on the run. And you know we hadda lotta men in the neighborhood looking. Couldn't even find the gun if he threw it away."

"Sometimes the perps get lucky. Look, Columbo, I know all this. What else can I tell you?"

Columbo looked down at his hands, then up. "You heard the shots and you broke down the door. Can I assume it was locked?"

"You can assume. I smashed that damn door right off

its hinges, right on the floor. I was in a panic that something really bad had just happened to Charlie."

"Hmmm. And then you went out the back trying to chase the perp."

"Exactly."

Mrs. Kincaid returned with the coffee. Columbo took it, slopping a little into the saucer. "Ah thanks, ma'am. Much appreciated."

"Will you be needing me, Lieutenant?"

"Oh no. Just your husband."

Looking a little less nervous, she smiled faintly and left the room.

Columbo set the coffee down on a side table next to him. He removed a sheaf of papers from his raincoat pocket and sifted through them. "Here it is. Sergeant Ramirez's report — he talked to the neighbors in the house next door. The husband heard the shots and saw you running past his house a few minutes later."

Kincaid sat down in a chair near Columbo. "And?"

"Well, Mace, if you chased the perp down the back alley how come this neighbor saw you running down the street in front?"

"Look," Mace said. "This is how it went down. I ran down the alley and circled around to the street, thinking I could find the perp. But I already told you all this."

Columbo nodded. "Just getting it clear in my mind." Kincaid got up. "No offense, Columbo, but I have the distinct impression you think *I* killed Charlie."

Columbo looked wounded. "Oh no, Mace, you got that wrong. Nothing like that."

Kincaid laughed. "You have to excuse me, but I've seen you play this routine time and time again. The paper shuffling, the distractions, the talk about your wife, or in this case your broken percolator. If you've got me in your cross hairs, you really have to do better than using all that crap."

Columbo got up, his hands outstretched imploringly. "That's gotta be all unconscious stuff, Mace. I do ramble around a bit, I admit, but that's no act, believe me."

"Yeah, right, as you always say. So I repeat—how can I help you?"

Columbo pointed his thumbs up. "You already have. I just wanted to check on that discrepancy about the front or the back."

Kincaid was his genial self again. "It was my pleasure." Then the dig: "So now I hope you'll be spending all your time trying to find Charlie's killer and I won't be seeing you anymore—I mean as part of your investigation."

Columbo's smile was ingratiatingly noncommittal. "You know I always like to see you, Mace. "

The following day, Kincaid was in the squad room on the phone when Columbo ambled in. The room was empty except for the two of them.

Columbo looked at some clipboards on the wall, waiting while Kincaid finished his conversation. Finally he hung up.

"My accountant's been bugging me," Kincaid said in despair. "Those Sacramento guys are always finding something stupid in your tax return."

He watched, his eyes wry question marks, as Columbo turned slowly from the wall: "*Another* discrepancy? I thought I wasn't going to be seeing you so soon again."

"Just one more thing, Mace."

"You talked to that semi-blind neighbor again? He saw me with the smoking gun this time?"

"Oh no, no, something else. I talked to Charlie's ex-wife the other day. She said Charlie said he was going to blow the whistle on somebody."

Kincaid saw an officer about to enter the room, waved him away. "That's interesting. Did Charlie say who?"

"No. But since he was such a good cop, and you know the force was his life, it must've been one of his colleagues."

"Strange. You think it was *me*?"

"I'm just checking, Mace."

Kincaid had no problem showing his skepticism. "Among Charlie's friends?"

"Or enemies."

Kincaid pounced: "He had no enemies. Don't bullshit me, Columbo. I told you I'm wise to your routine."

"Everybody has enemies, Mace. As a smart, experienced cop you know that."

Kincaid shifted uncomfortably in his chair. "So besides me, you're just 'randomly' checking around?"

Columbo nodded. He dropped down familiarly next to Kincaid in a chair, leaned closer.

"You know I'll check to see if you're really checking," Kincaid warned him.

Columbo nodded again.

"So you've started your 'duel.' "

"Duel?"

Kincaid shook his head in feigned frustration. "Here you go again. You think you've got your man, so the dance begins."

Columbo smiled disarmingly. "I thought you said it was a duel."

Kincaid did his best to look casual, indifferent. "Go right ahead. I didn't kill Charlie."

Columbo went back to Charlie's neighborhood. The winds had died down. There was yellow crime tape strung across the front of the house, the front door was open. He ducked under the tape and took a slow, thoughtful stroll through the small bungalow. He was always surprised by what he perceived as loneliness lingering in all the nooks and crannies in the homes of the divorced or the lifelong bachelors. Charlie's was no different. Sort of sad in a way.

He checked the back door leading into the tiny back-yard where Kincaid said he had run out to catch the perp. He went out himself, walking down the length of the alley behind the neighboring houses. When he came to the end he took a left leading back to the street and saw a mailman at the mailbox on the corner.

"Sir?" he called, walking up to the man, a youngish Hispanic wearing glasses. He had never seen a mailman before with glasses. You'd think some of the older ones would need them.

"Is this always your route, in the afternoon around this time?"

The mailman took offense. "Yeah, it is. Why do you want to know? Who are you?"

Columbo found his wallet, showed him his ID.

"Oh, you're investigating the murder?"

Columbo nodded. "So you came by after it happened. Did anything seem different about the neighborhood?"

"Sure," he said, the word weighted with sarcasm. "There was guys like you all over the place. One of them questioned me then, too. Don't you dudes talk to each other?"

Columbo smiled defensively. "Nothing different at all that afternoon besides all us dudes?"

The man was belligerently adamant. "Nothing at all."

Columbo backed away, waved a hand. "Have a nice day."

Late that afternoon, he was in his office when Kincaid came in, closed the door. "Like the switch?" he asked. "You don't come to bother me, the suspect comes and bothers you."

Columbo swung slowly around in his swivel chair. "What's on your mind, Mace?"

"Pagano said you were checking out Charlie's house. I was wondering what you found."

"Nothing at all. Had a brief talk with the mailman, nothing there either."

Kincaid's smile was ice. "I told you—you were going to have a hard time, didn't I?"

"I've got some work, Mace. Anything else on your mind?"

"Yeah, there is. Reason I dropped by. You've had men tailing me for the last few days. It's very annoying and I want to know why."

Columbo matched his smile. "You should know by now we never tell a suspect what we're up to."

Kincaid smashed his fist down on the desk in triumph. "So I *am* a suspect! Your main man."

Columbo was thoughtful. "What did you call it, a duel?"

"Right. So now that it's out in the open, let's shelve all your snide little tricks. Deal?"

Columbo didn't answer. Then: "I've got work, Mace."

"Well, you're going to fail, my friend. If I know you've got men on my tail, it's going to ruin your plan, whatever it is."

A long silence. Then: "Will it?"

"I said, the game-playing is over. This is *mano a mano* from here on in."

A careless shrug. "If that's what you want."

Kincaid's anger was escalating as he leaned down, both elbows resting on the desk. Not a muscle had moved in Columbo's impassive face. "I don't think you know how to operate without all those well-worn, annoying schticks of yours."

"Whatever it takes to get my man."

"You don't always 'get your man.' "

Columbo leaned back, linked his hands behind his head. "No, not always. That's true. Very true."

Kincaid went to the door. "It's airtight, Columbo. And you don't have a clue."

Columbo only shrugged again.

The next day, he returned to the Kincaid house in Culver City. It was less quiet than the first time, kids skate-boarding in the street. There was an older-model Chevy on the drive. Had Mace sold that nice Buick they had?

Mrs. Kincaid opened the door, still in a dressing gown at two in the afternoon. She was surprised to see him, but courteously led him into the living room where he was puzzled to perceive even less furniture than before.

"Ma'am," Columbo said, "pardon me for asking, but weren't there two silver candlesticks on the mantelpiece?"

She hesitated, tried to smile. "You're very—very observant, Lieutenant. Yes, they're out being replated. I inherited them from my mother after she passed on last year."

"Hmmm. And those nice old brass andirons in the fireplace?" She tried to hide her embarrassment, but it was a failed attempt. "We got rid of them because Mace never liked them," she said. "Can I get you something, some coffee, a nice cold soda?"

"Oh no, ma'am. Thanks, but I just had some coffee back at the station. Oh, and what happened to that nice wide-screen TV?" Before she could answer there was the unmistakable sound of a key in the lock of the front door.

He turned to see Kincaid coming in, stopping abruptly in his tracks when he saw his wife's visitor.

"Goddamn, Columbo. Isn't a suspect's house off-limits these days?"

His wife stared at him, obviously taken aback by the word 'suspect's'."

Columbo shrugged. "Don't they say all's fair in love and detection?"

"What the hell are you questioning Marion about? Behind my back, I might add."

"He wasn't asking me about anything really important, dear," Marion said.

He gave her a hard, probing look. "Are you sure?"

Columbo took a step in the direction of the door, which Kincaid had forgotten to close. There was the dull rumble of skateboards and kids' excited voices from the street.

"I was just here observing," Columbo said.

"Observing *what*?"

Columbo's answer was characteristically cryptic: "Things that aren't here."

Back out on the street, Columbo went over to an unmarked police car parked two houses down. Pagano was in the shotgun seat, Ramirez at the wheel.

"You start on the post offices?" Columbo asked Pagano.

"This morning. No luck yet. But give us some time."

Columbo watched the skateboarding kids coming back along the street. "Sure. But not *all* the time in the world."

He was in Commissioner Howland's office. Howland had his suit jacket off, his shirtsleeves rolled to the elbows. He looked unusually testy, tense. Is he going to have me on the carpet? Columbo thought with dismay.

"It's been free-floating all over the station," Howland said. "You boring in on Kincaid."

"But you've known that yourself, sir," Columbo gently countered. "I've been giving you daily reports."

"Yes, but I don't want the rest of the men passing around this kind of thing, buzzing about it at lunch and in the bars after work. It wreaks hell on discipline."

"I realize that. But we're all like a family around here, everybody's looking over somebody else's shoulder. It's human nature, isn't it?"

"I don't want a lecture on human nature. I'm told you've been harassing Kincaid and his wife at their home. That's stepping over the line, Lieutenant."

"Harassing is sort of a strong word, sir."

There was the sound of a cellphone ringing. Howland looked ominously at Columbo.

"It's mine. Sorry, sir." He dug the phone from his coat pocket, opened the lid, holding it like a lodestone to his ear. "Columbo. Yes. You're kidding! Boy, right in the nick of time. When are you coming back? Okay. Great."

He closed the phone, still holding it in his hand while he gathered his thoughts for a few seconds. The Commissioner was staring impatiently at him.

"Who was that?" Howland finally asked, more intrigued than annoyed.

"Sergeant Pagano. They just found what we've been looking for. It's a done deal, sir."

"That's what I've been afraid of," Howland said, sitting down morosely behind his desk. "When it's one of our own it plays havoc with every decent man on the force."

Columbo was about to go out. "Ah—just one more thing, sir. Don't forget—he killed one of our own."

Howland grudgingly nodded: a point, unfortunately, well-taken.

Columbo was back in his office at his desk a half-hour later when there was a knock on the door. He had already seen Pagano who had given him an evidence bag.

"Come in," Columbo called, glancing at the bag near the front of his desk.

Kincaid entered, wary, his eyes moving. He was in his usual blue suit with a darkly-patterned tie against a white shirt. "You wanted to see me?" he asked in a slightly strained voice. What had happened to the sarcasm?

"Sit down, Mace," Columbo said pleasantly, indicating a chair.

"I'd rather stand if you don't mind."

Columbo let a few seconds slip by. "The duel's over."

"You mean you've come up with a clue?" The sarcasm was back, having lost some of its force.

"You're an out-of-control gambler, Mace. Probably for years. I saw those no-nonsense enforcers leaving your house a few days ago. They're the hoods who threaten to break a few limbs if you welsh on a gambling debt."

"You don't know that."

"They were deep into you. That's what I assumed when I saw that the candlesticks, andirons, and the TV were missing from your living room. And you got rid of your Buick for a cheaper car. Whatever else your wife and you were forced to sell, I have no idea. That kind of obsessive gambling could've knocked you right out of the force and then you wouldn't even have had a salary to pay off your debts."

Kincaid shifted from one leg to another, but said nothing.

"Charlie Bevans found out. He was a righteous s.o.b and

he was going to blow the whistle on you. That's why you shot him to death in his house."

"Are you taping this?" Kincaid asked in a shaky voice.

"Nah. I don't have to. After you shot him, you ran down the alley and around to the street. You see, you knew if a cruiser came by quickly you would have to get rid of the gun, the untraceable .22 that you shot him with."

"The neighborhood was thoroughly searched," Kincaid said with an echo of his former defiance. "They found nothing."

"No, they didn't. That's because you had prepared a padded mailing envelope. You placed the gun in the envelope and deposited it in the mailbox at the end of the street. That's why you ran down there."

Kincaid had nothing to say.

"I had only one theory. Maybe you took a box at some post office in the vicinity so you could mail the gun to yourself and pick it up later when the heat was off. That's why I had you followed immediately after the murder. You caught on right away so you were afraid to get the mailing envelope from your box because the boys could pick you up and nail you with it. How'm I doing so far?"

Kincaid was still silent, looking out the window.

"My men had a court order to search boxes all over town. When you take out a box you have to give your real name backed up by ID. Just this morning they found out you had rented a box in Studio City, and they found the package with the gun."

He indicated the evidence bag on his desk. Kincaid gave it a hurried glance and turned back to the window.

"I haven't had time to send it to ballistics yet," Columbo went on, "but I'm sure it will be the weapon that killed Charlie. And it will probably have your prints on it and the envelope. But that's just a cherry on the ice cream sundae."

Finally Kincaid turned from the window, a smile frozen on his now hollowed-out face. "You were right: the duel is over. I fell into the same trap all of them make even though I knew your M.O. I underestimated you. You're good, Columbo. You're really good."

Columbo sighed, swiveling around to look out the window at the bright glowing day. "Only if I catch you and all the others."

REQUIEM FOR
A HITMAN

HYSON COPELAND MET HIM at a restaurant on Ventura Boulevard in Woodland Hills. She had given them an excuse at the office and arrived early, ordering a shrimp cocktail appetizer, no drink.

He came in, almost exactly on time, an ordinary-looking man in an ordinary sport-coat over unpressed khaki slacks. The only giveaway, it seemed to her, was a slight, almost undetectable scowl lurking at the distant corners of his slightly narrowed eyes.

He joined her at the table after a quick appraisal of the few other diners in the room. She had selected a table in a corner, perfect for a private conversation.

Almost as soon as he was seated, the waiter appeared, asked if he wanted a cocktail or a glass of wine. No.

She took this as a good sign—no drinking during a business meeting.

She realized that she didn't know what to call him. He knew her name and her husband's, but he hadn't volunteered his own. And he hadn't greeted her with her name when he sat down.

She watched him as he briefly, silently, scanned the menu and put it away.

"What do I call you?" she asked with a smile.

"Try Jack."

She knew he was lying. The waiter was back again.

"May I buy you lunch?" she asked.

"Just coffee. I don't plan to be here very long."

Allyson gestured to the waiter. "Coffee for my guest."

"Jack" closed the menu. "When do you want it done?" He had a hoarse, grating voice like that of a heavy smoker.

"How about tomorrow evening? Are you busy?" she added with another smile, brighter this time. You never knew about hitmen, she thought humorously, they might have a dentist's appointment when a client wanted it done.

"Not 'how about,'" he corrected her. "I want definite."

"Tomorrow night." She was beginning to dislike him, which was good.

"What time?"

"Eight o'clock. We'll have finished dinner and he'll be in the study reading, which he does every night when he's home."

"Where's the—?" he broke off as the waiter brought him coffee. He waited until the young man had moved off to another table. "Where's the study situated in the house?"

"When you enter the house from the kitchen you go straight back down the hall. On your right is the living room. The study is right off the living room."

She removed an envelope from her handbag, slid it across the table to him.

He picked it up, weighed it in his hand. "Key?"

"To the kitchen door. Make sure you take it with you when you leave."

He shot her a withering look, as if her order was questioning his competence. "You won't be in the house."

She shot him her own withering look, having fun, trying to taunt him now. "Of course not. I'll be establishing an alibi very much elsewhere." She paused. "Aren't you going to ask me why I want him killed?"

He shrugged.

"The old fool is seeing a much younger woman, a lawyer's aide. If he dumps me, I'll never get his money."

He obviously couldn't have cared less. He took a sip of the coffee. "Money?"

She was getting a little tired of his studied ennui. Sliding another envelope across the table, she said: "I added a little extra."

Wordlessly, he pushed the envelope down somewhere inside his sport coat. Not even a thank you for the gratuity. Then he pushed the coffee away as he rose from the table, and strode quickly, long-legged, toward the door.

"Can I count on you?" she called after him.

No response. He went out to the street.

At precisely seven-thirty o'clock the following evening, Judge Victor Copeland settled himself in his favorite chair in the study, and almost immediately engrossed himself in a book. He was at least twenty years older than his wife, with cloud-soft white hair that was sticking out from the back of his collar. His fleshy, jowly face was bland, innocent, belying what some defense attorneys called him, "the Injudicious

Judge." He had a well-earned reputation for shortness of temper and lengthy sentences. But he was just an old man now who probably enjoyed books more than sending the convicted to their destinies.

Allyson, upstairs in their bedroom, removed the judge's .38 revolver from the bottom drawer of the nightstand next to his side of the bed. She had checked it out the day before, and it seemed well-oiled, ready to do its job, even though she knew nothing about guns.

Weapon in hand, she went to the window that overlooked the back lawn. In less than a minute, a shadow moved there, almost invisible in the moonlight, and then she saw Jack approaching the kitchen door. She went quickly out of the room to the head of the stairs.

The hitman left the kitchen, gliding into the living room and then into the study. The judge glanced up from his book and had no time to register surprise before the bullet, through the book, shattered his heart. Without even crying out, he slumped in the chair, the book sitting impossibly placid, opened and bloody on his lap.

Jack went over to the body, kneeled down to check for a pulse. At just that moment, Allyson appeared in the doorway, holding the gun behind her back. She gave him a questioning look.

He stared at her, speechless. He got to his feet and she shot him. He tumbled to the floor, the gun still clutched in his hand.

Allyson scrubbed the .38 clean with a handkerchief, then placed the gun in her husband's right hand, curling his forefinger around the trigger.

Just to be on the safe side, she went to Jack's body, felt for a pulse. None. Then to be doubly sure, she slipped a hand inside his jacket to feel if there was a heartbeat. None. She found the key immediately in his sports coat pocket. Then she went to the kitchen, opened the window just a few inches. It was incredible—she hadn't even broken out in a sweat. As long as she didn't make a habit of doing things like this, she thought with a laugh.

She took the wall phone down, took a deep breath, and called 911.

She knew she had seen the investigating cop before—

going in to see her boss in his office or downstairs in one of the corridors, huddled with some of his fellow plainclothesmen. *Columbo.* It suddenly came back to her—that was his name. He looked shambling, non-communicative, peering around a little lost in this strange house.

The two bodies were being removed on stretchers and the tech team was moseying around, doing their Santa's Helpers' tasks.

The Columbo cop came over to her. "Why don't we go in the other room," he said, gently. "I think it best you get outta here, ma'am."

She nodded, bringing the handkerchief to her eyes, the same handkerchief that had wiped her prints from the gun.

The living room was dim and she liked keeping it that way, not turning on any of the lamps. The dimness didn't seem to bother Columbo.

"Why don't you sit down, ma'am," he suggested.

She collapsed into a wing chair, dabbed at her eyes with the handkerchief again. And she still wasn't sweating.

"You told the Sergeant you'd been upstairs napping in the bedroom when you heard the shots?"

"Yes. I was sleeping very deeply but they woke me."

"Uh-huh. And you said after dinner the judge always went to read in his study?"

"Yes." She forced a sad smile. "Victor always believed reading was good for the digestion. He was a murder-mystery fan, the more gory the better, and that didn't make sense to me." Stop the b.s. with this guy!

"Hmmm. And the gunshots?"

"Woke me up, as I said. I—I don't know where I got the courage but I came downstairs and found—" She broke off, bringing the handkerchief to her mouth this time.

"Two shots? One following the other?"

"Yes."

"Almost simultaneously?"

She nodded.

"I hate to ask you this, Mrs. Copeland, but I have to. What exactly did you see after you came downstairs and looked in the study?"

"I saw exactly what you and your men saw when you came here. That horrible man in the sports coat had shot my husband. And it looked like Victor had shot *him.*"

"That would appear to be what happened, yes." He groped around, steadied himself with a hand on the back of a chair.

"I'm sorry," she said, "I guess I should've turned on some lights."

"It's quite all right, ma'am. I don't think we should have any lights blaring in your face after what you've been through tonight."

"You're very kind. Lieutenant, was it?"

"Yes, ma'am. Lieutenant Columbo. I know we've seen each other before, exchanged hellos." He took out a notebook, realized it was too dark to read or write. Stuffed it back in his pocket. "If your husband was relaxing, reading, what was he doing with a gun? A .38 revolver."

"Victor said he was receiving some death threats as of late and he wanted to be protected even in his own home."

"Death threats," Columbo repeated. "Were they on paper or verbal?"

"He didn't say. But you know, Lieutenant, my husband sent up many, many men over his years on the bench. I guess many vengeful men among them."

Columbo was musing. "Yeah. I guess holding a gavel can turn out to be a pretty dangerous job."

She brought the handkerchief again to her eyes.

"I'm gonna let you go, ma'am. I know it's gonna be a tough night getting to sleep, but we have a doctor who can prescribe some sleeping pills if you need them."

"Very kind, Lieutenant. But I have some of my own." Another sad smile, this one wreathed in her very real tiredness. "Anything else you'd like to ask me tonight?"

"Nah, that's it." He still seemed disoriented in the dark room. "But we'll be in touch."

She woke up a little groggy from the sleeping pill and wondered if she had really needed it last night. It was Sunday and she didn't have to report to the office. After her husband was murdered, did she really think her boss wouldn't give her the week off? It's funny—she loved her job and continued to work after her marriage even though she never had to work another day in her life.

The house was pleasantly peaceful, cleansed now that that libidinous old man was gone. Around ten, after she made herself a light breakfast, she was interrupted by some members of the tech team who rang the bell. There were a few other details they had to check, they told her politely. She nodded wearily, and most of them went to the study, but two trudged into the kitchen.

Columbo came back while the men were getting ready to leave. He chatted with them and then went into the living room, looked around, trying to acclimate himself now that sunlight had taken possession of the space. He was surprised to see Allyson standing there.

"I'm really sorry to bother you so soon again, ma'am," he said. "Please sit down, this won't take long."

She sat. "Any way I can help."

"Did you manage to get some sleep?" he asked, genuinely concerned.

"Fitfully, but yes."

He paused. "Mrs. Copeland, do you have any idea how the intruder got into the house?"

"None."

"Did you ever see this individual before?"

She shifted in the chair. "Well, I only had a quick glance at him on the floor. But what happened was so horrendous, I really couldn't register much."

He handed her a photograph. "This was taken last night at the morgue."

She stared at it distastefully. "No, I never saw him before. Who is he?" She was going to add "ex-con?" but she thought better of it.

Columbo took the photo back, slipped it into his raincoat pocket. "We don't know yet. We're circulating his photo and prints to various law enforcements here and out of state."

"Well, you mentioned last night he might have been someone who Victor sentenced."

"We're checking that out, ma'am. But we don't have his name, anything. There was no wallet or identification on the body. There *was* a key in his pants pocket that might be to a motel room. The clothing label on the sports coat was from a store in New York City."

"May I ask you a question, Lieutenant?"

"Sure."

She gestured to the doorway. "What were your men doing in my kitchen?"

He decided to sit down across from her. "Kitchen? Oh

yeah, there was a partly open window next to the fridge. Did you know it was open?"

"No. A day worker comes in twice a week. Maybe she opened the window to let some air in. I'll have to ask her."

"They're some prints on the sill and the bottom wooden frame of the window. They just told me some of them are yours."

She stared at him. "How—how do you know?"

"Yours are on record. You know, the formality when you got your job?"

She was thinking furiously, trying to hide it. "Well, I *have* opened that window now and then in the summer. There's no AC in the kitchen."

"Uh-huh." He stretched out his legs on the carpet like he was comfortably at ease in his own house. "We think maybe the perp got in through that window. He might have checked around to find out if one was open."

"Were *his* prints on the window?"

"No. But he might've wiped them off." Columbo nodded gravely. "When we find out who he was we'll be one big step further in the investigation."

Now *she* nodded, matching his graveness.

Friends were calling all afternoon, wanting her to come over, join them for dinner. But she begged off, saying all she wanted to do was get some sleep.

That night she drove along the coast, had a nice dinner with wine at a steakhouse where she knew she wouldn't be seen by anyone who knew her. She paid in cash so there would be no record of any kind.

Why was she being so careful? she asked herself. It was probably because she didn't trust that cop. He seemed a little too non-attentive, almost detached, as if he was waiting to catch her making a mistake out of one of those sleepy, heavily lidded eyes. Like a deceptively lazy cat, secretly watching a bird alight on the lawn. If he caught a steakhouse bill he'd probably ask her how come she had such a good appetite the evening after her husband's murder.

She drove back home and hadn't been in the house more than ten minutes when the phone rang. She took it in the darkened living room. "Hello?"

"Mrs. Copeland?"

She didn't recognize the voice—it was a female but a little hoarse, grating on the ear. "Yes?" she said, trying to keep any tremor out of her voice. "Who is this?"

"I have a recording," the woman said.

"I don't know what you're talking about."

A harsh laugh. "No, I guess you don't. The recording was made by someone you knew as Jack. Ring any bells, dear?"

"I'm not your dear." She reacted with anger but her stomach told another story. "I don't know any man named Jack. So I think we'd better terminate this conversation right now."

"That's up to you, *dear*. You don't remember meeting two days ago at a restaurant called Arrigo's in Woodland Hills? You're too young a woman, dearie, to be suffering from Alzheimer's."

Allyson hung up violently. She stood for a long moment, swaying just a bit, trying to digest what she had just been told. It was the accuracy, the bull's-eye accuracy about the name and the restaurant that had set her thoughts and stomach churning.

The phone rang again. She stared at it, debating whether to answer or to silence it. If the woman kept trying, she knew how to shut off all the phones in the house so she couldn't be disturbed.

But her terrible curiosity made the decision for her. "Hello?"

"Me again, dear. Hanging up was very impolite of you. I mean, a distinguished judge's widow?"

"Get on with it. Who are you?"

A laugh. "Got you hooked, huh? The recording I referred to was made by the man you knew as Jack. He was a secret recording freak, especially all his business conversations and I guess his 'hits' too."

"I told you to get on with it." But she was rocked to her core. Swaying, losing her balance this time, she collapsed sideways on a sofa, the receiver still pressed to her ear. "Are *you* recording this call?"

"What did we used to say when we were kids? That's for me to know and for you to find out."

Allyson reached across with a shaking hand and put the receiver back in its cradle, cutting off the call.

She waited, thinking, thinking. Even if the woman was recording her, she hadn't said anything incriminating. And she had emphatically denied knowing this "Jack." But what if there *was* a recording that he had made in the restaurant?

The phone rang. It seemed louder this time, insinuating, intrusive. With a seizure of trepidation, she picked it up.

The voice said, "I don't think you're in the proper mood tonight, dear. You're probably grieving over the sudden and unexpected death of your beloved husband. I'll call you back tomorrow. And you'd better take my call." The phone clicked dead.

She sat there, brooding, her thoughts scrambled.

Now she was sweating.

She woke up the next morning, foggy again from the sleeping pill. She couldn't become a goddamn sedative addict with all this on her mind. She would have to go cold turkey tonight, even if it meant she wouldn't get much sleep, if any.

And then her memory really woke her up: that woman was going to call her again today.

Late in the morning, Columbo was back.

"What is it now?" she asked, letting him see the full extent of her irritation. He sat down again in the same chair as he had previously, as casual as ever.

"Just one question," he promised, "and I'll be outta here." He seemed upbeat, annoyingly oblivious to her mood. "We identified the man. Roy Prochek. He was a killer-for-hire outta New York. Somebody paid him fifty thousand dollars to kill your husband.'"

"How do you know all this?"

"The key I mentioned was to a room in a cheap motel in the Valley. He was registered as Clyde Thompson. Somebody told me that was the name of a hitman in an old movie. Guess he had a sense of humor. Anyway, there was nothing in the room much except a change of clothes and his suitcase. There was still an airline tag on the suitcase that showed he'd flown in from New York."

"You're very thorough," she said.

Columbo turned his head away from the strong sunlight. "Boy, my wife'll think I was goofing off, getting a tan sunbathing all morning." He moved away from the window. "Reason I'm here, the question I wanted to ask you?"

A tiny tinge of sarcasm: "A question? From you?" She

suddenly remembered she had to call a funeral home, get Victor tucked safely underground.

"You said two gunshots woke you up, one after another. How close were they apart?"

She stared up at the ceiling—what did he have up his sleeve, the sleeve on that disreputable raincoat? "A few seconds. I really don't remember."

"Prochek had one of those small recorders in his sports coat."

She should have guessed after what the woman had told her. "But you said you searched his body, only found a key."

Columbo didn't bother to respond to that. "We played the recording, ma'am. There was a gunshot, no doubt Prochek's and then, a good fifteen seconds later another shot—from the judge."

"I don't understand. What are you getting at?" She surprised herself with her quicksilver ability to appear confused.

"How did your husband manage to shoot Prochek if he had already been shot?"

"Maybe ... maybe he still had enough strength, even though he was dying."

Now Columbo turned to look directly at her. "Then do you really think, ma'am, Prochek just cooled his heels, waiting around fifteen seconds or so till your husband shot him?"

She shrugged, helplessly. "I don't know. I really can't figure that out."

Columbo was still gnawing on it, refusing to let it go. "We know the first shot had to be fired by Prochek when he took your husband unawares."

"Well, I guess it's just logical that the hitman fired first," she said.

"I think we can say that."

"You seem to be a pretty logical man yourself, Lieutenant. Am I right?"

He seemed a little embarrassed. "Yeah. Yeah, I guess you could say that."

Now she was directing her gaze at him. "Well then I suggest you figure out this whole time-discrepancy thing. But I wouldn't get bogged down in a lot of silly details."

Right after she had called the funeral director, the phone rang. She dreaded the call, her pulse starting to flutter.

"Good morning, dear," the woman said. "I'm not going to waste any time getting to business. As I told you yesterday, I have the recording of you and Jack."

"You mean Roy," she said.

"Correct. I guess the cops identified him." She hesitated just a beat, as if this news had surprised her. "About the recording—"

"How do I know a recording actually exists?"

A laugh. "Want to hear a sample, just a taste as the pot smokers say?"

Now Allyson hesitated, nervously grabbing the cord to the drapes, twisting it. "Go ahead, give me a 'taste.' "

Some fumbling on the other end of the phone, then her voice saying, "What do I call you?" It was definitely her voice.

Prochek's voice: "Try Jack."

Her voice again: "May I buy you lunch?"

She said to the woman on the phone, "That's enough."

"We guarantee satisfaction with our product," the woman said, more cheerfully intimidating than before. She had turned off the recorder.

"Where do we go from here?" Allyson had her composure back but she was still twisting the cord like a lifeline.

"I think a lunch is in order. How about Argil's?"

"Are you kidding?"

"Nope." The voice had gained a steely authority as if she knew she was firmly in the driver's seat. "How about tomorrow, 1:00 pm? I'll make the reservation."

"How do I know you won't be recording me there?"

"You don't. But we're way beyond that now, dear."

Allyson expelled her breath, flinging the cord away. "I guess we're at the money stage," she said grimly.

"We'll have a pleasant lunch, dearie. 1:00 pm." The connection died.

The following day, she was preparing to leave, checking that her BlackBerry was in her handbag when the doorbell rang. Who the hell could it be? But then, deep in her gut, she *knew*. Columbo was on the doorstep, a dead cigar in his hand. "Sorry again, ma'am, to interrupt your day—"

"1 have no time to talk to you right now. I'm late for a meeting."

"Suppose I drive you? We could talk on the way."

"No!"

Her vehemence surprised both of them. "How long will your meeting be?" Looking at his watch: "Is it a lunch meeting?"

"No, I don't know how long it'll be. You should come back here later in the afternoon." She tried to sweep past him, but he was innocently blocking her path.

"Well, I could follow along to where you're going, do a few things while you're having your meeting."

Now she had almost lost it, practically to the point of striking him. Get a grip, she warned herself. "I just told you I don't know how long it'll be."

"Yeah, you said. Sometimes I don't have enough coffee in the morning and I get a little slow. My father-in-law says—"

She interrupted him. "I told you I'm late!"

"Got it, Mrs. Copeland." If he had had a hat he might have bowed and tipped it.

She willfully banged his shoulder shooting past him.

When she entered the restaurant, a woman in the back crooked a finger at her. Allyson joined her at the table, gave her a hard, scalding look: late thirties, plain features, dishwater brown hair, wearing an ordinary pantsuit neither cheap nor expensive.

"How did you know it was me?" Allyson asked, looking around to see if people at the other tables were near enough to hear them.

"Just look at yourself," the woman said. "Very elegant as befits a judge's wife. Beverly Hills wife—widow, I should add."

"No more 'dears?' " she asked with a well-tempered acidity.

"Oh no," the woman said, placing her very steady spread fingers on the table.

The waiter came up, the same young man as before. He unleashed a dazzling actor's smile at Allyson. "Well, hello there. Back so soon?"

She nodded. Next he'd be telling her his name and reciting today's specials. "Menus," she muttered. To the woman: "Unless you'd like a drink?"

"No, no. A drink makes me sleepy."

The waiter looked faintly disappointed, left the menus with Allyson and sauntered away.

"Will you have lunch?" Allyson asked her.

"No, no. Just coffee."

Like Prochek. Wait a minute—she studied the woman more carefully. She hadn't caught it when she came in, but the woman had a definite facial resemblance to the hitman. She was his sister!

"Roy Prochek was your brother," she stated flatly.

There was a long pause and then the woman nodded. "A year older."

"Did you know what he did?" She tried to expunge the implied humor when she said, "I mean, for a living."

"I suspected. But I didn't really know for sure and I didn't ask. We come from a Polish family in New York. Our dad ran out when Roy and I were in grade school. He used to beat Roy something awful."

"Oh, Lord," Allyson said, picking up a menu. "The poor, abused, unloved son becomes a hired killer. Save me the Freudian cliches. What do I call you?"

"Jane will do."

"Well, I'm going to have lunch." Allyson signaled the waiter who came over. She gave him her order and coffee for her guest. She waited until he had gone off to the kitchen before she said, "What do you want from me, Jane?"

"You killed Roy," the woman said. "But you're not going to kill me."

Surprised: "I'm not?"

"No, you're not. You are going to pay me to sit on the recording and keep my mouth shut. You see, my brother gave me a small package for safe-keeping. After you killed him, I opened it and found a small recorder. I listened to it, made a CD, and now the CD and the recorder are with a good friend. The CD is sealed in a package with my name and return address on the front with a note inside explaining exactly why you had to kill me. The package will be sent to the Distract Attorney, a Mr. Willard. Edgar Willard."

Allyson was jolted—tried not to show her delight. This was beautiful, beyond her furthest hopes. She tried to look properly crestfallen. "You've really thought all this out," she said finally.

"You're a cold-blooded killer, dear. You think when I

blackmail you, you wouldn't hesitate to kill the sister after you killed the brother?"

"You make me sound like a rattlesnake."

She smiled; she wasn't wearing lipstick, in fact no makeup at all. "I read the cobra might be the deadliest. It spits its venom right in your eyes which destroys your sight in seconds. But some say the worst is the coral snake. It's found in Florida, although I don't know why anybody would want to find it. It's beautiful. Its skin has a rainbow of colors like that bracelet you're wearing."

"You're certainly an expert on reptiles, Miss 'Jane.' I guess you learned firsthand from that serpent of your own—your brother."

Before the woman could angrily reply, the waiter brought her coffee, told Allyson her food would be coming shortly. He moved off, mission accomplished.

"How much is this going to cost me?" Allyson asked.

"Fifty grand."

"And how do you want it delivered, since you're so afraid of my snake-like proclivities?"

"Right here in a roomful of people. But I don't think you'd be so stupid to kill me before or after or anytime for that matter, knowing my friend would send the CD to the D.A. What do they call it, a deterrent?"

She felt her inward smile radiating like a stiff warm drink throughout her body. "I think I can scare up the fifty thousand. When do you want it?"

"Tomorrow. Here. Same time, I'll make the reservation again."

"Tomorrow's Victor's funeral. I'll be tied up the whole day."

This did not disturb her. "Then two days from now for lunch. I wouldn't want you to miss your beloved's funeral." Her smile was infuriatingly crooked. "As I said, I'll make the reservation."

The waiter was looking over at them.

Allyson said, "You're sure I can't buy you a nice lunch? What do snakes eat— grass, other reptiles?"

She hadn't touched her coffee. "Nice meeting you, dearie." She got up and went straight to the door, exactly like her brother had.

Cobra, Allyson thought, moving the coffee over to her. What an efficient snake....

She had the funeral at Forest Lawn. It was one of those smoggy days that reminded her of London on a dreary winter morning. You could almost see the studios from the gravesite, which she knew Victor would find very displeasing. You're dead, old man, don't let it bother you.

On the way back to her car, after having said tearful goodbyes to friends, she saw Columbo lingering in the parking lot. He was smoking an evil-looking cigar, looking as even-tempered and watchful as always. For a man with no personal magnetism, there was something curiously compelling about him.

She warily watched him coming over to her. "No interrogation," she told him straight-out. "Not when I just buried my husband."

"Oh no, no," he said. "Absolutely not. I just wanted to tell you something."

"What happened to telephones?" She jingled her car keys to let him know she was impatient, had to be on her way.

"The night of the double murders? Seems there was one of your neighbors walking his dog past your house."

She stopped jingling the keys. "Who?"

"Guy by the name of George Harbeson, old guy, lives down the street."

"I don't know him. What did he say?"

Puff of cigar. "Says there was a period of time between the two gunshots. Maybe fifteen seconds or so."

"We went over all this." She angrily opened her car door.

"But it substantiates what we heard on the recorder."

She turned toward her car. "This is an interrogation! How dare you submit me to this on a day like this!"

He seemed impervious to her outrage. "You can see the discrepancy there, can't you, ma'am?"

She turned to face him, showing him the rampant anger in her face. "Lieutenant, the shots woke me up. I was still groggy, probably still half-asleep. Maybe there *was* a space between the shots, I just don't remember now. I've been going through a very trying time."

He nodded, glumly. "I realize that, Mrs. Copeland, and I'm really sorry that I had to ask you about this. But it's important."

"And are you sorry you even came here this morning?"

"I am. But you have to understand I'm just trying to

do my job." He shuffled a bit on the gravel. "Just one other thing."

She shook her head. The man was relentless, flypaper in a raincoat. "*What* other thing?"

"The gun in the judge's hand. The first joint of his forefinger was around the trigger. But when you fire a fairly heavy gun, it's the second joint that does the work. I hate to say this, but it's like the gun was placed in his hand...."

She held her temper. "Joints! Triggers! This is the silliest thing I've ever heard in my life." Now she got into the driver's seat. "When you come up with something substantive, I'll be happy to talk to you."

She turned the motor on and was gunning back in reverse, on her way to leaving the lot. He called something after her, but she couldn't hear, didn't want to hear.

She knew as she raced along the road through the smoggy green hills studded with graves, that everything he had said was true, right on target.

814 Willow. It was a modest, seen-better-days frame bungalow in a lower-middle-class neighborhood. He drove up, parked on the street, and went up the short path to the house, looking at the ragged lawn that cried out for a haircut.

He rang the bell. The door was opened almost immediately by a plain-featured woman in T-shirt and jeans.

"Oh!" she exclaimed. "I thought it was my friend Kim." Columbo showed her his ID. She let him in, looking out to the street to see if her friend was coming.

"I'm investigating the murder of your brother, Miss Prochek. I guess you know how he made his money."

They were standing now in the small, immaculately clean living room. There was the lingering smell of detergent in the air and a vacuum cleaner hugged the wall.

"Now wait a minute," the woman said. "I learned that in the paper. I had *no* idea what my brother was doing with his life. You could've knocked me over with a feather!"

"You weren't close?" He noticed an inviting ashtray on the coffee table.

"No. We came from what you would call a dysfunctional Polish family. My dad used to whale the daylights out of Roy." She ruminated, remembered something. "I always thought he made a living playing the market. Sometimes he gave me a stock tip, but I can tell you I got no money to gamble with."

He said, mildly defensively, "You mind if I smoke?"

"No, go ahead. My ex used to smoke. I loved the guy, but he dumped me for another broad. I hate to say it, but cigar smoke always seems to bring back one of the few happy times in my life."

Columbo took a cigar from his coat, smiling. "I'm happy to oblige, ma'am. You sure you don't mind?"

"Hell no." Now she was smiling, relaxing with this down-home kind of cop. "Anything else I can do for you?"

"Do you know if your brother had any enemies?"

She smiled sourly. "Does a man who kills people have enemies? If the families of his victims found out it was him, sure, some might try to get revenge. Isn't that possible?"

Lighting up: "Yeah, I would say. Was your brother ever married?"

"Not that I know of. He liked call girls, hookers. I don't think he really liked women too much."

"Did you know any of these prostitutes?"

"No. He didn't talk much about his 'dates.' That's what he called them, dates."

Columbo was silent, puffing clouds on the cigar.

"Is that it?" she asked.

Columbo hesitated. "You aren't scared, are you, that maybe the perp who killed your brother might come after you?"

"That's a hell of a question to ask," she said, grinning. "You're lucky I'm not paranoid or something. Answer to your question—no, I'm not scared. I had very little to do with my brother."

He was about to ask her something when she said, "But just in case—a friend has a little package of mine she can send to the D.A. if anything happens to me." Another grin. "So I wouldn't worry about me, Lieutenant."

"That's good to hear. I wanted to tell you we can release your brother's body whenever you want."

"I'll have to ship it back East if I can scare up the money. Bury him right next to his loving father."

Columbo went to the door, trailing a miasma of cigar smoke. He nodded at her, about to leave, when she said: "Well, at least he won't be killing anybody anymore."

Laughing: "If that's any consolation."

"Oh it is, ma'am," he said, saluting her with the cigar as he went out.

A few minutes later, there was a hard knock on the kitchen door. Was it Kim? she wondered. But Kim always came to the front door when she paid a visit.

Puzzled and curious, she went back to the kitchen.

Columbo was there again early that evening. He had been interrupted in the middle of his dinner, an elaborate meal his wife had spent most of the afternoon cooking, and he couldn't blame her for being really ticked off.

The body was on the kitchen floor, the head bludgeoned and bloody, the fingerprint team doing their routine with the lights on as the mauve twilight deepened at the window over the sink.

"What was the weapon?" Columbo asked Pagano.

"We don't know yet. Maybe some kind of hammer."

"Forcible entry?"

Pagano shook his head. "Doesn't look that way. She must've let somebody in the kitchen door. Probably somebody she knew."

Columbo nodded to one of the fingerprint people who was going back to the van. "Who found the body?"

"A friend of hers," Pagano said, "a young Asian woman, Kim something. You know me on those foreign names, Lieutenant. She was hysterical, but we got her statement. You can talk to her if you want, lives right across the street. Better take a big box of Kleenex."

It had been four days since "Jane's" murder. Allyson felt almost her old self now, sleeping well, beginning to think she might be finally out of the woods. The sister had overestimated her hand; those dumb, arrogant types always did.

She sat at work in the outer office at her desk, typing up letters for her boss, Edgar Willard, on her computer. Her eyes drifted now and then to the clock on the wall, her back stiffening with tension. The mail was always delivered by Randy, the mailboy, at eleven sharp.

Maybe—maybe today was the day it would arrive. The sister's friend had undoubtedly found out she had been murdered, unless she was vegetating on another planet. With the slow, inconsistent mail these days, you never knew when anything would arrive.

Sure enough, the door opened and Randy came in as the red hand on the clock edged toward eleven.

"How goes it, Allyson?" he asked, easily picking off her mail because it was practically the first office on his schedule. She dropped her glasses on their chain, peering intently at the stack he had given her. There was a mailing envelope a bit more square than the other pieces.

Randy was on his way to the door: "Hey Allyson," he said. "You're very quiet today. The D.A. chewing you out?"

"No, no," she smiled. "He's just waiting for an important letter," she lied.

He opened the door. "Well, I hope it's there." He winked at her. "Can't have you taking any crap from a public servant!"

She waited till he had left before she scrambled through the letters on her desk and separated them from the little package.

Her heart was beating like an out-of-rhythm trip hammer. There it was! She held it in her hands, staring at the name and address in the upper left-hand corner. *Anna Prochek, 814 Willow St., Los Angeles, CA. 90036.*

The door began to open again, and she thought it was Randy coming back in. But it was Columbo, a little hesitant as usual. He had been coming in the last two days around this time, chatting with her before he went in to see her boss.

She tried to slip the parcel under the other mail, but she saw he had caught her doing it.

"Good morning, Lieutenant." She tried to keep her voice on an even keel, not looking down at the mail.

"Morning," he said in almost a mumble. His hand moved casually down to the desk and he suddenly slid out the little parcel. He peered at the name and the return address.

"Anna Prochek, 814 Willow. Hmmm." He picked it up, looked at it more closely.

"Give me that!" she said. Now her voice was quavering. "That's Mr. Willard's confidential mail!"

Columbo thoughtfully kneaded the mailing envelope, feeling around its edges. "I think the District Attorney will be very interested in this. I know I am." His eyes came slowly up from the envelope to meet hers. She looked away, she had to!

Then he went past her desk, over to the door of the inner office. He knocked once, waited for the D.A.'s curt "Come in," and entered, parcel in hand. He never looked back at her.

She sat there for a long moment, feeling the tension slowly drain from her body as she awaited the inevitable. Did they allow you to bring a change of clothes to lockup? She would have to hire one of the best defense attorneys in the business, no matter what it cost. But what could he possibly challenge when Willard played that horrible recording to the jury in her trial?

She giggled, but it was almost a sob, when the thought struck her: she hoped she would get a much more lenient judge than her late husband.

MURDER ALLEGRO

LIEUTENANT COLUMBO WAS called to the Hotel Taki on Saturday night, interrupting his wife and him watching a movie, a good one, on Showtime.

The Japanese hotel was on La Cienega, a beautiful white sandstone building that seemed discreet and unassuming in the coolish night. He had never been there before, only passing by it now and then in the course of his duties. Now there was a clot of police cruisers and vans parked out front, jellybeans flashing and glaring against the white facade like maybe there was a movie shooting.

The lobby was a shock—all white like he was walking into a bottle of milk. Guests were talking in clusters, a few wearing white terrycloth robes and white spa slippers. The impassive young man at registration guided him to the elevator and politely pressed a button before he left and the doors closed on a somewhat disoriented Columbo.

Suite 601 was where he had been directed. It was a short trip from the elevator and the long corridor was white, although relieved with islands of shadow between the overhead lights. There were cops and plainclothesmen at the door. A few hotel guests were whispering and milling around further down the hall. One of the cops told Columbo that Sergeant Pagano was expecting him in the suite.

Columbo was glad to see the place wasn't white. The tech team was there, a photographer shooting shots, lighting up the tasteful furniture and Japanese prints on the combed-beige walls. The body was near the door, covered now, and white-clad paramedics were readying a stretcher.

Sergeant Pagano filled Columbo in while others continually interrupted him with questions. "The victim's a young woman, Elaine Morasaki. Appears to have been strangled. This is probably gonna get a lot of attention, Lieutenant."

Columbo looked over at the paramedics. "Don't move her yet, okay?" To Pagano: "Sorry, Sergeant. Why a lot of attention? I guess you mean media?"

"She was a violinist in a famous group, the Allegro String Quartet. They've been rehearsing here, going to play tomorrow night at Disney Hall."

Columbo palmed a cigar, realizing he couldn't smoke in there. "I guess they're going to have to cancel."

"I guess they are, unless they can find a quick substitute." He gave Columbo a wry glance. "You maybe play violin, Lieutenant?"

"Actually back in high school, yeah. I never followed it up and it practically killed my father. He was a big Paganini fan." He looked over at the covered body. "The victim was married?"

"She was registered with her husband, Arthur. We don't know where he is."

"Who found the body?"

"Maid came around eight to turn down the bed and I guess leave a chocolate."

Columbo motioned to the man at the body. "I want to take a look."

He went over and pulled up a corner of the sheet. Beautiful young woman, probably in her thirties, smooth black hair, bruises and discolorations around the neck area. Even fully clothed you could tell she had a slender but muscular body.

He let the sheet drop back, went to Pagano who was listening to someone on his cellphone.

"Bad connection in here," he said to the phone. "Okay, I think I got it."

He hung up and said to Columbo, "My man downstairs, says the husband's in the bar. You wanna go talk to him, Lieutenant? I know you'll take it easy."

Columbo looked puzzled at him.

"Well he probably doesn't know what happened up here—to his wife."

Columbo's smile was faint. "I try hard not to make assumptions, Sergeant."

The bar, the Taki Room, was right off the lobby. Columbo was going toward the checkroom when the young woman behind the counter called to him: "Sir?"

"Yes?"

She gave him a friendly smile, "Your shoes, sir."

Columbo halted, confused. "What about them?"

"The rule, sir. Please check your shoes, it's a very old Japanese custom. We follow it here in the hotel."

"But I'm a policeman."

Another smile. "I'm afraid you must check your shoes."

Columbo groaned, knowing he was beaten, bent down and

began tugging off his footwear. The shoes were scuffed, almost battered-looking, hadn't been shined in probably a year or more. He handed them over to the woman like they were some kind of very fragile orphans. She didn't seem to notice their deplorable condition. Handed him a claim check.

"Thank you," he mumbled, mentally thanking her for her polite disregard.

The bar was typically dark with no white walls, Japanese samisen music low and unobtrusive from the Muzak. There were a few couples, and only one threesome, a Japanese male with two women, one young, one older.

He went over and introduced himself, showing them his open wallet with badge. "Are you Arthur Morasaki?" he asked.

The man nodded, frowning. He had shining black hair and an intense pudgy face. Columbo usually found that pudgy was rarely intense.

"What can we do for you, Lieutenant?" he asked, casting a worried glance at his companions. The older woman was in her sixties with soft features and slightly unkempt gray hair, looking like an amiable grandmother festooned with lots of jewelry but no wedding ring. The other was young and pretty with longish wheat-blonde hair.

"And who are you, ma'am?" Columbo asked the older woman.

"Sylvia Rosenstadt. May I ask why you're inquiring?"

"Police business." He looked at the younger woman. "And you, Miss?"

"Jennifer Adams." She was wearing a tailored tweed suit, much too warm for L.A. She had a recorder near Morasaki's glass on the table, its record button on red.

"Mr. Morasaki," Columbo said, "I'm afraid I have some very bad news for you." Morasaki stared up from his drink. "Your wife was found in your hotel suite." He hesitated. "Someone has strangled her."

Morasaki shrunk back silent from the table, his face frozen, the women exclaiming out loud. Columbo put a consoling hand on his arm. "Maybe you should have some more of your drink. And I can get you another."

The man nodded no, fiercely. Sylvia moved closer, draped a maternal arm around his shoulders.

Jennifer asked, "Do you have any idea who did it?"

"Not yet, it's much too early." To Morasaki: "When was the last time you saw your wife, sir?"

He took a generous pull of his drink. "Before—before we came down here, eight o'clock or so."

"And you've been here with the ladies—all that time?"

"That's correct," Sylvia said. "I'm Mr. Morasaki's agent and Jennifer is interviewing him for a story in *The New Yorker*. This is a terrible shock, Lieutenant, especially for Arthur."

Morasaki's hand covered hers on the table. "It's all right, Sylvia, I want to help this man as much as possible." He said to Columbo, "I have to see my wife."

"That's not possible right now, sir. She's been taken away to—" He stopped himself from saying morgue. "You can visit her sometime tomorrow morning."

Now they could see that Morasaki's composure was close to crumbling. He was handsome with a proud, erect bearing, but now he was slightly bent over the table like an old man. Sylvia pushed a glass of water toward him, made him clasp his fingers around it.

Columbo got up, almost slipping in his stocking feet. "We'll talk tomorrow, sir. I'm awful sorry about what happened."

Morasaki only nodded.

Columbo conferred with Sergeant Pagano, feeling much better with his shoes back on. The fingerprint men were still dusting things down, but the rest of the tech team had departed. It was nearing midnight, the room perfectly silent now as if it were holding its breath.

"Morasaki didn't want to come back here tonight?" Pagano said. "Who can blame him, I guess. They're putting him in 312 if you want to talk to him again. You get anything out of him?"

"No, not really. He's been with his manager and this young woman who's been interviewing him since around eight, and at seven he had an hour-long radio interview."

"He's completely covered then. So why does that make me suspicious?"

Columbo smiled, looking out to see if there was a terrace where he could smoke. "Maybe because you're a cop. Always look at the husband first, isn't that what we've learned over the years?"

Pagano yawned, glancing at his watch. "Well, I'm heading back—"

"How do you think the perp got in here?"

"Probably she opened the door to somebody she knew. They told me the couple took only one key to the room and her husband's probably got that. Funny."

"What?"

"I'm told the victim was an expert in karate. So I'm thinking how did somebody overpower her, get his hands around her neck?"

Now Columbo was yawning himself. "Just another thing to keep us up thinking all night."

Columbo arrived at nine the next morning. He had told his wife about his ordeal taking off his scruffy shoes and she had insisted he wear his loafers today. They were pretty beat-up too, but what could he do?

Sylvia Rosenstadt cornered him in the lobby almost as soon as he entered. She still seemed bedizened with jewelry and he wondered if it was all real. His wife ordered the fake stuff from Home Shopping and for the life of him he could never tell the difference.

"Let me buy you a cup of coffee," Sylvia said. She was one of those take-charge, New York types, but Columbo didn't mind.

In the downstairs coffee shop, they had to relinquish their shoes outside the entrance. They sat down at a plastic table in the all-white room under the tranquilizing hum of fluorescent lights.

"I don't have a lot of time," Columbo said, "I have to start questioning the other members of the quartet."

"That's going to be hard, Lieutenant," Sylvia said, tearing her own little quartet of sugar packets into her coffee after having ordered a hearty breakfast. "They're already in rehearsal for their performance tonight."

"Gee. You'd think that would've been called off."

"You don't know musicians. Arthur insisted they all go ahead. It's like what they say in the theater, the show must go on."

He stirred his coffee. "Well, it's certainly good for Mr. Morasaki, takes his mind off things. But how are they going to perform with a missing violinist?"

"Arthur's brother flew in this morning from San Francisco. He's a world-class musician and he knows their repertoire. Tonight they're playing the Bartok 1st and 2nd string quartets. I could get you some tickets if you want."

"Thanks, but I gotta ask the wife. We're opera fans, used to go all the time when the tickets were cheaper." He laughed. "Now it's two arms and two legs to get seats practically in Iowa."

Sylvia's face darkened imperceptibly as she pushed her empty coffee cup away. "I probably shouldn't be telling tales out of school, but it might not be all peace and love this morning. Arthur and his brother have always been enemies, you know, older brother, younger brother. The classic sibling rivalry thing."

"Who's the oldest?"

"Arthur. A string quartet needs exquisite cooperation, precision give-and-take. Neal would probably be a bit obstreperous for the mix."

The waitress brought Sylvia her bacon and eggs. "How do you know the brother knows the Bartok music?" Columbo asked.

"He knows everything." She pushed her cup over to the waitress for a refill, her gold bangles jangling. "Arthur and Neal are both professionals. Oil and water maybe, but they would never disappoint their audience. Sure you don't want anything to eat?"

"Already had breakfast, ma'am."

"Arthur told me a curious Japanese proverb. If you enjoy a food you never had before, you lengthen your life by 75 days."

Columbo laughed. "I don't think I'd try sushi even if they promised me I'd live forever!" He rose from the table. "Sure I can't help you with the check?"

"Lieutenant, have you any idea what this quartet grosses a year in Europe alone? I get a fifteen-percent commission." A smile threatened to take over her face: "I think I can cover this."

He leaned over to her, very confidentially. "Can I ask you a personal question, ma'am?"

She gave him a mock-flirtatious flutter of her eyes. "It depends on what that is, Lieutenant."

"Is all that jewelry real?"

Her sumptuous smile was now regal. "I already answered your question, Lieutenant. Fifteen-percent commission?"

"Wow. Guess I'm in the wrong business."

The room commandeered for a rehearsal hall was next to the hotel gym, and Columbo dutifully left his loafers in a long row of shoes at the entrance. He had on inappropriate white socks, but they were the first thing he could grab that morning!

The quartet was in the midst of a wild brutal movement when he entered the big, white, echoing room. Jennifer Adams was sitting against a wall, the recorder on her lap.

The violin player was obviously Neal, who looked like Arthur with the same straight black hair almost down to his shoulders, framing a perspiring but impassive face. Arthur was playing and a tall, lanky young man was working hard on his cello. An older man with untamed white hair integrated his violent viola in the brilliantly controlled chaos. The music ended abruptly, surprisingly, in a crashing crescendo.

Arthur rested his violin. "Neal," he said, "I know you just got here, but I have to go over the score with you. There're lots of things we've got to look at."

"You're lucky I can play *anything*," Neal countered with a slight sneer. "You're not my goddamn conservatory teacher."

"I just lost my wife. You want to cut me some slack?"

"All you deserve. But if I'm going to bail you guys out tonight I want some breathing space and some respect."

Arthur didn't respond, turned abruptly away, and walked over to Columbo. "That's my congenial brother, brimming with sympathy. You have any brothers, Lieutenant?"

"Nah, only child." He grinned: "Guess I was spared." He watched the lanky cellist and the older violist getting themselves coffee from a setup near the door. "I'd like to talk to your friends over there. What are their names?"

"Kober. Steve Kober, the cellist. And Monroe Miller, who plays the in-your-face viola. Why them?"

Columbo shrugged. "I just want to talk to the people who knew your wife and were here at the hotel last night."

"I hope you don't think they had anything to do with Elaine's death." Pause: "Do you?" He wiped a tendril of sweat that was running down from his hairline.

"Have to start someplace, sir."

"Well, we are going to begin again in a few minutes, Lieutenant. Think that's enough time for your interrogatives?"

"That's a new one on me, sir, never heard it before. *Interrogatives*." He nodded to himself, smiling. "I promise I'll get all my interrogatives over in a few minutes!"

Columbo ambled over to the coffee drinkers, introduced himself, showed them his ID. "Just want to get your take on what happened last night," he said.

"Terrible," Kober said. "Still can't believe it. Who would want to kill Elaine?"

Columbo's eyes were on the older man, Miller, who seemed to be sublimating a cynical smile. "Who?" he asked rhetorically. "Maybe all of us, maybe?"

Columbo was interested. "Why do you say that, sir?"

"She was an angry woman, Lieutenant. Brilliant musician, but it didn't seem to satisfy her."

"Come on," Kober said, "how many of us are really satisfied? Are you?" He looked back at Columbo. "She was threatening to break up the quartet."

"But Miss Rosenstadt tells me it's very successful. Why would she want to do something like that?"

"Elaine didn't care," Kober said. "She had played in the San Francisco Symphony and the Los Angeles Philharmonic. Maybe she had her eye on New York— more prestige, more money."

"You're forgetting," Miller said, "she came from a very wealthy family. Her father was in the real estate business. He died, left her millions, I'm told. Maybe she was just trying to screw up Arthur. Who knows?"

Columbo poured himself some coffee. "Why do you say that, Mr. Miller?"

Now the cynical smile surfaced. "I'd rather not go there, Lieutenant, if you don't mind."

Columbo said amiably, "But that's the kind of thing I get paid to find out."

"Let's just say they've had their differences like most married couples."

Columbo was looking off at Arthur who was talking into the journalist's recorder. "Like maybe if he played around?"

"Did I say that?" Miller joked, looking comically up, down, and around. "Who said that, who?"

They saw Arthur was pointing to the wall clock. "Time to resume, gentlemen," he called out.

"Whew!" Miller breathed to Columbo. "The task-master's

back on our backs. Gets me out of answering any more of your impertinent questions."

Columbo grinned. "Don't forget I can always get your room number, sir."

But Miller and Kober were already walking away, chatting.

Columbo had gone straight from the rehearsal hall to the third floor and stood near the elevators, sizing up the housekeeper who was working her way down the corridor. It would probably take her a few minutes to get to Morasaki's new suite, so he killed time on his cellphone. Pagano told him the medical examiner's estimated time of death was anywhere between seven and eight the previous night.

"Any interesting prints?" Columbo asked.

"Just the Morasakis' and some partials. We'll print the chambermaid who cleaned the suite."

"Any evidence of a sexual attack?"

"No. None. Someone strangled her, someone with strength. Probably a male."

That ended their conversation and Columbo saw the housekeeper had finally moved into Morasaki's suite.

Columbo made a quick call to his wife, catching her in before she was off to meet some friends. She told him to stop at the grocery, bring home some veal, some angel hair pasta, and two jars of their favorite marinara sauce, the spicy kind.

"I'll try to do that," Columbo said, "if I can get out of here before the store closes."

He hung up and gave the housekeeper a little more time before he went into Morasaki's suite. He flashed her his badge and stood looking out the window at a courtyard with a single cherry tree near a quaint tea house. The housekeeper finished her work, left the suite, casting him a sour, suspicious glance.

In the bedroom he was wondering where to look first when he heard the door to the corridor opening, low muted voices coming into the suite. He went over to the partially opened door to hear—and reared back, realizing a man and woman were coming directly toward the bedroom.

The door jerked open when Arthur and Jennifer Adams came hurtling into the room in a passionate embrace, tumbling onto the bed.

Columbo cleared his throat. Loudly. *Very* loudly.

The two tore themselves apart, to see—"Columbo!" Morasaki exclaimed. "What the hell are you doing in my suite? You've got no goddamn right to be here!"

Columbo was cool. "I was waiting to talk to you, sir. I didn't want to disturb you during your rehearsal. Say—I thought you were still supposed to be rehearsing—"

"Don't try to divert me. I got into a fight with my brother and everybody thought we should resume later."

"Oh. I'm sorry to hear that, sir."

The young woman got up from the bed, awkwardly, her eyes locked on Arthur's.

"Yes, I'm sure you're *very* sorry," Arthur said with a scintilla of sarcasm. "But you're going to be more sorry when I sue your department for the invasion of my privacy."

Columbo's tone was conciliatory: "Oh I wouldn't do that, sir. It's really not necessary. I mean not in the middle of a murder investigation of your wife. It could be a little embarrassing, not only for me."

Disgusted, Arthur blew out his breath, turned to Jennifer. "Why don't you go back to your room? I can handle this here." She rose shakily from the bed, but Columbo held up a restraining hand. "Ah, I wouldn't go yet, Miss Adams. I've got a few questions for you too."

Arthur decided belligerency was the proper mode. "What *kind* of questions?"

"Well sir, it's obvious that whoever killed your wife had a key to the suite."

"Why do you say that? Maybe she let somebody in who she knew."

"We've just about ruled that out, sir. Your wife was a physically powerful person, had karate training. I don't think the murderer wanted to confront her face-to-face, I really don't."

"So maybe a hotel worker or somebody else had a passkey." Columbo shook his head. "Nah, don't think so. Nobody on the hotel staff would've had a motive. And besides, they guard keys pretty good around here."

"So what are you getting at?"

"Well, you had a key, Mr. Morasaki. Did you give it to anyone?"

The belligerency hadn't left. "Of course not! Why would I give my key to someone?"

Now Columbo's attention had shifted to Jennifer who had

sat back down on the bed. "That was a question I wanted to ask *you*, Miss Adams. You were with Mr. Morasaki all day yesterday."

She was adamant: "From the second he left his suite at eleven that morning."

"And you were with him the rest of the day?"

"Yes. It's all on my recorder. I can testify, Lieutenant, that he never gave his key to anyone."

Columbo mulled this over, shuffling around in a small circle on the rug, his hands laced behind his back. "You've been having a romantic relationship with Mr. Morasaki...."

"Columbo!" Arthur said forcefully.

"You got to admit, sir, what I just saw was pretty—what's the word I want?— explicit." Morasaki didn't answer. "Has this relationship been going on for a while?"

Arthur was about to speak, but Jennifer signaled him to keep still. "Yes, it has, Lieutenant, and it's nothing we're ashamed of. Arthur's marriage hasn't been a marriage for a long time. But their involvement in the quartet kept them together in the business sense."

"Right." Columbo was mulling again. "But you got to admit, Miss, that when you tell me he never gave his key to anybody you might be lying to protect him or the person he gave it to. Am I way off base here?"

Jennifer came up off the bed, almost hitting Columbo. "*He never gave his key to anyone.*"

Columbo stepped back, a little embarrassed at her flare-up. He smiled. "You know something? I believe you, Miss Adams. I really think you're telling me the truth."

"Good," she said with a relieved smile, looking over at Arthur. "I pride myself in telling the truth. It's sometimes gotten me into a lot of trouble in my job, but so be it."

Columbo gave her a slight bow, a subtle inclination of his head, and went to the door. "Mr. Morasaki," he said, "I have to apologize for interrupting you the way I did, but I think I learned something that might be important. I must admit this little meeting was productive."

Arthur studied him. "I'm trying to get your perspective on this. You thought I gave my key to someone so they could murder my wife? Is that it?"

Columbo shrugged. "Just one of my theories. Sometimes I have a lot of them, too many. And I have to tell you, sir, most are wrong."

Arthur mimicked his slight bow. "So I'm no longer a suspect?"

Columbo opened the door. "Oh no, sir. I don't remember saying that."

And with a brisk wave, he was gone.

Columbo came into the hotel restaurant after relinquishing his shoes early that evening. Members of the quartet were having light dinners or snacks before the impending concert at eight. He spotted Neal Morasaki at the bar and headed over.

He introduced himself with the badge in his wallet. "Lieutenant Columbo, Mr. Morasaki. I'm investigating the death of your sister-in-law."

Neal nodded morosely. "You want a drink?"

"No, thanks. I don't want to be judgmental, sir, but should you be drinking before you're playing tonight?"

"You sound just like my mother." He smiled a humorless smile. "No, a drink or two calms the nerves. But no more than that."

"So you're helping your brother out tonight. You flew down here from San Francisco this morning?"

"Yes, United Airlines, Lieutenant. What else can I do for you?"

"What will happen to the quartet after tonight? They'll go back on the rest of the tour—with you?"

"I have no idea. That is all up to my distinguished brother. Why don't you ask him?"

Columbo waved the bartender away. "Well," he said to Neal, "break a leg before the concert tonight."

Another humorless smile, but he raised his glass to Columbo. "*Kanpai!* That means 'Cheers' in Japanese. I've never been wished good luck before by a cop!"

Columbo passed Arthur and Jennifer at their table. The recorder was on as always, and Arthur was answering a question while he speared a shrimp.

Columbo dropped by Miller and Kober who were sharing appetizers. "Anything new?" the older man asked.

"Not really. But we're working on it."

"I hope you're coming to the concert tonight, Lieutenant," Kober said, pouring cream in his coffee.

"Wouldn't miss it, sir. Bringing the wife too."

"Boy," Kober said jokingly to his colleague, "we better be at our best!"

Sylvia Rosenstadt gestured to Columbo that he should join her at her table. He did, observing she was enjoying a more than substantial dinner with wine.

"The old lady's allowed, Lieutenant, seeing as she's not playing tonight," she humorously pointed out. "Can I order you something?"

"Oh no, ma'am, thank you. I was wondering where your people move on to from here."

"San Francisco, then Seattle. I'm working on Tokyo." She looked up, worried, from her prime rib. "You're not going to keep them here, are you?"

"Oh no, no. I have no authority to do that."

She put down her fork. "You have a suspect?"

"Not yet, no." He looked pained, uncomfortable.

"What's wrong? You think you know who it is and you can't prove it?"

Columbo reached down and massaged his foot. "I don't know, without shoes my feet keep itching."

Sylvia laughed. "I'd recommend using some good foot powder. Or at least solve this damn thing and don't ever come back here!"

Columbo rose slowly from the table, wincing. "That's what I'm trying to do, ma'am."

At the checkroom he had another problem: he couldn't find his shoe-check. The young woman was amused, but sympathetic. "Happens more than you think. What do your shoes look like?"

"They're old," Columbo said. "Sort of beat up. I mean, they probably stand out like some sore toes with all the elegant shoes you got there."

"These?" she asked, pulling down a battered pair.

Columbo smiled. "Those are the babies."

It was weird: by the time he reached the lobby, he suddenly knew how the whole thing had been worked.

After the concert that night, he went backstage and was directed to Arthur's dimly lit dressing room. Arthur sat at a makeup table, dabbing sweat from his face, and then downing a full glass of water. "Well?" he said when Columbo entered. "What's the verdict, Mr. Critic?"

"Very, very good, sir. Could anybody tell that your brother had never played with you guys before?"

Arthur turned from the mirror to look at him. "You must realize this wasn't like our regular audience tonight. I was told we sold out. No tickets left unless you wanted to hang from a chandelier."

"I guess you mean because of your wife's murder."

"My, but you're particularly astute." His laugh was sarcastic. "Vultures. People who wouldn't know a string quartet from a string *bean*. I thought we played a bit too, shall we say, frenetic? Perhaps hysterical is more the word, but I think Bartok might have enjoyed it. Although I really don't think music and murder mix. Do you, Lieutenant?"

There was a hard rap on the door followed by Pagano's voice: "Columbo?"

"Come on in."

Pagano entered, nodding at Arthur who was pouring more water from the ice-filled pitcher. "May I offer you gentlemen some scotch?" Arthur asked. "A bottle came courtesy of the management."

Both policemen declined. Silence.

Arthur looked from one to the other. "In music we call this a rest. What are we waiting for, Maestro Columbo?"

Columbo frowned at Pagano. "Did you send someone to get him?"

Pagano nodded. "Detective Boland. They should be here by now."

Columbo was looking at his watch when there was another sharp rap on the door.

"We're here, Officer," Pagano called, opening the door.

Boland came in with Neal Morasaki, his bowtie open and askew. He looked drained but reasonably cheerful. Arthur gave him an unreadable glance, then looked away.

"Well, now you've got the Brothers Morasaki," Neal said. "Sounds like the Japanese version of the Brothers Karamazov."

Columbo said to Boland, "The witness is on her way?"

"Yeah. I told her to wait outside when she gets here."

"This is all very mysterious," Arthur said. "Would you mind explaining, Lieutenant? I have an aversion to being kept in the dark."

"I do too," Columbo admitted. The room was growing hot and with a forefinger he loosened the knot on his tie.

"I'd like some water," Neal said. "You have another glass, Arthur?"

"How about some scotch? I have a premonition we're going to need some. Am I right, Lieutenant?"

Columbo didn't answer and Arthur removed a bottle and another glass from a drawer in the makeup table.

Pagano's eyes met Columbo's as he turned to face the two brothers. "I'm placing both of you under arrest in the conspiracy to murder Elaine Morasaki."

"Interesting," Arthur said, unfazed. Neal groped for the bottle, almost overturning it in his haste to open the cap.

"You can pour yourself a drink, Mr. Morasaki, but I want both of you to keep your hands visible," Pagano said.

Arthur kept his hands flat on the table. "Haven't I seen something like this once in a movie?" His eyes snagged Columbo's in the mirror. "I'm still waiting for an explanation, Lieutenant."

Columbo flexed his fingers. "You wanted your wife out of the way, Mr. Morasaki. I think she was not only threatening to leave the quartet, but she wanted a divorce. Her death would serve a double purpose—you would get her family inheritance and then your brother would join the group and your professional life would go on."

"So I enlisted Neal to do the dirty work?"

"Yes, sir. He drove down here from San Francisco so there'd be no record of his coming and going. You needed him to get into your suite and wait for your wife to come back there while you established an alibi with your interview and in the bar with Miss Adams and Miss Rosenstadt."

Neal had poured a drink and Arthur took the bottle. "Why did Neal have to wait for Elaine?"

"Because she was a very strong woman, adept in the martial arts. He was relying on the element of surprise to overpower her. But you had a problem—how were you to get him a key to the suite when Jennifer Adams was with you all day and nobody was supposed to know he was in the hotel?"

Arthur poured himself a drink, topped his brother's glass. "Sounds like a real stickler. What did I do, Lieutenant? You're the expert."

"When you and Miss Adams went to the bar and you checked

your shoes in with the checkroom girl—you left the key in one of the shoes."

"That's what gets me," Pagano said to Columbo. "How would Neal get the shoes if he didn't have the claim check?" Columbo said to Neal, "Suppose you tell us."

Neal remained silent, staring down into his glass, avoiding their eyes.

"I think he told the checkroom girl that he had lost his claim check. But he told her he had put his key in one of his shoes."

"Now wait a minute," Pagano said. "He actually *said* that to the girl? That would incriminate his ass when we talked to her."

"But why would we question somebody like her after the murder? Why would we suspect anything like that had happened?"

Pagano wasn't satisfied: "But he had to put on his brother's shoes. How would they fit?"

"Look at their feet," Columbo said. "Very similar in size, they're brothers."

"Okay, but let's go back: he uses the key to get in the suite and murder Mrs. Morasaki when she arrives. But then how—oh, I get it. He hangs around until much later, then slips the key under the door of his brother's new suite."

"Right before he drove back to San Francisco," Columbo said. "When Arthur called him the next morning he took a plane—because then there would be a record that he had actually left from San Francisco if we checked."

"Very clever," Arthur said. "But you're forgetting something, Lieutenant. When I left the bar with Jennifer, how could I get my shoes back if my brother had gone off with them?"

Columbo pawed through his raincoat pockets, found a recorder and placed it on the table. "Miss Adams' habit was never to turn off her recorder during an interview so she wouldn't miss anything. You left the bar and went right past the claim check room without asking for your shoes—it's on the tape."

"Come on, Adams would've noticed," Pagano said. "That's pretty strange, a guy not getting his shoes back."

Columbo smiled. "I spoke to her before the concert. Arthur told her he had foot trouble, sometimes he liked to walk around in his stocking feet on the carpet, work the muscles. He said no problem, he'd come back later for his shoes."

"That's ridiculous," Arthur scoffed.

Columbo nudged the recorder. "It all on here, sir. Should I play it for you?"

He was silent. "Just a minute, Lieutenant. What did my brother do with his own shoes?"

"Put them in a briefcase, or a little travel bag, a shopping bag, who knows?"

"That's still ridiculous." But his eyes dropped down from Columbo's in the mirror.

Columbo said to Neal, "You've been very quiet, sir. You know it would be in your own best interest to make a statement."

Neal stolidly finished his drink and started to pour another. "Statement? Is that a cop euphemism for confession?" He downed the glass. "I've listened to all this garbage," he said in a tired voice. "*Alice in Wonderland*. No proof, Columbo. You're strutting around a load of crap, especially about me. My lawyer will handle you guys."

Columbo nodded at Officer Boland, who went to the door, opened it. "You can come in, Miss," he said.

The checkroom girl came in, a little frightened, blinking in the dim light at the hulking group of men.

"Nothing to be afraid of, Miss," Columbo said. "All we want is your identification of a certain individual. Do you see the man who told you his key was in his shoe? Take your time, Miss."

She slowly looked from face to face, her hands tightly gripped at her waist. "Yes," she said finally in a barely audible voice. She brought up a slender arm, her finger pointing. "That's him. That's the man. I especially remember him because he gave me a very big tip."

"You're lying," Neal said, "you never saw me before. Besides, the light's too dim in here."

Columbo went to the switch on the wall, turned on the overhead light. "How's that?" he said to Neal. Then to the woman: "Well, Miss?"

She wasn't frightened any longer. "That's him. I found him the shoes with the key. Plus the big tip. That's not something you forget."

"No," Columbo said, "you don't." He motioned to Officer Boland, who came over to read the two brothers their rights.

Arthur shook his head. "You're a real piece of work, Columbo, you know that?"

"You should talk to my wife, sir. She'd agree with you. But I gotta tell you, sir, she *really* enjoyed your concert tonight."

PHOTO FINISH

MRS. IRIS BLACKMER WAS HAVING coffee in the living room when Janelle, her housekeeper, brought the day's mail to her. Almost three-thirty for a mail delivery these days. Slowly but surely, Iris thought, we are becoming the United States of Barbados.

She sorted through the letters, the usual bills and trivia, and then stopped when she saw one from the Department of Motor Vehicles, addressed to her husband. Traffic ticket? She tore open the envelope, slid out its contents—and almost dropped the stack.

It was a summons all right, for speeding near their beach home. She had paid enough speeding tickets herself. It was accompanied by a photo taken by one of the mounted traffic cameras that had caught Scott, her husband, behind the wheel. It also caught, to Iris's shock, a beautiful redheaded young woman seated very cozily next to him in the passenger seat.

While she sat paralyzed, the incriminating photo on her lap, Janelle looked in at her from the hallway. "More coffee, Mrs. Blackmer?"

Her response was delayed. "Oh, no—no. I'm fine, thank you."

It was then, staring down again at the photo, that Iris Blackmer made the decision to kill her husband.

It was working it out that took time. First, she had to destroy the letter and photo from the Department of Motor Vehicles. Then she went to check out Scott's obvious place of assignation, their summer and weekend beach house a little south of Long Beach on the ocean.

She drove down to the house the next weekend while Scott was playing golf at the club. Sure enough, she found two cigarette butts with incriminating lipstick stains on the filter tip. The bed was rumpled too, and she noticed some suspicious stains on the sheets that made her turn her head away in disgust. He would no doubt clean up before they came down again.

She had been suspecting him throughout their twelve

years of marriage. She remembered complaining humorously to her best friend Marcy Kramer: he saw his shadow today so I guess I'll have to endure another six months of marital nuclear winter! But it wasn't funny any more.

She left the house from the kitchen, walked out on the beach, seeking the bright, cleansing air, leaving all of Scott's filth behind. She would inherit the business, the stocks and bonds, millions. Was it worth it, dear Scott? The furtive phone calls, the sneaking around, the classic excuses of working late at the office at night?

There was a hard, raking breeze off the water, probing like fingers through her hair. She inhaled deeply, enjoying the day and her decision, and then remembered something crucial that she had to check in the house.

Yes, the Smith and Wesson .38 Airweight was still in the bedside table in the back of a drawer with its box of bullets and some match folders. Maybe if that woman smoked enough she was guaranteeing an early death down the line. But Iris knew that sooner was better than later.

Back home in Beverly Hills, Iris checked the calendar. Next Tuesday night, Scott's fortieth birthday, would be perfect. Birth and death day combined. He would take the day off as usual and she would treat him to a lavish lunch at Armand's, his favorite restaurant. But the real gift this year would be after lunch when she drove him to the beach house, promising him an exciting surprise. Was there anything she hadn't thought of? Any crucial detail? Why does murdering someone have to be an on-the-job learning experience?

The plan almost failed when he had an attack of indigestion during his birthday lunch and wanted to go home. Okay, okay, she thought, she could put everything on hold until the following day or even later, but she would rather not postpone it.

The waiters scurried around, until one gave him a special concoction that settled his stomach within minutes. I need some of that stuff myself, Iris thought. She had been suffering from what she called "killer's jitters" since she had awakened that morning with a grinding headache.

In the car on the 405, Scott said, "Come on, honey, tell me. You know I hate surprises."

"I promise you," she said, "this will be the last surprise

I'll ever give you. How's that?" She lifted her sunglasses and gave him a dazzling, heart-swelling smile that she hoped would put his soul and stomach to rest.

In the living room of the beach house, Scott collapsed in the Eames chair, bridging his feet across to the footrest. "Don't make me a drink," he said. "The ol' digestion track's still not A-okay."

Iris looked around the room, everything was spotless. Scott must have sent Janelle down to clean up his mess.

She went calmly into the bedroom, quietly opened the drawer of the bedside table, removed the revolver.

"I hope I'll be up for the 'matinee,'" Scott called. "We *are* going to have a 'matinee' on my birthday, aren't we?"

"Of course," she called back, checking that all the bullets were staring at her from the holes in the cylinder. "What's a birthday without a hot matinee?"

She went back into the living room, the weapon tucked in the waistband of her skirt in back. Scott, grinning, said, "So where's the big surprise?"

"Three guesses," she smiled back.

"You know I'm a lousy guesser. Twenty questions— smaller than a breadbasket?"

"Not small and not that expensive. Give me your cellphone."

Scott dug it from his pocket, handed it to her. Amused: "You going to call the store where you bought it or what? Or am I going to call somebody?"

"Yes. Me."

Now he was truly dumbfounded. "But you're here."

With one hand she punched in their home number, held the phone out to him, close to his mouth. Waited while the number went through, got the leave-a-message message on the answering machine.

She brought the gun around, pointed it at his stomach. Then she aimed the cellphone at him.

"My God," Scott cried out. "Get that gun away! What the hell are you doing with that thing?"

She raised it, aiming at the center of his forehead.

"Is this a joke?! Aren't you—?"

She lowered the gun and shot him twice through the heart. He died instantly, sinking down in the chair, the blood quickly forming an abstract explosive painting on the front of his coat and shirt. She clicked off the cellphone, and placed it in his hand, firmly closing his fingers around it.

Her eyes panned the room. The neighboring houses were probably abandoned until the summer season began. She took a magazine, *Business Week*, from the magazine rack and left the house by the back door that fronted the beach.

The ocean was serene and shining, not a surfer in sight. There was a helicopter, but it was only a sun-soaked metallic bug on the horizon, too far away for the pilot or the passengers to see anything.

She took a tissue from her pocket, wiped the gun clean. Then she slipped the gun into the magazine, kept it reasonably flat, and dug out a small excavation in the sand with her fingers. She buried the magazine with the gun in the hole and covered it over with more sand, brushing most of the excess particles off her hands. Now came the most important part.

She returned to the beach house and called the police department. They came within minutes, followed by the homicide boys with the tech crew. An ambulance came, removed the body, and the police began their questioning.

Well over an hour later, a friendly plainclothesman in a raincoat arrived on the scene and approached her, with a small notebook in hand: "Ma'am, I'm Lieutenant Columbo." He showed her his ID. "You mind if I ask you a few questions?"

"Of course not." She explained in a tremulous voice how they had celebrated her husband's birthday at lunch and then had returned to their house in Beverly Hills.

"So he drove down here, to the beach house by himself?" Columbo asked, his notebook at the ready.

"Someone must've picked him up. I was busy upstairs at the house and the next thing I knew he had left." She hesitated. "I have to tell you something—something very, very personal."

"Only if it pertains to the case, ma'am."

She moistened her lips. "I suspect Scott had women or a woman on the side. I was determined to catch him with one of them. It—really embarrasses me to admit this."

He nodded. "I understand."

"So I figured he used this place as a, well, place of assignation—I know that's such an awfully old-fashioned term these days. That's why I raced down here, thinking I could catch him with someone. When I got here—I found Scott. Certainly not the way I wanted to find him." She faltered, looked around desperately for a chair.

"Here, ma'am, here." Columbo pulled a chair over, helped her sit down. "You want some water? Is there a fridge here? I can get you some cold water."

"No, I'm all right. Thank you, Lieutenant." She brought a hand to her forehead. "Where was I?"

"You had just found your husband's body. Do you remember what time that was?"

"Three, three-thirty. Something like that."

The tears came and Iris hunted for a tissue in her handbag.

Columbo looked disturbed himself.

"Are you sure," she said through her grief, "*you* don't want a glass of water, Lieutenant?"

He faintly smiled, sympathetically. "No, I'm fine, ma'am. Thank you."

"I remember I almost had an accident on the highway getting down here," Iris continued, subtly gauging his eyes, "but I always drive too fast anyway. Unfortunately I wasn't in time to prevent—what happened."

Columbo nodded, putting the notebook away. "And when you got here there was no one around, the house was empty?"

"When I saw Scott ..." Where were those very important tears again when she needed them? "I—I was so ... shocked, disoriented, I didn't even think of checking the rest of the house."

"That's all very normal, ma'am." He squeezed the bridge of his nose, thinking. "There was no gun on the premises, far as we can tell, but his cellphone was in his hand."

"I didn't touch anything. I learned that from television."

"Oh yes, ma'am, sometimes television can be very instructive." He paused. "I'm wondering who he was calling on the cellphone. Probably you, asking for help. We can check on that."

She didn't know how to get a bead on this guy. He seemed so regular, just a nine-to-fiver doing a job that happened to be murder. But she didn't know if she trusted those seemingly non-observant eyes under a head of hair that was just as rumpled as his raincoat.

"You wanna wash your hands? I notice you got some sand on them."

She glanced down, noticed she still had some sand on the back of her hands. He was looking at her as if he needed an explanation.

"Oh. When I was getting out of the car I dropped my keys. Must've got the sand on them when I picked them up."

That seemed to satisfy him. "Okay, Mrs. Blackmer, I'm not gonna bother you any more today. You should get some rest."

"You mean you'll be bothering me some time later?"

Was she being too humorous, under these terrible circumstances? How did the movie actors summon up the goddamned tears when the camera was rolling? Special effects?

"I never try to bother people, ma'am. I mean, not intentionally. I just might have a few more questions."

When she left the beach house, there was a young man standing near the clutter of police cars. He looked vaguely familiar but she couldn't place him.

"Mrs. Blackmer?" he called.

"Yes."

He came over to her. He was no more than late thirties, good-looking, sun-streaked blond, very California in his T-shirt and shorts, loafers and no socks. "What's going on in there?"

"Who are you?"

"Your neighbor? I live in the house over there. I think maybe we met a few years ago when you and your husband bought the place, and threw a little party?"

She put on her sunglasses in the intense white sunlight. "My husband was murdered. That's what's going on in there."

His amiable expression crumpled, darkened. "I—I'm very sorry to hear that. Do they know—?"

"Nothing so far."

He looked away from her, down the little roadway that ambled past the beach houses. "There was a car here, earlier."

"A car? It couldn't have been my husband's, it was home in the garage. What kind of car?"

"A green Corvette, older model. A great-looking babe, a redhead, came out of the house. Do you think—?"

His squeeze, Iris thought, she must have come right before we got here.

"What time was that, do you know?"

"A while ago. No reason to check my watch."

"You didn't know this woman, did you, Mr. ...?"

"Rosen, Dale Rosen." He looked like he wanted to shake hands with her. "No, I never saw her before. But today I had just started a jogging regimen so when I passed the house I saw her and the car."

"This is very important, Dale," she said, lifting her sunglasses to look at him, impress him with the urgency of her concern. "You must tell all this to the police. Go in and ask to see a cop named Columbo." She nodded gravely. "I think this redhead might've killed my husband, Dale."

Late that afternoon, she called the police station, asked for Lieutenant Columbo.

He wasn't there so she asked them to leave a message for him, that it was important, *very* important, that he come to her home in Beverly Hills as soon as possible.

He got there a little before six, chewing on a dead cigar. She took him into the study, a beautiful, well-kept room, one wall lined with family pictures.

She motioned him over to a message machine next to the desk. "I want you to listen to this, Lieutenant. I realized the machine was blinking with a message a little while after I had gotten home from the beach house."

Columbo nodded, leaned in close to the machine. She turned it on, hit the Play tab.

Scott's voice: "My God, get that gun away! What the hell are you doing with that thing! Is this a joke? Aren't you—?" The sound of two quick gunshots. Silence for seconds, then a click.

She left the machine on, looked at Columbo, whose expression hadn't changed but tightened. "He must've called you, got the message machine—"

"Because I was already driving down the coast to the house."

"Right. Yeah. But why'd the killer let him actually punch a number on the cell, make the call?"

"Hard to say. You said you were going to check out his cellphone with the company."

He had his notebook out, but it seemed just a habit. "Haven't had time yet, ma'am. So somehow he managed to call you for—what, help? You were miles away, how could you possibly help him?"

"Is anyone threatened with a gun thinking clearly?"

"No. No, I guess not." He gestured at the machine. "Could you give me that? It's part of the evidence chain."

She nodded.

"Something else's been bothering me."

She smiled. "You seem to be a person who gets bothered quite a bit."

"It's the little things, ma'am. I guess I'm sort of hung up on the little things."

She would have liked a cigarette, but she wasn't desperate. "So what's the little detail this time?"

"Either your husband or the murderer turned the cellphone off. And if your husband was mortally wounded, how would he have the strength to turn it off? Especially if he wasn't thinking clearly. Why turn it off? I'm sure the murderer didn't hang around after the murder. Got out of the place in a hurry. So why not leave the cellphone be?"

"I don't know. That *is* strange." She knew exactly why she had turned it off. She was scared that he might have cried out her name.

Columbo was wandering around the room, looking at some of the pictures on the wall. "Something else," he said on his little circuit past her.

"What's that?"

"The cellphone was in your husband's left hand."

Oh God, in her anxiety she had moved around the chair, put it in the wrong hand!

Columbo pointed to a photo. "Very beautiful picture. Taken at your wedding, I guess?"

She came over to look at it over his shoulder. "Yes. One of my favorites."

"You're both raising, I would guess, champagne or wine glasses. Your husband's holding his in his right hand. I take it he was right-handed, Mrs. Blackmer?"

"Well ... yes. When you're with people so long you forget things like that."

"Yeah, I couldn't agree more. Somebody asked me once what were the color of my wife's eyes and for a whole minute I couldn't remember! Can you believe that?"

Was he trying to distract her now? She knew he had uncovered something and there seemed no way he was going to leave it alone.

"Your husband was right-handed, so what was the cell-phone doing in his left hand?"

"That's truly puzzling, Lieutenant." She paused. "Well we know he called me and left that message right before he was shot, so he must have taken the phone from his pocket in his right hand, put it in his left so he could dial with his right. Don't we right-handed people do that?"

He was looking at her with, what seemed, a genuine new respect. "I gotta hand it to you, that's probably exactly what happened."

"Should I sign up with the department, Lieutenant? I think we'd make a terrific team, don't you?"

Columbo chuckled. "I'll talk to the Captain about it."

She looked at the electronic clock on the desk. "If that does it for now, I've really got to make a few calls."

"You go right ahead. And I thank you, ma'am, for your time."

She went into the office the next morning, wearing the approved L.A. widow's weeds: black pants, black T-shirt, and her dark black sunglasses. Everyone was sweetly consoling, and she quickly escaped into Scott's office, but not before she met, for the first time, his secretary-assistant, Lucinda Brenner, in the reception area. Lucinda had been only a crisp, efficient voice on the phone for the past few years.

Early thirties, wasp-waisted, athletic-looking, with ample, ambitious breasts in her tight, form-fitting blouse. And she was definitely the woman with Scott in the photo from the Department of Motor Vehicles. And she was a redhead, no less.

Iris introduced herself and the young woman seemed cold, hardly offered any condolences. Her attitude was not exactly ice, but Iris felt she needed an electric blanket in her presence. She excused herself to go into Scott's office.

At the desk, she looked up Lucinda's address in the Rolodex. Such a quaint, old-fashioned name for such a sexy secretary. There was a gentle tap on the door. "Come in," Iris called.

Lucinda entered, stood like a recalcitrant schoolgirl in front of the desk. "I—I just wanted to say how sorry I am," she said. "I have a really hard time handling someone's ... death. Especially Mr. Blackmer's."

But you didn't have such a hard time handling the deceased in his cheating life, did you, you little bitch?

"That's quite all right," Iris said. "I understand. I've got a problem like that myself."

"I've been out the past two days with the flu," Lucinda said. "I only spoke to your husband a few times on the phone. He was so kind, said I should take a few more days off till I felt better."

"Yes. He was a very kind man. Are you married, Miss Brenner?"

"No."

"So you had no one to take care of you while you were ill?"

She noticed the woman was studying her more closely now. She had beautiful green eyes. And Iris thought *if Lucinda had driven down to the beach house before the Rosen guy had seen her, she would certainly be a suspect. Interesting—if the green Corvette was her car.*

"I'm going to need you," Iris said. "With Scott gone there's going to be lawyers all over me, coming out of my ears. And it's all going to be when I'm so exhausted, so depressed."

The woman actually reached across the desk and patted her hand. "I'm here for you, Mrs. Blackmer. You can count on me for anything, I want you to know that."

Even if I pin this thing on you? Iris thought, suppressing a smile. "That's good to know, it really is."

In the underground company garage, she found the stall with Lucinda's name on it. And her car: a turquoise older model Corvette. The color even matched her eyes, the slut. She had been Scott's squeeze all right, and now she was going to pay for it. In spades.

That afternoon she was trapped in the house, bogged down with the legal work and phone calls, when Janelle brought that bothersome cop into the study. "Bad time for a meeting, Lieutenant," she said by way of greeting.

"This is important, ma'am. Can we go somewhere away from your phones?"

"I guess. But it better not be too long. I've got to get through a ton of paperwork the attorneys gave me dealing with my husband's business, and you know how difficult that's going to be."

"Yeah. When my uncle Carlo died ... He had a little hardware business and that was tough, really tough on the family working things out with the lawyer and trying to find somebody to run it or buy it."

She led him out to a tiled patio adjoining the house. Bougainvillea climbed the mansion wall like a clinging pink net and birds bickered in the trees, everything pleasant, but this cop gave her a slight chill. It was his offhandedness; he was always going off on a tangent about non-essentials in a murder investigation. If it was an act, it was a pretty good one. *Be careful.*

"Now what's so important, Lieutenant?"

"I guess I can smoke out here?"

"I guess you can. Give a few robins lung cancer, see if I care." *God, watch the callousness, your husband just died!*

Columbo took his time lighting an already half-diminished cigar. "I was just thinking, you know, what a brave lady you are."

"No more so than probably most people. Why do you say that?"

He took a few introductory puffs. "Well, when the police arrived at the cottage yesterday you weren't outside."

"No, I wasn't. That makes me brave?"

"Well, to stay in the room with your, ah, husband "

"For your information, Lieutenant, I stayed in the kitchen. I dearly loved Scott, but I wasn't going to stay there and hold his cold hand." Luckily she didn't say the one with the cellphone!

"But you were in the living room when the boys came in."

"I had heard their cars and I went back in the living room so I could open the door for them."

Columbo nodded, still puffing.

"You don't inhale that thing, do you?" she asked, frowning.

"Oh no. My doctor says don't do that." He smiled. "He's a smoker, by the way. My wife yelled at me, how could I

get a doctor like that, and I had to remind her that she rec-
ommended him."

"How very nice for you. Now Lieutenant, you can see what
a busy day I'm having. What else is on your mind today?"

"Well, actually, it's your husband's gun."

She wasn't ready for this. She had wanted it to look like
the killer had shot him with the killer's own gun. How the hell
did he know that she had used Scott's .38? "What about it?"

"We checked and found out he had a registered weapon,
a Smith and Wesson Air-weight .38 revolver. But we won't
know until this afternoon whether it was a .38 that killed
him. He kept it at the cottage, didn't he?"

"I have no idea. My husband likes—liked guns. There's
probably one around here too. I just don't pay attention to
them."

Columbo nodded. She noticed he did a lot of nodding.
*How smart was he? He was the kind of person she always wanted
to shake by the shoulders—they took a year to think out things she
had figured out in a second.*

"There're shells, shells in a box for a .38, in the bedroom
night table. I guess you didn't know that, ma'am."

"No, as I said, I don't pay much attention to guns. Especially where they're kept."

"Well, it looks like the murderer knew right where to
find the gun—"

"But you don't know yet if that *was* the gun that was
used to kill him."

"True, very true. If Mr. Blackmer kept the gun in that
drawer then the killer knew exactly where to get his hands
on it."

Damn! She should have realized he would have registered
the gun, he was such a decent, by-the-book citizen. "So—
you're saying it could have been someone who had been in
the cottage before, knew where to look?"

"Maybe. Who cleans the cottage, ma'am?"

"Janelle, my housekeeper, the woman who let you in.
Lieutenant, Janelle *adored* Scott." Indignant: "Janelle is no
murderer."

"Oh no, no, I'm not saying anything like that. No, not
at all. Who else has been in the cottage? You've had parties there?"

She breathed easier. "Of course. We're there a lot in the

summer, sometimes with friends on weekends. You know how it is in the summer."

Columbo had a sudden, slightly yearning look on his rumpled face. "Yeah, I do. My wife and I would love to go to a friend's house on the ocean when the city is broiling." He laughed. "Trouble is, we don't have any friends with a place like that."

No, that's for the wealthy, little man, she thought. *You and your friends would have to work a lifetime or two to afford a house on the beach.*

"Another thing that's bugging me. If the gun was your husband's, why'd the murderer take it away after the murder?"

Why indeed. She would have liked a glass of white wine, but that wouldn't have looked good.

Columbo was studying his cigar. "Can I tap these ashes on the patio, ma'am?"

"Please go ahead. You're right, why *did* the murderer take it?"

"You see what's bothering me? All the killer had to do was clean his prints off the gun and leave it there for us."

"How very thoughtless of him to take it." *Watch the sarcasm.*

"Holding on to a weapon can be very stupid for a murderer," Columbo said.

"Why is that?"

Columbo moved over to tap his ashes on the patio. "Unless he intends to use it again to kill somebody else. We searched the area. No weapon."

She was relieved they hadn't found the gun and was delighted with this wrong detour his cop's mind was taking. "You have a very devious imagination, Lieutenant."

"Yeah, that's what my wife says. And she doesn't mean it as a compliment."

She smiled at him. "Well I wouldn't worry yourself to death thinking about the man murdering somebody else. Why haven't you asked me who I think the murderer is?"

He looked quickly over at her. "Who do you think? Ma'am?"

"Did a young man named Dale Rosen speak to you?"

"Yeah, nice young fella, lives right near you. Says he saw a redheaded young woman come out of the house and drive off in a green, older model Corvette."

She laced her fingers together in her lap, almost as if she were praying. She looked down at them, her face serious, sad. "I told you, Lieutenant Columbo, that Scott was not faithful."

"Yes, ma'am, you did."

"That redhead Rosen mentioned? She could have been the one who drove him down to the cottage."

Columbo touched a finger to his lip. "So then Mr. Rosen saw her leave the cottage."

"That's what he said. That's what he told you. Didn't he?"

"Yeah, we were glad to get that information. We're working on it. There're a lot of redheads in Los Angeles, lots of older model Corvettes too."

Her smile was gently skeptical. "You can't find her with all your new technology?"

"You been watching television again, ma'am. This is still a shoe leather business, plug away, one step at a time."

Yes, she thought, that fits you, Columbo, to a T. or a C. One slow, dragging, cautious step at a time. "Well it's certainly something to pursue, Lieutenant."

"I was wondering—why would the redhead want to kill him?"

"Oh, good heavens, I don't know—maybe jealousy because he had other women besides her, angry because he wouldn't divorce me and marry her. Or maybe it was some kind of terrible accident. Who knows."

Columbo got to his feet. "Well, thanks for your time again. I'll let you get back to your lawyers."

Another smile, this one a shade acidic. "I don't know what's worse — talking to an attorney or getting grilled by the police."

Columbo had started toward the door to the house, but he suddenly stopped, turned back. "Oh. Just one more thing, ma'am."

The man was definitely getting to be a drag. "What's that?"

"The tech crew found a little strand of hair on one of the pillows on the bed in the beach house."

"They did?" She kept her face placid, hiding the surge of her expectations. "My husband's—or a woman's hair?"

"Too early to tell yet. But they'll have it under the spectroscope tonight."

"A red hair, Lieutenant?"

Slight smile. "Cross your fingers, maybe we're getting lucky."

He turned back toward the house to go.

"Oh no, Lieutenant—not through the house with that stogy. Would you please go around to the drive and down to the street?"

"Much obliged." And he was gone.

She drove down to the cottage that night. There was yellow crime tape strung across the front door, but there were no police in sight. She drove down and back along the road, her headlights the only illumination, just to make sure. No patrol cruisers, no one on foot, no walkers on the beach, nothing.

She parked and went around the side of the house.

The ocean was querulous and dark, but the moonlight was like bright, scattered pollen on its surface. On the beach she knelt down and dug the sand away with both hands. It was hell on her nails but who cared?

The magazine with its cargo was gone.

God, was she looking in the right spot? No doubt of that, it was 60 feet away from the edge of the lower kitchen step, exactly where she had buried it.

It was at that moment that the phone rang in the cottage. Who would be calling at this late hour—it was almost ten o'clock?

She scrambled to her feet, let herself in the kitchen door. She grabbed the phone on the counter. "Yes?"

"Good evening, Mrs. Blackmer," a pleasant male voice addressed her.

It sounded familiar, very familiar, but she couldn't quite place it. "Who is this?"

"Your neighbor—Dale Rosen."

"Oh yes." She paused, getting control of herself. "How are you, Dale?"

"Fine and dandy. Wasn't that a song way back when? Why don't you come over for a drink? Facing the ocean I'm the house on your right."

"Well, it's a little late and I should be getting back to town "

"Five, ten minutes. Get to know each other a little."

She had a passing chill again, but this time it wasn't

because of Columbo. "How—how did you know I came down here?"

"Because I saw you," he said simply, no inflection. And she knew then, with a sick spasm, that she had better go see him.

He answered the door before she had time to ring again. He was in his casual uniform, different T-shirt, loafers, still no socks.

He took her back through a short, lightless corridor to what looked like a work room, dominated by a floor-to-ceiling window that looked out over the somnolent black seascape. There was an easel near the window with a canvas and a crude work table with a smattering of brushes and tubes of paint. The abstract was a work in progress, bold, brutal slashes of white and black like an embryonic Franz Kline. It was ugly.

"So you're a painter," she said, unnecessarily.

"Yes. I have a New York dealer and so far I'm making a living."

"Very good. It's a tough profession."

Dale was at a collection of bottles on a table under the window. "Scotch?"

"Just a little. I have to drive."

And then she saw the magazine, a little worse for wear, lying near him on the work table. It looked bulky, like the gun was still inside.

She was at a loss at how to play this out. And then she made her decision. Tentatively touching the magazine, she scrutinized him as he brought her the drink. "Where did you get this magazine?"

He was unfazed, cheerful, handing her the glass. "Where you put it."

"And how did you know where I put it?"

"Saw you. The afternoon your husband was killed and before the guardians of the law arrived. I thought it very interesting, you hiding the murder weapon."

"How do you know it was the murder weapon?"

Dale shrugged. His shoulders were thin, almost bony, under the T-shirt. "I think it's a very solid assumption. I think that Lieutenant Columbo would be very happy to receive it—the gun, I mean."

"Plus your accompanying eyewitness account."

He sipped his own drink. "That all might be averted," he said genially, with a wink.

Good. He had brought it up himself, she didn't have to play any sly, labyrinthian games. "How?"

"Well, I'd like to have a patron. An art patron like maybe da Vinci and some others had during the Renaissance."

She laughed at him. "Da Vinci?" She jerked a finger at the canvas. "And you're the new da Vinci? You have the audacity to even suggest that?"

Dale flushed, moved reflexively to block her view of his painting.

"You're a filthy blackmailer," she said. "You want to bleed me to death while you paint those dumb, untalented little nothings. Or should I say *big* nothings."

Now his face was almost blood red. "And you're a filthy murderer. I *will* go to that cop!"

She was still touching the magazine and she knew she was right: *the gun was still inside.* She quickly withdrew it and he backed away in fear, almost knocking over the easel.

"Now wait a minute—" he cried.

She shot him just once, through the head. And this time he did overturn the easel on his way down. Well, at least she had saved the world (at least the Art World) the horror of viewing any more of his abominations. Both times she killed with an amazing accuracy. This both surprised and delighted her.

She deposited Scott's gun in her handbag and remembered to wipe her fingerprints from her glass and the doorknobs before she left.

It was two days later when Lieutenant Columbo called on her again in Beverly Hills. This time they talked in the living room, two stories high, with a towering, white brick fireplace and a spacious window filled with the slowly dying late-afternoon light. He had a gnawed cigar in his mouth, knowing she would never grant him permission to smoke in her house.

"Some more bad news," Columbo said, in his usually placatory tones. "You've probably seen it on the tube, ma'am."

"Yes, if you're referring to another murder in a beach house near our own. Who did they say was the victim?"

"It was that young man we talked about—Rosen, Dale Rosen?"

"Very sad." Then: "My God! Someone broke into his house?"

"No, no forcible entry or anything. He was shot with a .38,1 just got the ballistics report. You're not going to believe this, ma'am—"

"Believe what?"

"He was shot with the same gun that killed your husband." She waited what she thought was the proper amount of time while Columbo removed that awful stump of cigar from his mouth.

"No," she said finally, "I don't believe it. Is this some kind of serial killer who likes to prey on people with beach houses?"

"It might be a little more complex than that."

Here he comes with another one of his left-field head-snappers: "Explain."

"There was a magazine near the body, a copy of *Business Week*."

"Yes?"

"Your prints were on it."

She got up, drew the curtains to close off what was left of the lingering light. She had wiped the glass and the doorknobs, but not the damn magazine. God, what an amateur! "Then it must've been one of our copies. Scott subscribed to *Business Week*."

"His name and address were on the copy." He put the butt somewhere in the jacket pocket of his suit. "That doesn't seem to be the problem. What was the victim doing with a copy of a magazine that came to you?"

She should've taken the magazine along with the gun. That's what happens when you're ad-libbing everything, including murder. "Were there any other fingerprints on the magazine?" she stalled.

"Yes, ma'am. Your husband's and Mr. Rosen's."

She came back from the window, hands clenched in the pockets of her skirt. "That is a puzzler, Lieutenant. How did this Rosen get a copy of our magazine?"

"Another puzzler, ma'am. Why were *your* prints on the magazine? Didn't you tell me you hated anything about business?"

She really had to watch her step with this guy: he didn't forget a goddamn thing!

"I probably took it in from the mailbox when it came. I

assure you, Lieutenant, I don't spend my time poring through boring business magazines."

"Hmmm." He went into one of his semi-deep, meditative moods, but she noticed he still had his eyes fastened on her. "But that still leaves us with the biggest puzzle of all."

"Yes. How did that magazine get into Rosen's house." She sat down again, facing him. "Probably Rosen came over, chatted with Scott, and borrowed the magazine. Who knows? Maybe Scott wanted to show him something in the magazine and Rosen took it with him."

"Were you aware of Mr. Rosen's coming to the house?"

"No. But as I told you, Scott went down to the cottage by himself, presumably to 'unwind' after a particularly hard work day. And obviously, he brought women—like that redhead. I loved my husband, Lieutenant, but it wasn't idolatry. Scott had his flaws."

He was silent and she congratulated herself. Thrust and parry. She was beginning to almost enjoy playing his tricky little game. But just don't get cocky!

Another "hmmm." Then he looked at her matchbook on the table. "Could you lend me your matches? I won't smoke here, I promise you, but after I leave I'd like to light up in the car."

Amused, she pushed them over to him. "Anything I can do to help a man find my husband's murderer."

He took the matchbook. "Thank you, ma'am." He paused. "You know, when you mentioned your husband's women—"

He let it hang there and she felt compelled to prod him: "What about them? Have you done any checking on the redhead with the Corvette?"

"We have, yes. Were you aware that your husband's secretary, a Miss Brenner, is a redhead?"

"Yes. I only just met her. I tried to stay away from Scott's business, although now I'm going to be drowning in it while we clear up the estate."

A very sage nod. "I'll be questioning her first thing in the morning."

"And the hair you found on the pillow?"

"A woman's red hair, ma'am. Maybe we'll get lucky again."

She smirked. "I'm trying to remember the first time."

After he left, she bided her time while a tardy twilight

took its time evolving into darkness. She told Janelle to leave dinner on the table and go home.

She sped down Wilshire to the company building. It was after-hours now, everyone had left, and the lobby guard, recognizing her, waved her smilingly to the elevators. She was carrying her handbag, nothing else.

The cleaning crew was already at work and they paid her scant attention as she quickly proceeded to her husband's office.

Once there, she laid her handbag on Lucinda's desk in the reception area, making sure the door was closed to the outside corridor, and removed the .38. She hunted through various drawers in the desk until she found a stack of large manila mailing envelopes. Wiping the gun clean of her fingerprints, she slid the gun into an envelope, took care of any prints on it, and secreted it near the bottom of the stack, closing the drawer with her elbow.

She went into Scott's office, planting herself down in his chair behind the desk. She swiveled around to look out the window at the light-bejeweled folds of downtown Los Angeles under the usual dirty scrim of smog. Then she swiveled back around to survey the vastness of his office. Not his anymore—*hers*.

She stayed away the next morning and let the cop conduct his interrogation. When Lucinda became a "person of interest" they would probably get a warrant to search the woman's apartment, car, and anything else, including her desk. She was sure the tenacious Columbo would be hounding the woman.

It took him almost five days before he showed up again. This time she was finishing a late lunch, having a desultory cigarette and coffee on the patio. "Good afternoon, Lieutenant. Are you coming over to cadge lunch from me?"

"Oh no, ma'am. I grabbed lunch on the way. My wife always says a good lunch is more important than a good breakfast."

"Sounds like you have a smart wife who really takes care of you. I'd like to meet this woman."

"Well, I'm not saying she's reclusive or anything, but she really likes to stay away from my business."

My God, he was amusing. "Trying to pin murder on somebody is just 'business?'"

Unfazed: "I don't think anybody's trying to pin murder on anybody, ma'am."

"That's very reassuring, Lieutenant. Since lunch is so important, may we at least get you some coffee? Maybe a chocolate chip cookie to go with it?"

He waved her offer away. "Thanks, but I came over to bring you up to date."

"How thoughtful of you." Wry: "Did we get lucky *again*?"

"I told you I was going to question your husband's secretary? Well, I'm sorry to report this, ma'am, but she admitted she *did* have an affair with your husband."

It was getting easier and easier to play the despairing widow: "Yes...I suspected that when you told me she was a redhead. And does she own a green Corvette?"

"Yes, she does." He took an uneaten roll from the bread basket. A little sheepish: "You mind?"

"Certainly not. Enjoy."

He took a big bite out of the roll before he continued. "We also have another incriminating piece of evidence. We found your husband's gun hidden in the drawer of her desk."

Iris set down her coffee cup very slowly on the saucer, trying not to be too dramatic. "Really. And do you think that's the same gun that killed Mr. Rosen and Scott?"

"We're pretty sure it is; ballistics is checking it out. But if Miss Brenner killed your husband, why did she kill Mr. Rosen?"

"You're the detective, Detective." This should be interesting. "Hard to say at this point. He saw a redhead leaving the beach house that afternoon."

She watched him take another bite of the roll. "He reported that to you." He looked like he was already coveting another roll in the basket.

"Maybe he thought he could blackmail her," Columbo said, "And didn't realize how risky that was, how dangerous she could be."

"Fascinating. And maybe she was forced to kill him.... Knowing you, I'm sure you'll come up with a definitive answer." She pushed the bread basket closer to him. "I guess that almost ties everything up in a neat bow—am I right, Lieutenant?"

"It would seem."

"You don't sound very positive."

He was about to answer when Janelle came out to them

with a handful of letters and magazines. "The mail came early today, ma'am."

"I don't believe it. Do you usually get late mail deliveries, Lieutenant?"

"I don't know. To tell you the truth, I'm never at home during the day."

Janelle grunted, went back in the house.

Iris thumbed through the letters, stopping at one. It was a letter from the Department of Motor Vehicles, addressed to her. She knew she hadn't paid the fine sent to Scott, that had him with Lucinda in his car, but if they were checking up on him, why did they send it to her?

"Excuse me, Lieutenant," she said, tearing open the envelope. "You know all the bills we get these days."

But as she extracted the letter and a photo, she realized his eyes were tight on her face.

She glanced quickly at the photo and she felt a sharp, stabbing pain in her gut. It was another traffic camera shot that showed her driving with *Scott beside her*. She started to innocently slide it back in the envelope when Columbo said, "That's what's going to put you away, Mrs. Blackmer. I had the DMV send me anything they had on you and your husband. I saw that photo yesterday and they told me your copy was already in the mail."

She felt the blood draining from her face. She grabbed at her cigarette in the ashtray, but it had gone out.

Columbo reached across and took the photo from her. "I have to tell you," he said, "that I was sort of on to you from the beginning. Something just didn't add up. You said you raced down to the beach house where you thought he was with one of his women. But how did he get there? Lucinda Brenner said she never drove him. You drove him, ma'am, and you killed him down there. I checked your driving record with the DMV—a lot of speeding tickets over the years and you told me yourself you drive too fast." He flicked the photo with a finger. "You sped that afternoon and a traffic camera caught you, proof positive he was with you—and look at the time and date which proves it."

She nodded. The photo of Scott and his secretary had triggered this whole thing.... And now this second photo was the ironic finish. Her finish.

Columbo sighed as if he felt just as depleted. "You're a very smart person, Mrs. Blackmer. I'm sure you would've

been a terrific business woman.... But you had no business killing two people."

ABOUT THE AUTHOR

William Link created, wrote and adapted sixteen on-the-air television series, a record to this day.

Called "Mr. Rolls and Mr. Royce of American television" by the *New York Times*, William Link and his collaborator, Richard Levinson, created, wrote and produced many successful mystery/ crime television series, including: *Columbo*, *Murder She Wrote*, *Ellery Queen*, *The Bold Ones*, *Mannix*, *McCloud* and *The Cosby Mysteries*. Sadly, Richard Levinson died in 1987.

Link was also known for his numerous mystery/crime movies-for-television, *The Savage Report*, directed by Steven Spielberg, *Guilty Conscience*, starring Anthony Hopkins, *The Judge and Jake Wyler* starring Bette Davis, *Murder by Natural Causes*, *Rehearsal for Murder*, and is proud of his ground-breaking television movies, including *My Sweet Charlie*, *That Certain Summer*, *The Execution of Private Slovik*, *The Gun*, *Crisis at Central High*, *Terrorist on Trial*, and the autobiographical *The Boys*. Movie credits include *The Hindenburg* and the cult classic *Rollercoaster*.

In addition, Link was well known for his humorous show-biz cartoons, a fly-on-the-wall perspective of one of the world's craziest businesses, which have been shown at the Cartoon Art Museum in San Francisco, Hollywood Entertainment Museum and Writers Guild West, in Los Angeles.

His awards include four Edgars, two Emmys, two Golden Globes, Paddy Chayefsky award for Lifetime Achievement in Television Writing, the Peabody, the Ellery Queen, the Raymond Chandler Marlowe, to name a few. Link has served on The Academy of Television Arts and Sciences Board of Governors; as National President of Mystery Writers of America; and in 1994, Link and Levinson were inducted into the Academy of Television Arts and Sciences Hall of Fame. In 2018 he received a fifth Edgar Award: the Grand Master, in recognition of a lifetime of sustained achievement.

Link published two novels, two non-fiction books and wrote the Tony-nominated book for the Broadway musical, *Merlin*. His play *Columbo Takes the Rap* was a major hit at the International Mystery Festival and *Prescription: Murder* toured the UK in summer 2010.

William Link died of congestive heart failure on December 27, 2020. He was 84.